THE *Tortilla* STAR

ABBEY CARPENTER

Black Rose Writing | Texas

ISBN: 978-1-68433-434-6
PUBLISHED BY BLACK ROSE WRITING
www.blackrosewriting.com

Printed in the United States of America
Suggested Retail Price (SRP) $18.95

The Tortilla Star is printed in Calluna

*As a planet-friendly publisher, Black Rose Writing does its best to eliminate unnecessary waste to reduce paper usage and energy costs, while never compromising the reading experience. As a result, the final word count vs. page count may not meet common expectations.

To Mama-San

Josephine Van Wey

Storyteller extraordinaire

1938-2013

THE Tortilla STAR

PROLOGUE - 2018

Bette ground the gears in the faded silver Toyota looking for third while listening to the president rant on about The Wall. She jammed the radio off until he was done spewing. Why such focus on an ineffective barrier? Why not more pressing issues like climate change, the perverting of democracy by foreign powers, voter suppression? The list was endless, and he did nothing about any of it. Just the wall, the wall, the wall. She was wall-weary. The steel monstrosity shimmered up ahead in the haze of the early morning heat. Bette touched her belly. Yes, all there tucked in safely – passport, credit card, dollars, pesos.

She flipped the radio back on. "...invasion, drugs, human traffickers, criminals..." What about family separations, child detentions, asylum seekers, Bette wondered. The crossers now were mainly women and children fleeing from violence, but a decade ago it had been men and boys seeking work, trying to provide better lives for themselves and their children.

Bette saw Enrique dancing in her living room with his nephews, Fernando and Nemecio, both so innocent and young, full of wonder and still quiet as they took in the new life around them. Rosa and Felipe and their children had crossed ten years ago in 2007 not to bring in drugs, but to protect their children from them in their own country. A smile lit up Bette's face at the thought of Isa and Gerardo. And their cousins too, *los tres tres.* Who would she be today without having had them in her life?

And Marco. Her hands lost their tight grip on the steering wheel. She extended her arm to the passenger seat, imagining running her fingers through his lush black hair. Marco.

CHAPTER 1 – 2008

---

la suerte (SWEHR-the)   2008
luck

~~Yo no~~ *Tengo mala suerte.*
I have bad luck.

I'm have god luck.
Bicause I'm have you. (Bette)
        has

Friday/*viernes*   **13**   July/*Julio*

"Marco," she had asked in Spanish, "¿What's a polite word for these?" Bette was sitting at the kitchen table, cupping her breasts over her tank top, smiling at him. She loved the way he said breast. Just like she couldn't make her 'dr' and 'tr' roll, he kept reversing 'st' and 'ts'.

He dropped the round green *tomatillo* he was holding into the blender and moved toward her. "¿You're not going to teach them *that*, are you?" he asked in Spanish.

"Uh-huh, it's important to learn. It's not a...a bad word." She was planning her English as a Second Language lesson and wasn't going to leave out many body parts. She hated that her Spanish-English dictionary didn't have the word for breasts. *Tits* maybe made sense, but *breast*? What was obscene about that?

He looked over her shoulder at her book and slid his hands where hers had been. "*Senos,*" he said. She let her head drop back on his chest.

"Say it again, please."

"*Senos. ¿*How do you say them in English?"

"Breasts."

"Breats." Marco tried.

"Brea*st*," Bette said, emphasizing the last two letters.

"Brea*ts*." He did his own emphasizing.

Bette chuckled. "¿What's this?" She turned and put her hand on his chest.

"Breats."

"No, these are breasts," she said, putting her hands on his shapely pecs. "Here, above your breasts." She waited a second while he thought. "Chest," she said.

"Chets."

"Che*st*."

"Che*ts*."

"You better go finish my dinner, *Señor* beautiful chets."

Later that night in bed, Bette sat with her English and Spanish books around her, finishing up the lesson she would teach. She had met Marco in her English as a Second Language class that spring of 2008 when he had just arrived from Mexico. Her two semesters of Spanish had been all they had between them for communication, but it hadn't kept them from finding a way to let each other know they were interested. They still always spoke in Spanish except for a few English words, but Marco was picking up more in the ESL program and at his construction job. Houses couldn't seem to be built quickly enough in Arizona, and many of her students were employed in some aspect of that profession. Bette much preferred the small, older house she'd found to rent, especially since no neighbors could see in her bedroom windows which were all open to take advantage of the cool night air. Even in the mountains of Arizona with the summer rains, the heat could create a restless night.

As she finished practicing drawing the outline of a man to be recognizable as a human on the whiteboard, Marco came in from brushing his teeth. His white cotton underwear hugged his firm butt and contrasted sharply with the coffee brown of his body.

"¿What's this?" She pointed to various body parts.

"Arm," he said.

"Good. ¿This?"

Leg. Head. Lips.

She stroked his neck, tickling up to his hairline, and he said, "Knee."

"No. Neck. This is a knee. Remember those last sounds, like in can and can't. Very different."

"¿How do you say this?" Marco asked, slipping his hand under the sheets, between her legs.

"Relax," she said, and they laughed together.

The first time she'd given him a back massage, he'd kept himself propped up on his elbows. His back was sore from a day of lifting sheets of plywood up on the roof of a four-thousand-square-foot house. The new owners would be able to fit five of her house into their one. What did a retired couple need with all that space?

Bette had said *relax* in English and pulled his arm out from under him and pressed on his elbow to help him stretch it out and lie flat. Marco had relaxed his arm and let his body sink into the bed. His arm reached down to her pubic hairs as she squatted beside him, rubbing his shoulders. His fingers wiggled, searching for more, and she swatted his hand and laughed. "Hey," she'd said, "relax." From then on, whenever she'd massaged him and said *relax,* his hand went straight for her crotch.

"¿What do you call the *relax*?" he asked again.

"Vagina."

"Bañina."

"*Va*gina." She stressed the hard g sound.

"Ba*sh*ina," Marco tried.

The phone rang, and Marco gave her a quick kiss before she hopped out of bed. It was Tracy. The sound of her friend's voice made her smile. They'd met ten years ago on a birdwatching outing sponsored by the local Audubon group. Over the years they'd supported each other through a few heartaches with the healing often taking place under the stars on camping trips.

"What's going on?" Bette asked.

"Oh, Don and I are thinking about getting out of the heat this weekend, and I couldn't remember what road goes to White Horse Lake. When we went last summer, you drove so I wasn't paying attention."

Bette gave her directions, remembering the route they'd taken, then filling the canoe and paddling up the lake to set up a private camp. No room for three in the boat now with Don in Tracy's life.

"What're you doing?" Tracy asked.

"Working on my ESL lesson. Marco's here."

"Is he living there now? Want me to call back?"

"No, he can't understand what we're saying. Plus I talked him into reading a book of short stories written in both English and Spanish." Bette looked in the bedroom at Marco. He normally just lay in bed while she read or wrote in her journal, and she was ashamed how much that bothered her. How could a person spend so much time doing nothing?

Bette's father had judged her on how much she could do and how efficiently. Although she tried to switch his harping of *Don't just sit there, do something*, to a more Buddhist mantra of, *Don't just do something, sit there*, the seeds he had planted were firmly rooted in her psyche. She had not been able to break free from her tendency to judge others with the same harsh standards.

"He must be helping you get over Mike."

Bette sucked in her breath. She had thought Mike was the one, finally, but he had ended the relationship saying he couldn't live with never feeling good enough, constantly disappointing her. She'd always been the one to end relationships before, so it was a double wounding. Bette had just been trying to get him to make small changes so they could get along better. Wasn't that part of the give and take of a relationship?

"He's got to be a distraction."

"Marco? Yah, that's putting it mildly." They chuckled as Bette told her about the fun language mix-ups they kept creating.

"I'm learning to cook some new foods, too. When Marco's housemates come over, I look at everything differently." Bette remembered the first time she had invited them when she was newly involved with Marco. She walked around her house trying to imagine how it would look to someone who had never been in the home of a *gringa*. Even knowing she wasn't a typical over-consuming American, she was embarrassed by her riches. She had a two-bedroom home all to herself. Though her furnishings were hand-me-downs or from thrift stores, her bookshelves were full, her cabinets brimming with food, and her music shelves tight with CDs. She had a lot of stuff. "I'm seeing the world with new eyes. Pretty cool."

"Do you worry about driving him around?"

"That ridiculous law. No." But in reality, it did niggle at her every time he hopped in the passenger seat. Would they actually fine her for transporting an undocumented immigrant? Could she claim she didn't know? "My life's more complicated now. What with Marco and ESL. But I like it."

"It's part of your personality. You like complexity and newness," Tracy said. "How many jobs have you had since I've known you? Three? Four? And boyfriends?"

"I know," Bette said, cutting her off. "I should quit whining. I'm pretty happy even though I don't know what people are saying around me most of the time."

Bette slipped into bed beside Marco. He turned sideways and slid his muscular legs under the tent of her own. She stroked his smooth skin, still thrilled at the contrast of her white hand against his mocha flesh which was one of their many differences that added spice to their time together. She had six inches on him, and her pale hair was long and wavy compared to his black spikes. Though she'd always felt like a big-boned gal, she experienced thinness compared to his solid bulk. They did have their age in common, thirty-eight.

"You and Don still doing great?"

"Yes. He got in at Shalom Yoga. He's scheduled to teach two classes a week."

"That's a start. I bet he's a good teacher. Mr. Vivacious. Fun to watch at your barbecue last weekend, flitting about like a colorful hummingbird. 'Can I get you more wine? Another ear of corn?'"

"Yes, Mr. Social. Sometimes it annoys me how much he focuses on himself."

Bette reassured her that it didn't seem like that from outside the relationship.

"You and Marco looked sweet together," Tracy said. "Why aren't Don and I more touchy? We should still be in the infatuation stage."

"I can't remember being like this with other sweethearts either," Bette said. "Both of us seem drawn to touch one another." Bette pictured herself coming up behind Marco in the kitchen, putting her arms around him, and just standing there talking while he put vegetables into the blender to make salsa for the barbecue. One arm over his shoulder, the other around his waist. It might bug another person to be constricted like that, but Marco seemed to love it. Bette looked at Marco beside her in the bed. "It's how we're talking to each other, what with my crappy Spanish and his five words of English."

"Well, girlfriend, you do seem awfully happy."

"I am. Even though it's frustrating at times. But it's also like a ride on a big, powerful horse. I don't know where it's taking me, but I've got my head thrown back laughing."

***

The next evening after work, Bette drove to the Catholic Church and was the first to arrive in the classroom they were given for the English as a Second Language lessons. She had just finished drawing her long-armed, big-handed man on the whiteboard when Catalina arrived. Bette sat between her and Elizadet, and the three of them visited in broken English and Spanish while they waited for more students to arrive and Gretchen, the main teacher. Catalina worked the day shift at Taco Bell.

"¿How is your job? ¿Do you like it?" Bette asked in Spanish, giving Catalina's brain a break before the class started.

"It's okay. I'm tired." Catalina was in her early twenties and at least thirty pounds overweight. She wore it with confidence, unlike many *gringas*, but it had to add to her discomfort standing on her feet all day.

"¿Is the work difficult?"

Catalina rubbed her neck. "It always hurts here."

"Neck," Bette said, forgetting she was giving them an English break.

Catalina tilted her head back and demonstrated looking above her at the order screen, then lowered her head and mimed making a burrito. Up and down, up and down, she bobbed her head, her arm reaching out right then left. Bette wondered if OSHA knew about these working conditions of scalding hot oil, sharp knives, and their focus constantly shifting. People in offices got ergonomic keyboards, cushy chairs with lumbar support, but she also knew anyone without papers would never complain.

Catalina said something to Elizadet in Spanish, and they both laughed. Bette missed it, as usual, and asked her to say it again, "*Otra vez, por favor.*"

"There was a guy at our house who said, *Estoy llanta*," Catalina said in slow Spanish.

"¿What's *llanta*?" Bette asked.

Catalina shrugged. Bette guessed that she probably knew the answer but was shy and unsure in using her English. Bette reached for her Spanish-English dictionary, smudged dark in the middle of the pages from where her thumb had flipped through looking up a thousand words. She wished her students used their dictionaries as much as she did.

"It means tire," she said. She wrote the word on a piece of scrap paper lying on the coffee table.

"He meant, *Estoy cansado*," Catalina explained.

Then Bette got it and laughed with them. She wrote *tired* on the paper below *tire*. "He..." Bette couldn't think of the Spanish word for 'confused.' She tried again. "He think *tire* is *tired,* so say in Spanish, I'm a tire. *Estoy llanta.*"

Catalina nodded and giggled. Bette flipped open their book, *English for Latinos*, and found Secret VI. "Remember, *la ultima letra* in each word is important, like Ben, a man's name, and bend, *doblar.*"

When the men started to wander into class, some braver ones practiced their budding English without being prompted. Mateo said, "Good evening, teacher. How are you?"

"*Estoy llanta*," she replied, and she and Catalina snickered again.

That evening for her part of the lesson, she used those similar words as an example of the importance of enunciation, and it became a class joke. She'd loosened them up by making them laugh, and the class went better with more of them willing to try speaking out loud.

Most of the thirty or so students were single men, but there were a few women, some with children. That night an entire family arrived together, Rosa and Felipe with their son Gerardo and daughter Isabella, nicknamed Isa.

Bette's parents had divorced when she was little. Her last vision of her mother had been in her second-grade classroom when she was about Isa's age. All heads had turned as the door opened, and her mother's white high-heels tapped into the room. She wore a tight, turquoise blue dress, her long blond hair cascading around her shoulders. "Who's that?" a boy near Bette whispered.

"That's my mother." Bette rose and walked to the teacher's desk where her mother hugged her for the last time until she was a teenager. She had gone to the coast with her lover. Bette's father had continued moving from one state to the next, always searching, never quite satisfied. The sweetness Bette saw in the new family was not even a distant memory for her.

When they broke apart for small group work, Bette pulled her chair close to the family.

"Welcome to the ESL class," she said. The kids smiled and talked over one another in broken English with the parents sticking to Spanish. Isa was in first grade and had straight, shiny black hair that Rosa had pulled off her forehead with tiny barrettes. Bette didn't know where Isa got her bubbly personality. It couldn't have been from her reserved parents. Perhaps it was just the difficulties with the language that hobbled their communication.

Gerardo at ten still wore his hair in a pageboy and hadn't succumbed to the fashion of shaving it close to his scalp.

Felipe and Rosa looked to be in their early thirties, quiet and respectful of the teachers. Felipe had a job so was gaining a smattering of English. He leaned over and whispered assistance to his wife with his few words. Bette smiled, watching Isa help her mom from the other side. She loved hearing them call their kids *mi amor, mi vida, mi tesoro.* The thought of her parents calling her their love, their life, their treasure was as foreign as the language she was trying to learn.

When Marco moved to sit near Felipe to help with some of the body words she'd taught him the night before, Bette felt a warmth rising inside and guessed that others could see her glowing with pride.

He came home with her that night, and while she refilled her bird feeders with thistle and black oil sunflower seeds, Marco poured them iced tea from her sun tea jar.

"I made ah...sugar water for you," Bette said, not knowing the word for syrup. Pour? How does one say *pour*? "Put it in..." Instead of? Ugh. Spanish. "Uh...put it in, and no sugar." She hoped he was understanding. She'd watched the three spoonsful of sugar in his tea sink to the bottom even after stirring and had made him a simple syrup so that it was already dissolved. When he came out of the kitchen smiling and nodding, she guessed he'd figured it out.

"Marco, ¿Remember our relationship is a secret from the class?"

"It's not important if they know. They're not paying you to be a teacher."

Bette turned away from watering her small garden plot. "*Sí, soy volunatira*, but it's the same. Teachers and students shouldn't be together. The ethics aren't...good."

"¿No?" Marco turned the water off and recoiled the hose. "¿Is it wrong to look at you with affection?"

"Affection, no. Passion, yes." She pointed her index finger at him, but when he laughed, she remembered that had a different meaning in Mexico. It was a swear word. They sat together on a bench seat on the deck.

"¿No, I shouldn't do this in class?" He placed his hand on Bette's thigh and slowly inched it upward.

Bette gave it a playful slap. "No."

"¿And this?" Marco lifted up so he could reach her neck and nibbled from her ear down to her collarbone. He was headed toward the hollow in her neck when she pulled away, her pulse already quickening.

"You are a bad boy. Go to my room." Finally, a joke they both understood.

Marco kissed her, then headed inside to prepare for bed. Bette sat outside a while longer, savoring her tea and the cool night air. Was it more than the ethics of being with a student?

The neighbors' backyard was dotted with ponderosa pines and Arizona oaks that provided the shade for her long, wide deck. Some of the trees were so old that their bark had stretched and flattened so they looked like pumpkins. When Mike was in her life, they spent many evenings here in their private world within the city. Now there was Marco. Did her hesitancy have just the tiniest bit to do with the fact that he was undocumented? Bette found her outside broom, with the bristles worn down to three inches, and swept the pine needles down the deck and swooshed them off the end where they fell onto granite boulders.

CHAPTER 2

To neiht diner. Me house you do like? Or here in you house. Dinner
  Marco

Bette was usually the first to arrive in the finance department and, as usual, she plugged in her teapot and turned on the computer. As the grants accountant, she kept track of the expenditures from the funds the research institute received. Their work on aging was financed solely by these grants. They wouldn't keep getting them if Bette didn't do her job well. She had built a little nest of an office and now rolled her comfy chair up to the wrap-around desk, which allowed her to have papers and printouts on three sides.

She was flipping back and forth between two different computer screens and down to papers on her desk, trying to find what was keeping her report from balancing, when she heard someone say, "Excuse me, Betty?"

"Hi, it's just Bette."

"Sorry." He smiled and stuck his hand out. "I know what that's like. I'm just John. From IT."

"Not Jonathan?"

"Nope, just John."

"Hey, welcome to our club." She gave him a full grin and one firm shake, sealing the pact. John smiled and tilted his head.

"We're The Justs. When I told a woman I was just Bette on my birth certificate, not Betty, not Elizabeth, she said she was just Cathy, not Catherine, not Kathleen. She brought me into the club."

"Cool." He nodded his head. "The Justs."

"We have a just Bill, not a William."

"My friend is just Vicky, not Victoria."

"Tell her she's in our club." It had been a sore spot growing up, explaining to each teacher that she was just Bette, but it irritated her less now.

"You put a ticket in? Your system keeps freezing?"

"Oh, right." Bette brought her attention back to her office. "Whenever I have Banner and Ap-Extender open at the same time, everything locks up." She stood back and maneuvered around him as he settled into her chair and squeezed his long legs under her desk. Must be two or three inches taller than her.

"Are you new?" Bette asked.

"Just moved up from Phoenix. And, yes, I'm glad to get out of the heat."

"I guess you get asked that a lot," she said.

While he was working on her computer, Bette watered her cactus plants and a long dangly pothos that were along the bookshelf under her window. It was open to let in fresh air before it got too hot and the building's air conditioner kicked on. Out the window in the courtyard, her bird feeder swayed on a branch of a scrubby bush.

"What kind of birds do you get?"

A bird watcher? Bette thought. Be still my heart. "Oh, mostly just house finches."

"Don't apologize for them on my account," John said, sitting back and smiling. "They have a beautiful song and cheery red markings."

Bette nodded but refrained from saying her standard line that all birds could use a little help as their habitat was being reduced and fragmented by the housing developments sprouting up like painful beige warts around Warren. What if he lived in one of those homes? Didn't want to piss off the new IT guy before he fixed her problem.

She leaned her hip against the file cabinet and watched him click around on her computer. He was thin enough that he might be a runner. Brown hair curled down his neck. His goatee was trimmed close and had auburn and gray highlights. Forties, maybe. It looked soft around his lips. Tortoise-shell glasses. A fellow reader?

"What were you doing here?" He was pointing at the large bulletin board on the wall beside her desk which was covered with cards, sayings, Chinese fortunes, and pictures.

Bette leaned over to see that he was indicating a picture of her swinging on a vine, her mouth wide open in a Tarzan yell. A woodsy scent rose off of him, and she took a discrete sniff before answering. "Hanging on English ivy trying to get it to come loose from a fir tree. I was volunteering in a park."

"Looks fun."

"It was a blast. You wouldn't believe how tough that stuff is. Big around as my wrist."

"Where were you?"

"Seattle. With so much rain, non-natives can aggressively take over."

"I worked on a project to get rid of Russian knapweed in Montana."

"Really? Cool. Where?"

They talked about the various attempts his group had made to combat the tenacious weed, including using a carpet cleaner to kill it with hot water and goats to munch it down. He'd worked with an animal rights organization and was volunteering with the trails association in town.

"Whatever it takes to help our beleaguered environment stand up to the abuses we humans pummel it with."

Bette stared at him, open-mouthed. She could have said the sentence herself.

As he was leaving her office, he paused by her file cabinet that was plastered with artwork.

"Did your kids do these?"

"No. Friends' kids. I volunteer teaching ESL, English as a Second Language. Some of the children tag along with their parents." Being single and never having children, Bette had sought out volunteer opportunities over the years to take up some of her free time. It felt good to help others and the environment. The ESL program was a world away from her more physical outdoor volunteer jobs. She loved how teaching the immigrants encouraged her to move out of her all-white life. She'd been living in the Southwest for years, and it was time to learn Spanish and to get to know more of the residents of her adopted state.

The phone rang on Bette's desk, causing them both to jump a bit and step apart from where they'd been shoulder to shoulder. "Thanks for fixing my glitchy system, just John."

"No problem, just Bette." They stood still a moment longer, eyes locked in a gaze. "Call me if anything else comes up."

She nodded, then reached for her phone.

"Hi, Bette," Cindy, the receptionist said. "There's someone on the line speaking Spanish. Could you take the call and see what he wants?"

Bette had gone through this with her before. Why didn't she read the sentence Bette had written for her rather than pass the call along? "My Spanish isn't good enough, Cindy," Bette groaned, "especially on the phone."

"You teach English to those Mexicans."

Those Mexicans. Bette's insides clenched. "Alright." But she was going to go down there afterward and tell the receptionist that you don't have to speak a foreign language to teach English. There was a couple from Viet Nam in her class. Did she think Bette spoke Vietnamese? And maybe she'd enlighten her about a few other things, too.

Bette tried but failed to understand what the caller wanted. As soon as he heard her few words of Spanish, he rattled away, and the words went right through her, not stopping to identify themselves. She'd ended up telling him what they did at the institute, in slow choppy Spanish, so he would figure out he'd called the wrong number. She hoped. He could sure use an ESL class, so she ended by telling him about the ones offered at the Catholic Church and the community college.

***

After work, Bette pulled Marco's note off the front door, smiling as she dug for her keys in her backpack. She liked when they ate at Marco's house once in a while instead of always at hers. Her senses seemed to open and come alive when she was with him and his Mexican housemates, and she relished being surrounded by it all, the food and smells, constant noise, their different habits, and the poverty which they did not seem to notice. It was such a mystery and more than a little intimidating as usually she didn't know what they were saying. It made her feel hyper-aware, though, like when she was the new kid in school, seeing everything for the first time, taking it in. It was a dance between trying to figure it all out so she'd know how to be in this foreign world and appreciating the differences, even if she didn't fit.

Since Marco didn't have a phone, she dialed his housemate Enrique's cell number to see about dinner. Enrique was on his second stay in the U.S. and had been here six years this time. His English was much better than her Spanish, and Bette knew he enjoyed being the intermediary.

"*Bueno,*" he answered in the characteristic Spanish fashion.

"*Hola Enrique. Soy Bette.*"

"Hi Betty," he responded in English. Like all of her Mexican family, Enrique pronounced her name with a *y* and a strong *t* sound. "How are you?"

"I'm good," she answered Enrique. "Thank you." She no longer cringed when she said that. Well, only slightly. The English teacher in her wanted to say *I'm well,* but her ESL students knew the word *good,* and she wasn't about to confuse them with nuances. Theirs was a class of survival English, not college grammar. "How are you?" she repeated, as she'd learned was their custom.

"I'm good," Enrique said. "Are you coming for dinner tonight?"

"Who's cooking?"

"*Yo.*"

"Well then, yes." She could imagine his chest puffing out. Enrique was still a bit of an oddity to her. For one thing, he liked to cook. Her mouth watered, remembering the *camarones a la diablo* he had made. Enrique also dressed more *gringo*, the nerdy kind of *gringo*. When he came to her house, he wore tan slacks with one of several thin pull-over polyester sweaters in various hues of beige. It didn't flatter his growing potbelly, but he never showed concern about that, flirting with the younger volunteer teachers with their flat bellies peeking out below short tee-shirts. There was always a cross on a chain around his neck and a gold ring with a purple stone which he wore turned around, so it looked like a wedding band. Was he ashamed to be a Mexican and not yet married at the ripe old age of thirty-five?

"Do you want Marco?" His question brought her back to her call.

"*Si, por favor.*"

After confirming her visit with Marco, Bette changed from her work outfit to a sundress. She knew it would be stifling hot in Marco's house where broken windows were covered with plywood. The landlord hadn't bothered to replace them, and even with the front door open there was never much of a breeze. No air conditioning, of course.

Bette parked and locked her car in the pothole-riddled dirt lot at the base of the hillside crammed with white trailers of various sizes. The "Park in the Pines" had been a desired place in its heyday but was now suffering from years of neglect. She walked up the dusty road past several trailers, self-conscious about how she must look as a tall, dishwater blond in an all-Mexican neighborhood. Little kids zipped past on bikes headed toward the bottom of the hill, jumping their cycles over chalk-dry mounds. Backing her car up to leave was always a little worrisome, but she liked seeing them play outside.

The house where Marco lived was the only non-trailer in the complex, and she approached it by squeezing past three cars in various states of repair. Marco always grumbled about those vehicles, but she wasn't sure if it was because Enrique was making money on them – buying cheap, repairing, and selling – or because they were an eyesore. More than the cars, it was the trash that rankled. Didn't the sight of litter bother them?

"*Hola,*" she called when she was near the door. With six people living in a one-bedroom house, she wanted to give them time to arrange themselves before she appeared in the open doorway leading to their main living space.

"*Pasale,*" she heard and entered.

The smell was always the first thing she noticed, a strong, pungent *chile* with meaty undertones mixed with a strand of male sweat and all overlaid by a faint propane odor from the stove. Her hair often had this scent when she arrived home.

Fernando was lying on a double bed watching TV when she walked in but hopped up and pulled on a tee-shirt. Like Marco, his chest was a lighter color than his sun-darkened arms, but his long torso was not as sculpted as Marco's. Usually Fernando wore an un-tucked western shirt opened as low as the weather demanded. Today he locked eyes with her, and she had second thoughts about wearing the sundress. Where was Marco? On the bed to her right was Fernando's cousin, Mateo. He had his English book open and was writing in a spiral notebook. Bette had thought he was twenty-three until right before his birthday when she overheard him telling Marco he was turning nineteen. "¿Hey, I think you are twenty-three?" Bette had said.

"That's what my ID says." He had grinned at her.

Like his uncle Enrique, Mateo liked to wear necklaces, and since she had known him he'd gone from a gold cross to a heart with a ruby-handled sword through it to what now dangled on a chain around his neck, a jagged-edged half of a heart. She loved his sweet temperament, willingness to help out around her house, and his unwillingness to get drunk. He always had his hair stylishly cut, combed, and jelled so that the front stood up in curls. She wished he could find a girlfriend but knew he had a pretty slim chance of that here. He wasn't as brash as his uncle Enrique, flirting at school, so that wouldn't help. Without already having a husband, few Mexican women attempted the treacherous crossing into Arizona, so the number of available single women was minuscule.

Bette leaned over him to see what he was studying. Question words. "*Hola*, Mateo. Where is Marco?" she asked in English, emphasizing *where*.

"In bathroom," Mateo answered in English. Bette glanced over toward the bedroom door. She'd had to walk through there in the past to get to the bathroom but now chose to wait until she got home because she hated to invade the privacy of the three men who slept there. Now she could see Luis and Gustavo lying on top of their beds watching TV. She hoped Gustavo didn't look her way. She had somehow thought all Mexicans had dark eyes and his green ones made her sink into them, sort of like Just John's. She pushed away the image of his smile.

"It's good that you are studying," she said to Mateo. "Do you want help?"

"You can help me," Enrique said from the kitchen where he stood at the stove, about ten feet from the bed. "You can cut the onions."

Bette joined him there, glad to know what to do with herself in this tight space full of men but no Marco. In order to find room on the counter to chop the onions, she pushed aside a tall stack of eggs in flat purple trays, plastic bags of onions, oranges, and apples, a huge bunch of bananas, a jar of Nescafé, and a large plastic container full of sugar. Beside her, Enrique added salt and squeezed lime juice into the pot on the stove.

"*Calienta las tortillas*, Fernando. *La comida está lista*," he ordered his other nephew. When Fernando opened the refrigerator, Bette glanced in and saw at least five bags of tortillas, each bag about six inches high. There were also gallons of that fake orange juice she saw sold at grocery stores as fruit punch. Maybe it was no worse than the Kool-Aid she had drunk gallons of as a child, but what about all those plastic jugs, how many zillions were adding up at the landfill? Mike used to buy cases of bottled water before she had been able to talk him into getting a filter for the faucet. She finally convinced him to see the benefits, and he had come around. She bet John didn't use those because of his environmentalism.

Marco emerged from the bedroom, and her heart made a little jump. His orange tee-shirt set off his golden-brown skin and highlighted his muscular chest. He had on a pair of the shorts they'd bought at *una yarda*, which was what she now called them. Yard sales didn't exist in the part of Mexico where Marco was from but he'd quickly gotten the hang of them. They went out every weekend as he collected things to bring back to Mexico. She bent down to give him a kiss, not minding the half a foot difference in their heights, his five-four to her five-ten, and caressed her cheek along his. She loved the smoothness of his skin rather than those stubbly *gringos* with their five-o-clock shadows that turned her chin red.

If her hands hadn't been onion scented, she would have run them through his hair. She was fascinated by how it stood up on its own accord and had a shock of white in the front. Her friend Tracy had told her it was a sign of wisdom. His intelligence was one of the things that had made him stand out from the twenty other men in her English class. That and his thighs like tree trunks and his Aztec nose. Best not think about those right now.

Marco checked out her dress, raised his eyebrows, and smiled. Then the seven of them squeezed around the table sitting on wooden benches, white plastic chairs, and one of the beds. Enrique had prepared chicken and potatoes in red *chile*. He served her a bowl and showed her how to top it with the onions she'd chopped then squeeze more lime juice over it. The taste was delicious but getting the hang of eating a soupy item with bones in it with tortillas wasn't easy. Or tidy. The guys would hold a chicken leg with a tortilla, slurp the soup with a spoon, then eat the chicken with another tortilla or two. A roll of toilet paper was passed around when it was time to wipe fingers. Bette also used it to blow her nose because the meal was very spicy.

"*¿Está picosa?*" Gustavo asked her.

"*Sí, pero muy rica*," she replied.

Marco piped in and said that Bette liked fiery foods. He was proud of the fact that she could eat foods hotter than some of his friends, and enjoy it. The conversation continued around the table, and she gave up trying to follow it. She was still at the ping pong stage in her Spanish, needing to look at people's lips to help her understand what was being said. When a discussion hopped back and forth between people she got lost and couldn't find the thread again. It was okay with Marco and Enrique, his best friend who spent a lot of time at her house, but marginal with the others.

She thought of John and whether he'd been offering to be her personal computer repairman. What a gift that would be. Rather than have to submit a work order electronically and wait, she could just pick up the phone for instant service. Were there strings that went along with that? No computers here. She let her focus drift around the room. Marco's twin bed mattress was on the floor beside Enrique's which sat on a frame, making it about a foot higher. That must give them some small measure of privacy since their beds were side by side.

Marco's dresser was topped with a black stereo system and on top of that were two dolls in boxes, about twenty-four inches tall. One was a redhead dressed in a green plaid Scottish dress and the other a blond wearing a white Swiss pinafore. Beside them were toothpaste and a toothbrush, Old Spice cologne like she used to buy her dad for Father's Day, a jar of Vicks, sunblock provided by Bette, a hairbrush, and a jar with peacock feathers in it. Next to Marco's dresser was Enrique's topped with a laundry basket, two shoe boxes, and more toiletries. Little worlds, side-by-side.

The corner of the room was filled with a tow bar, tire chains, tools, a case of motor oil, various pieces of lumber, and cans of paint. Mateo's low black bureau on the near side of the door held a television, still going at quite a volume, another stereo, his English book and notebook, more tools, belts circled around a tray of jewelry, another laundry basket and yet another assortment of toiletries. Mateo's double bed was the one the men sat on to eat dinner. Men? They were more like boys. Marco was the oldest at thirty-eight, and three of the six were under twenty, here working away their youth to have money for a future in Mexico.

Her gaze settled on the broken glass in the windows with the plywood behind it. She felt like a voyeur and dropped her eyes to the table. Did she think she was an anthropologist? Why not just take photos? Her curiosity about this new world permeated and shamed her. She heard her name called and looked up to see all eyes on her. What was she doing here? Could they see through her to the thrill she got amongst all this strangeness? She guessed she was just as much an oddity to them as they were to her and hoped the exchange was balanced. Mateo smiled, and she asked him in English, "What did he say?"

"Want more food?" He lifted his chin toward Marco, standing at the stove.

"*No, no más,*" she protested when she finally understood the question. She struggled having to put her vegetarianism on hold. Their one-pot cooking usually included meat or chicken, and it didn't always go down easily. She'd been deeply affected by reading *Animal Liberation* and had quit eating meat except when it was unavoidable like visiting someone's grandmother. Visions of chickens living their lives out in cages stacked one on top of the other, their feet growing around the wire, haunted her still. Recently her choice became even more important to her after learning about the environmental damage of factory-farmed meat, chicken, and fish. She hadn't gone against her values with Mike over this, but if she didn't bend a little now, what would she eat when she was with Marco and his friends? Why had she ever thought Mexicans lived on beans and rice?

"*¿Poquito más?*" Marco asked, standing with a spoon hovering over the pot.

"No, *gracias.*" She was already getting to know this dance.

"*Aqui, más papas,*" he said, now beside the table with pot in hand, holding up a spoonful of potatoes.

"No, *gracias. Estóy satisfecha.*" She patted her stomach with her hand and looked up smiling. Once she'd said, *Estóy llena,* proud to have figured that out by herself with her dictionary. I'm full. Marco had been quick to correct her, stating that glasses are full and cups are full, but not humans. It was not *educado* to say you were full. You were satisfied. Bette had argued that it was quite normal to hear that in English but he wouldn't hear of it in Spanish. That wasn't the first time that he had made a strong point separating himself from less educated Mexicans. Bette never heard Marco tell others that in Mexico he had been a veterinarian, but his language showed he took pride in being educated.

"Betty," Enrique said. "*¿Para que están papas?*" He was speaking in Spanish for the benefit of the others, and she knew she was being set up.

"*Para más nalgas,*" she replied on cue and got the expected laugh. And it was true. The more potatoes she ate, the bigger her butt got.

Bette washed her bowl and spoon like the other men, then Marco pointed out where he had hung the large black velvet painting of the Taj Mahal with peacocks in the foreground that they had found at *una yarda* the weekend before. He had debated with himself over spending two dollars for it. It was definitely worth it because it hid some of the scars and holes in the walls as did the calendar from Ranch Market, the giant Mexican grocery store in Phoenix.

She was sweating and started to take off her sandals, but Mateo said, "No, no," and showed her how the carpet was lifting up where it joined the linoleum. "*Puede cortar los pies,*" he said, running his fingernail across his palm to show her what he meant, grimacing at the imaginary cut.

Later when Bette reflected back on that night, she remembered *Señor Cuentos* most of all. He had come over after dinner and been introduced, but she didn't catch his name. She dubbed him Mr. Stories after sitting around the table and bed, drinking fruit punch and listening to the older man tell stories. He had a thin moustache and wore a beautiful high-sided cowboy hat, western shirt, and boot cut jeans, so she assumed he was telling ranch stories. She hadn't understood even one of them but loved watching the others laugh. They would throw their heads back, all at the same time and out would pour hoots and chortles in different tones. His words sounded like *cala cala cala*, only music to her, and they were the dancers, moving together in perfect rhythm. At one point she understood him when he'd asked, *¿Ella puede entender español?* Marco assured him that Bette couldn't understand much, even though she was smiling at him when he said it. Sure enough, she missed the bulk of that story, too, which must have been racy. That was okay. She would have her own risqué time with Marco later that night.

CHAPTER 3

The packing list
Camare
Short
Water
Cooler (phonix)
Naps
Sun bloque
Hat
Tee
Hat pot
Swame an sut
Home workh
Chocat
Phon, charge

Bette rode her bike to work almost all year except for in the summer when she either got too sweaty riding home in the heat or drenched from the monsoon rains. Since her town had no public transportation, she walked those few months to stay dryer, only driving on the days she would teach ESL classes after work. The entire route was on sidewalks except for where it passed *el desempleo*, the pick-up spot for workers which was kitty-corner from her two-story office building. Warren, the town of forty thousand, considered itself a retirement Mecca, not too big, not too small. And being in the mountains it had four seasons, not too hot, not too cold. By the tone of frequent letters to the editor, however, some of her fellow residents thought the Mexicans who stood or squatted on the hard-packed dusty earth looking for work were causing a blight to grow in their Shangri-La. Did they even know there were Central and South Americans here besides Mexicans?

This morning there were thirty men and boys stretched out for about a quarter of a block. As Bette walked by she tugged at her linen skirt and dropped her eyes, occasionally raising them to glance at the guys to her right.

"*Buenos dias*, Gilberto," she said to one of her students she recognized in the crowd of black-haired men. "How are you?" she changed to English.

"*Estoy llanta*," he replied, smiling.

She hated walking in front of groups of men, Anglos or Mexicans, so being able to have a little conversation made her feel less self-conscious. They became individuals rather than a silent, intimidating mass. The letter-writers should come to her ESL class to get to know these hard-working men as humans, not *illegals*. Maybe hearing the unintelligible joke – I'm a tire – was not such good advertising to get more of the men to come to class, but on the other hand, Marco had told her it was a point of pride for a Mexican to be with a white woman. Besides being a sign of assimilation, the others knew he might have it a little easier in this foreign country. If the guys looking for work wanted to imagine that students who learned English at the church had help from the teachers when needed, let them. It was true, and they could certainly use the assistance.

The finance department was in the throes of preparing for their annual audit, and there had been many people coming and going from her office, trying to make sure they had everything in order. Audits could be a little stressful, but Bette had capitalized on her father's training to be efficient, improve systems, don't make mistakes. She was ready for the auditors. It was the challenges that came in human form that stretched her. People were late with their travel documents, used the wrong account codes, and made exceptions where they didn't understand the repercussions. Nothing to do about that but clean up their messes and move on. She'd worked at the Bowman Institute for three years and had her systems running smoothly.

"Hi, Just Bette." John stood in her doorway, smiling broadly. She stood and rolled her shoulders back, loosening the tension.

"Out patching problems, Just John?" she said.

"One after the other. People are kind of freaking out."

"You're getting a trial by fire being hired at audit time."

"No better way to learn," he said. "You ready?"

Bette nodded. "I like shaking up my normal routine. Boredom's the worst." Bette had a shelf-life of about two-to-three years on a job and was nearing the expiration date at this one. "Why stress and worry about what you tell the auditors? Do your job well, work with them, and you can learn a great deal from their expertise."

"Sounds like a solid plan."

"And afterward, my mini-vacation." If Bette hadn't felt self-conscious standing so close to John, she would have done a little happy dance. "I'm going to Tucson for training on the new database."

A scowl traveled across John's forehead. Bette tilted her head at him. "What?"

"I wanted to go, but they're sending someone with more seniority."

"That's only fair. There'll be others. And it'll be hot."

"That's right." He gave a half-smile.

Bette remembered her manners and didn't rub in that she would be poolside when not in the training. And that Marco was joining her.

"I heard that Spruce Mountain's a nice place to hike in the summer. Cooler at the higher elevation. Would you like to go for a hike when you're back?"

What a treat from hiking alone. Tracy was now focused on Don, Cat usually doing things with her husband, and Marco would never hike for fun. Before she'd thought it all the way through she'd agreed. It was okay. They were just friends. It was a hike, not a date. And besides, it was on the other side of her adventure to Tucson with Marco.

It would be fun at the swimming pool, finding more authentic Mexican food, and spending hours in bed with Marco. But playing tour guide was what she truly looked forward to. She had left home as a teenager and found a place to live in the liberal city of Portland, Oregon. Her two housemates at the time which she found in the classified ads of the Oregonian newspaper could just as easily have led her into drugs or religion but instead they took her under their wings and introduced her to the topics from their generation: Cesar Chavez and the farmworker boycotts, reproductive freedom, gender equality, animal rights, and environmental protection. Advocating for the underdog struck a chord in her that resonated with her early experiences of being the new kid in class and not belonging. She'd gone to a dozen schools in more than twice that many moves before she made her escape and left home.

Teaching ESL was an outgrowth of her early experiences. Her students were carpenters, landscapers, and service industry workers here to try to make a better life for their families. Helping to smooth their transition into the United States allowed her to re-imagine a different childhood for herself.

Bette remembered her first-day, mid-year in eighth grade, getting to the corner an hour early, not exactly sure when the school bus would arrive and not daring to miss it. She waited shivering in the cold, her legs turning bright red between her white knee socks and where the hem of her dress rode. Even so, when the bus pulled up she left the cold reluctantly and climbed in to look for an open seat. Holding her backpack close to her chest she sat in the first available spot then heard some boy say, "That seat's taken." Bette popped up and went back a few rows and was lowering herself when she heard, "Can't sit there," this time followed by snickers. The bus driver was not any help as she moved toward the back, accompanied by, "Not there," and rough laughter until she finally slumped into the last row and dropped her head on her backpack.

With Marco, she felt like the guide she had always yearned for in the schools and towns she passed through. Though with him, it sometimes felt like being with a visitor from another planet. The first time he helped her put gas in her car, she had to teach him every step from orienting her debit card the right way and whipping it in and out of the machine, to selecting the grade of gas, all the way through to washing the windshield. He never really got the hang of that, always leaving big streaks from not pressing hard enough and wiping downward instead of across the windows. At least he no longer put the squeegee back with the handle in the water.

"*¿Qué estás haciendo?*" he'd asked once when she'd pulled over to the side of the road.

Not knowing the words for *fire truck* or *siren*, she pointed to her ear and said, "¿Can't you hear the noise?" They waited until the fire truck passed then all the cars drove back into the lanes.

"No one ever stops for *bomberos* in Mexico," Marco said. He spoke some more which Bette didn't understand, but she recognized what his arm was indicating as it wove in and around traffic, getting stuck, honking its horn.

"And all the *semáforos*," he said, throwing his head back. "And people stop for them here."

It took Bette a little while to understand what *semáforos* were, what with driving and trying to decipher another language, but she figured out they were traffic lights. Marco said there weren't very many in Mexico and that often people would stop for them but then go through if it was clear. Even if they had the red. Bette had never been to Mexico, which only added to the magic and mystery of her new life. What was it really like?

Marco and his friends found out the hard way about the differences in laws between the countries. She heard pieces of it in ESL class, and Marco went over it when they got home, explaining and embellishing.

"You can't pay off the police here," he said, a tone of incredulity creeping into his voice. "In Mexico, if you don't have insurance or a light is broken on your car, you..." He used his fingers to demonstrate giving a bribe. "And the policeman lets you go."

"Not here." she said. They didn't have *the bite*, or at least she'd never lived in a place where that was done.

He had been to movies in Mexico, but taking Marco to his first theater production turned out to be a joy for both of them. Bette chose *Annie* because he might be able to understand some of it. Also a colleague's daughter was one of the orphans. She was a little concerned about him becoming sad seeing all those little kids since he had left two young daughters behind in Mexico. Marco's wife had died of cancer, and he and his children had been living with his sister, who helped care for them, along with her own three teenage children.

When Bette was first getting involved with Marco, she had asked him to tell his story of crossing the border. It ended up taking several tellings as her Spanish wasn't good enough to grasp it all. Marco said his sister Perla had tried to talk him out of it. She knew that Marco's friend Enrique had been bugging him for years to come to the U.S. and Perla wanted to know why now.

"I want to make money so *mis niñas* can go to a good school and learn English," he told his sister.

Perla had agreed that it was better than working in a factory like she did.

"With English, they'll be able to work in a bank and make a good living."

Bette hoped that Perla had said she would miss him, but didn't know if they spoke in terms of affection. Marco had been three when their mother died, and he told Bette he had trouble talking about feelings.

When retelling this story, Marco said he knew Perla was worried about her own life without Marco as she had become more and more dependent upon him after her husband had left. Marco drove her to *el centro de abastos*, helped with money where he could, and was a strong presence in her children's lives. Bette knew firsthand how strong a presence that could be when she had heard him lecturing one of Perla's daughters. His niece must have been glad when Marco's phone card finally ran out, and the call was cut off.

Now in Arizona, six months later, Marco was soaking up his new world, starting to send money home with his lucky full-time construction job, and feeling special with his American girlfriend. Bette was excited about taking him to his first hotel, showing him the little soaps and shampoos, the coffee maker and ice bucket, and the TV with the remote at the foot of the big, plush bed. Unfortunately, it didn't work out as she'd planned due to *la migra* – the border patrol.

***

"Marco," Bette asked, "¿Will you start a list of things we need for our trip to Tucson?" He was sitting at the kitchen table sipping a cup of coffee while she cut up and stir-fried vegies and tofu. "The hotel where we're staying is old but very beautiful, *pero muy bonito.* The swimming pool is huge. It's like a park. There are orange trees and...and...that other fruit... yellow and big." She showed him the size with her hands while holding the knife.

"*Toronja*," he said.

"And *muchas* palm trees. And *verde*..." She moved her hand level with the floor, trying to indicate grass.

"*Pasto*. Put the knife down, *chaparita*," he said, shaking his head at her.

"*Es muy tranquilo. Con mucho paz.* It's rare in Arizona. And pink bougainvillea, too." The birds at the hotel woke her every morning, and she started her days smiling. "And they give you breakfast with *muchisima* fruit and eggs and..." How to say toast? "...And bread and potatoes."

Marco was smiling at her now. She went to him, held his head in her hands, and gave him a kiss. "Okay. We'll need the camera and our shorts. It'll be hot. Let's bring the big jugs of water. Oh, and the cooler for Phoenix." She always stocked up at a Trader Joe's market when she headed south, and Marco was developing a taste for his own favorites, too. "Maps," she added. "I need my maps for both cities."

"And your sunblock and hat, *mi güerita*," Marco added, referring to her pale skin.

"I'll take you to see the snake that is a..." She used her hands to show him how big it was but gave up when she couldn't figure out the word for 'bridge.' If he'd loved birds, she would take him to the wastewater treatment plant which was a magnet for thousands of thirsty birds. They could go to the big used bookstore which had an entire section of books in Spanish. Had he ever been to a bookstore?

After finishing dinner they started piling clothes and items from Marco's list into the spare room, which served as office and craft room, occasionally a guest room, and now a staging area.

"¿You're sure you can get off work? *¿No está un problema con tu jefe?*" Bette asked.

Marco had been searching for work for months at the pick-up spot for day laborers, getting a day here, two days there before he landed a full-time job as a carpenter. Both of them were thrilled with his good luck. He didn't have a car, so Bette drove him to a grocery store parking lot in the morning where the foreman, Scott – or eScott as Marco pronounced it, seemingly unable to start a word with an S sound – met him in his huge truck. She would leave him there with his tool belt and jumbo lunch of a Dagwood sandwich Mexicanized with slices of avocado and *chiles*, chips, fruit, a baggie full of cookies, an energy drink or two, and a gallon of water.

"No," Marco said. "eScott told me it's not a problem." She imagined it wasn't. They were probably glad to offer him something to keep him happy so he would stay working for them. His body was hard with muscles, and when they worked around her yard, he was a dynamo. She guessed he toiled like an ox for the carpenters and they would have to pull their own weight for a day. But then again, maybe they would miss him as much for his sense of humor as for his strength.

Last week they were sitting in her car having just pulled in from what seemed like a day of errands when he said, "Pleeeease." He was trying to get her to go back out one more time to get avocados which they had forgotten. Marco wanted to make *coctel de camarón* for dinner and couldn't think of eating it without its traditional topping of chopped cilantro and avocados.

"No," Bette said. "It's delicious without those." She knew he thought she was just being lazy, and selfish, but it had more to do with being opposed to driving for one item that they could do without. She didn't know if it would be better or worse if he got his own car. She would probably drive less, but they'd still be harming the environment as much.

"*Por favorrrr*," Marco said, making two fingers kneel on the palm of his other hand. The stubbiness of his fingers turned into little legs looked just like his short, stout body. It was too cute for her to say no.

"You win," she said laughing and started the car.

The night before they were scheduled to leave on their mini vacation, Enrique invited her over to their house for dinner. "*La migra* have been showing up in Tucson," he said.

"I've been going there for years. I've never seen the Border Patrol," she argued, but as she said it she realized that she had never specifically looked for them. Those were her pre-Marco years. Doubt crept into her confidence that he would be safe. "When were you in Tucson?" she asked Enrique.

His jaw clamped. They both knew he never went farther south than Phoenix. "My friend tell me they are there."

Bette turned and looked at Marco. He was not helping her challenge Enrique's opinion that it was unsafe. He likely didn't understand the conversation. Because Enrique had been in the U.S. the longest, he knew the ropes. Marco must be wavering between fear of getting caught and his desire for special time with her. Her feelings exactly. She wanted to talk with him but instead inwardly railed against her rotten Spanish that intimidated her into silence in front of the other four men in the house.

She looked at Enrique again and tried to get inside his head to see if he was being truthful and protective of his friend or just jealous and trying to ruin their plans. She walked outside and wanted to scratch Enrique's ailing cars with her keys as she squeezed through to her own.

***

That night Bette wouldn't allow herself to talk Marco into going – she would never forgive herself if he got arrested and deported. Instead, they made slow and sweet love with Bette crying quietly and then she drifted off to sleep with Marco spooning her. She tried to get her friends to go to Tucson with her, but it was too last-minute. Tracy and Don had another couple coming for dinner, and Cat and Jeff both had to work. What fun it would have been to have Rosa and Felipe's children with her but she couldn't risk them being deported either.

Sitting alone beside the pool in Tucson, Bette wrote Marco a letter. It was her attempt to connect, even though she only knew the present tense in Spanish. She threw in occasional indicators that meant past tense – *pasado*. When she got home, they would be able to decipher it together, sitting side-by-side at the kitchen table.

> *Quierdo Marco,*
>
> *¡I wish you are here! Enrique is not correct. There is no migra here. Only me and a lot of happy people. It is hot, but I hop in the swimming pool when it is too much. Brincan, brincan los borregos. In the past, I am in Tucson many times and never see la migra. But, I do not (pasado) want to put you in danger. I prefer (pasado) that you stay in Warren where it is more safe.*
>
> *I am sorry. It is a huge pool with about thirty children and fifteen adults. Everyone is bilingual, and I do not know where they are from. If you are here, we play in the pool and the bed. We lie beside the pool, and you can read your new Harry Potter book.*
>
> *I miss you, Marco, and I am sorry I listen (pasado) to Enrique and take (pasado) his advice.*
>
> *Con cariño, tu Bette*

On the drive home, Bette saw a Border Patrol SUV and a police car beside a broken-down truck on the north side of Tucson. Two Hispanic men were standing together on the shoulder of the highway. Surely Marco would be safe with her dependable Subaru. When she got home he was at work, and she found a note on the kitchen table. With the help of her dictionary, she interpreted it.

To: Bette
From: Marco
With much affection, I say these words to you that I miss you so much. How I need you by my side because you are mi compañera, my reason to live. When I go to our house I miss you because I cannot find you and I desire to hug you, kiss you, sleep with you, talk, laugh.

Now that you are not here, I am alone and sad. I wait with great anxiety that we are together. Many kisses for you, my love. Marco

Bette made a cup of tea and checked her voicemail.

"Hey, it's John. Just checking to see how your time was. Hope you had fun in the sun. Let me know when you want to go for that hike."

He had left his number, but Bette needed time to think before she called him back. She found another note on her pillow.

To: Bette
From: Marco
Hi, my love. It is good to come to our house, our nest of love and passion. The days that you were not here were very sad and very solitary. I have a great need to be together with you, with your voice, the color of your body, to touch your very soft and warm hair, to listen to your voice during your dreams.

I like it when I come to your home, and you await me, you ask me what I want to eat or what food I prefer for my lunch and if I want sex now or later. This is muy bonito and significant. It is as if you are my new wife. It has been only a little time since we have been together, but it seems like years. Bien venida otra vez a mi vida Bette.

The meaning of that last line eluded her and her efforts with her red dictionary, but she wasn't worrying over it now. More immediate was figuring out her own feelings in English and finding the willingness to communicate them to Marco and John.

CHAPTER 4

The next week, Bette and Marco awoke at five to the ringing telephone. It was Rosa asking if Bette would take her to the emergency room. As she put things into her backpack, Marco complained about her helping Rosa.

"I spend plenty of time at the hospital with your friend when his daughter cut her arm."

"Make Felipe take her."

"He has a job."

"So do you."

She yanked the door open and left, wondering why he was so upset.

When she arrived at Rosa's home, all the bedding had been picked up off of the living room floor, and Felipe was sitting on the two-part sectional blue couch. The living room/bedroom combo was about twelve feet square and had stucco walls rounded at the corners. There was a border of flowered, maroon wallpaper circling the room close to the ceiling. Rosa had tried to make use of the color by putting up lacy, maroon curtains in the front window and the doorway leading to the kitchen. Felipe had laid a beige carpet over their previously torn, stained indoor-outdoor flooring which had increased the livability of the space a hundred-fold.

Rosa was ready to go and grabbed her purse hanging on a nail in the wall.

"Tell me again what the problem is," Bette said as she drove them to the hospital. She was preparing herself for having to interpret so wanted a jumpstart on the Spanish terminology.

"*Lo siento, Betty*," Rosa said, pronouncing her name with the same y and strong t that Enrique did. "It hurts so bad I couldn't wait any longer." She went on to explain how she had been having blood in her urine for several days, using *pee-pee*, the universal term, and hoped it would go away with lots of liquids. It had only gotten worse until Felipe had convinced her to call Bette.

"*Está bien*, Rosa. There are not going to be many people at the hospital..." How to say *so early*, Bette wondered. "We should see a doctor..." *Quickly?* "...rapidly." She and Rosa had become friends through their contact at the ESL class and often went to garage sales on Saturdays when Marco was working. Now Bette tried to distract her by asking what she had found while Bette was in Tucson. Rosa hadn't felt well enough to go.

Bette explained to the receptionist what Rosa's problem was and then they found a seat in the waiting area as far away as they could from the man who sounded like he was hacking up pieces of lung. When they were called into the interview room, Bette was relieved to see that the hospital had upgraded their interpreting services since the last time she had been there. Two blue telephones were now on the desk, and the woman questioning Rosa spoke English into one and Rosa, Spanish into the other. Somewhere out in the world was a bilingual person helping them to understand one another. Bette doodled the two phones on a notepad while listening to the three-way medical interview. There were times with Marco when she had almost been desperate enough to ask Enrique, or even a bilingual stranger off the street, to interpret in an argument for them. Someone, anyone to help her express herself. Marco seemed able to get his intentions across with body language, but Bette craved the logic of words. Where could she buy one of those blue phones?

They were led into an examining room, and Bette settled into a corner chair as Rosa put on the flimsy tie-in-the-back gown. Bette looked away but caught a glimpse of Rosa's black push-up bra. Too bad that's one of the things their cultures had in common, using cleavage to appear more attractive.

Both the nurse and doctor used Bette to assist them in interpreting rather than use the blue phone on the wall behind Rosa's bed. Bette guessed they knew quite a bit of Spanish and were only relying on Bette to confirm what they had heard Rosa say. Or maybe they were just trying to keep costs down. She saw how vulnerable Rosa was in the U.S. to have to depend on Bette's poor Spanish to relay medical information to a doctor.

The nurse returned with the results from the urine test. "We're going to give her antibiotics intravenously." She hung the bag of fluids and laid out her supplies for the needle. "We rarely see an infection this bad. She must be in a lot of pain."

"Yes, she is." Bette raised her hand and made a fist to relay the nurse's instructions to Rosa.

"We'll also give her a scrip of antibiotics that she should continue when she's home." The nurse leaned over Rosa and said, "You're going to feel a poke."

"*Va estar dolor,*" Bette explained. What the heck was a poke? A stab? Would she ever get fluent in Spanish, she wondered. It seemed overwhelming at times, the learning curve so steep she kept sliding backward. If only she had started when she was younger.

As the nurse was adjusting the flow of liquids and injecting the antibiotics, Bette said, "Your pants look like utility pants for nurses." Oh so easy in English.

"Aren't these great?" the nurse asked. "There's a pocket for everything – scissors, tape, pens, gauze pads." She looked competent and comfortable in her hiker-type pants and sturdy tennis shoes with her hair pulled out of the way in a tight ponytail. "It'll take about an hour for the meds to work their way in. Does she need another blanket? Her bed raised a little?"

After the nurse finished adjusting Rosa and they were alone again, Rosa told Bette that the nurses in Mexico were nothing like the ones in the U.S.

"¿How?" Bette asked.

"They jab the needle in your arm. They're rude. They don't do anything to make you feel better."

"It's not like that here," Bette said. "My sister is a nurse, and she can be...*fuerte.*" Strong. Bette searched her mind for a word for *demanding.* "And...*serio.*" Serious. She scrunched up her brow. "But it's to help the person, not to be...." What was the word for *mean?* Bad? Not quite it.

"I understand."

They drifted into silence and could hear the man with the phlegmy cough in the room next door. Bette glanced at the full bag of liquids dripping into Rosa's vein.

"¿Would it be okay if you told me your story of crossing the desert?"

"*Si*, Betty, *sí*."

"¿Why do you want to come here?"

"I missed Felipe." Bette looked at Rosa and remembered her posing in the crook of his arm at the Grand Canyon, sitting close and listening to him pronounce words for her in ESL class. They were both in their early thirties and had almost been married longer than they'd been single. Felipe had gotten a good full-time job as a welder and knew he would be here as long as it lasted or until they had enough money saved to build a house in Mexico. Rosa thought she could speed up their return if she also worked in the U.S.

"¿Do you cross with anyone else you know?" Bette knew that Rosa was translating her words into past tense.

"Amaya and I came together." The sisters-in-law had taken the bus up from central Mexico to a border town with Amaya's two-year-old son and Gerardo and Isa who were nine and five at the time.

"I hated Nogales," Rosa said. Bette knew that if her arm wasn't immobilized by the IV, Rosa would have crossed it over her chest. "All these coyotes were pawing at us, trying to get us to go with them. ¡*Señora*! ¡*Señora*!" Rosa grimaced. "I wanted to go into a hotel, lock the door, and never come out." But she told Bette how they had to make the rendezvous with the woman who would drive the children across the border and up to Warren where their fathers were waiting for them.

"¿Do you know the woman?"

"No." Rosa dropped her eyes then raised them to look at Bette and shook her head ever so slowly. Bette's heart ached for Rosa having to give her children to a complete stranger. "We paid two thousand dollars each. When we said goodbye we expected to see them the next day." Like all the others Bette had talked to, the men who guided the immigrants across the desert – the coyotes – promised the hike across the desert would only take a day.

A male nurse dressed in navy blue scrubs came in to check Rosa's IV and take her temperature and blood pressure. Bette left the room and called her supervisor, leaving a message saying she might be a little late that morning. When the nurse left, Bette turned to Rosa and said, "*Dígame*."

"It took us three days. *Tres días. Gracias a Dios*, that Felipe told me to wear sturdy boots. At first, I felt ashamed when the other women looked at my boots then glanced into my face. Later I felt sorry for them. They must have expected trails." She used her one free arm to weave a path to help Bette understand the word. "Their stylish shoes were scratched and torn, and some didn't have heels at the end."

Rosa told Bette how she'd imagined the desert would be flat, but it was only like that for a little while. "There are mountains near my town, but I've never walked in them. We hiked up and down. *Eterno*. And it was..." After seeing Bette's scrunched brow, Rosa rocked her hand side-to-side to show Bette what the word meant.

Unstable. She nodded. Bette had learned the hard way not to step on big rocks when hiking if she could find another route around them between the pokey cactus bushes and the spiny, piercing trees. The rocks looked stable, but some rolled anyway, and she would have to do a dance shuffle to maintain her balance.

"¿Do you or Amaya get hurt?"

"*Si, muchas* scratches." She dragged her clawed painted nails across her arm. "The trees were like giant rose bushes without the beauty – dark, gray, and threatening." Flesh-ripping mesquite, Bette thought. Rosa told her how they grabbed at her hair and arms and tore her jeans. It was terrible having to walk at night.

"And there were balls of yellow cactus dangling off the sides of my boots like lemons on a tree." She told Bette she'd never seen anything so tenacious. If she kicked at it with her other foot, it just stuck to that boot. When she had time to knock it with a stick, it left half its spines behind on the leather. She tried to avoid those soft-looking vicious pincushions. Jumping cholla, Bette told her.

"But Amaya had it the worst," Rosa continued. "She had her menstruation and walked hunched over with her arms folded across her stomach with a..." Rosa squeezed her face into a frown, "on her face." Rosa told her how she carried Amaya's food to lighten her load but even so, every time they stopped for a moment Amaya curled into a squat. "*Gracias a Dios* that on her worst night we didn't have to run from *la migra* with their devil-red laser lights."

"Then we ran out of water." Of course. Bette had heard this before. Rosa told her how a few men went off to find some while the others waited. What they brought back from a cattle tank was cloudy and rank. "Amaya got sick when we arrived in Warren, but it didn't affect me, only a little nausea."

"¿Do you have any trouble with the men or the guides?"

"No. Felipe was worried, too, but that part was fine." She laughed and said, "When I got here, I didn't think he would recognize me." Rosa told her how her face was scratched from bumping into things during the night, and she smelled like Felipe did when he came home from work.

"But you're not happy here," Bette said.

"No." Rosa's gaze shifted downward. "I miss Mexico and my sisters and my parents." Bette knew that Rosa hadn't been able to find a full-time job in Arizona and only worked once in a while cleaning houses and a doctor's office.

"¿When will Felipe be ready to go back to Mexico?"

"I don't know. ¿When's Marco going to return?"

"I don't know, either."

A third nurse came in and while unhooking Rosa from the IV gave instructions for the antibiotics but lost patience when Bette couldn't interpret fast enough. She began rattling off the instructions without giving her time to interpret, as if Rosa wasn't in the room with them. Bette wrote everything down and went over the instructions while driving Rosa home, then headed into work.

Bette stepped into her boss's office around nine. One wall was covered by black four-drawer file cabinets. A second was wall-to-wall bookshelves stuffed with wide black binders. Along the third wall were two chocolate brown chairs with an end table between them. Her supervisor sat at her desk beside a large window. She was focused on her oversized computer screen, great for looking at columns of numbers all day.

"Hi, Lynn," Bette said. "I'm sorry I'm late. I took a friend to the hospital. She had a bladder infection."

"It's fine, Bette. Is she okay?"

"Yes, she was in a lot of pain." Bette related the ER visit to Lynn, leaving out the part about the cloudy urine thick with infection because Lynn had a touchy stomach and wouldn't have been able to stand hearing the details. "I'll make the time up this evening." She was glad her supervisor was so accommodating. It helped that Lynn's schedule required flexibility because of her three active kids.

"Was she one of your students?"

"Yes, and now a friend. Her husband couldn't take her because he starts work at six. And they needed someone who spoke English."

"Who pays for that?" Lynn asked. She swiveled slightly in her leather chair behind the polished mahogany desk.

"I don't know. The person at the payment area spoke Spanish, so I wasn't involved. I know Rosa paid cash when she had her tooth pulled."

"Maybe she has Access."

"What's Access?" Bette asked.

"Insurance coverage for poor citizens."

"Maybe. I don't know how that works." Bette felt her chest tightening, so she took a calming breath and told her boss how Rosa's husband had state and federal taxes withheld from his check that he would never see.

"How did he get a social security number?"

"They can buy counterfeit ones." Bette watched Lynn's eyes move right then left and wondered if she was running through a mental list of the company's employees. "Undocumented workers paid six billion dollars in taxes last year but can't get refunds and will never be able to use their social security." Bette had read her students' letters from the IRS stating their name didn't match their social security number, and they needed to correct that if they wanted to collect in the future.

"Your volunteer work has been an education for me," Lynn said.

"And for me."

***

That evening Bette worked at clearing the kitchen table because Enrique, Mateo, and Fernando were coming over for dinner, and her paper piles were getting out of hand. The last time they had been over for dinner she had been standing at the stove heating tortillas when Fernando had asked her in Spanish, always in Spanish, how tall she was. She told him in feet and inches. Though none of them could convert it to the metric system, that didn't deter Fernando, and he'd insisted, "I'm taller than you."

"No, you're not." She wondered briefly if she was using the correct form of the *to be* verb but let it go. "Stand up." He shook his head no. "*Sí.*" He walked over from the kitchen table and stood beside her. He was the youngest of Enrique's nephews and Marco's friends, and she had to remind herself of that fact. His height and good looks made her see him as a man. He had broad shoulders narrowing to thin hips, an expressive mouth, and an open gaze that did not break contact.

"Hey, take off your boots," Bette said as she looked levelly into his eyes.

"No, don't let him." cried Mateo. "*¡Fuchila! ¡Huele a queso podrido!*"

"I'm taller," Fernando said again.

Bette waved Marco over, and he took over flipping the corn tortillas and placing them in a red-and-white checked dishtowel sitting on a plate. She pointed at Fernando's boots and waggled her fingers. "Take them off." She got a pen from the counter and backed up against the doorframe.

"*Tu cabello*," Fernando said.

"¿What horse?" Bette asked, and the others laughed.

"No, *cabello* means hair," Marco said. "*Caballo* means horse."

"Oh, that's sure clear," she said, rolling her eyes. Her hair was piled on top of her head and would have added an inch to her height. She took out the clip and let it fall about her shoulders.

Enrique leveled the pen over her head and made a mark on the doorframe. Fernando sat on the floor and tugged off his round-toed work boots, then stood against the wall, sucked in his breath, and stretched upward. As he stepped away, Bette said, "*Dicho y hecho.*" Said and done. "Sorry, Fernando. You're only fifteen and still..." She moved her hand up in increments. "Maybe one day."

Today as she finished setting the table, she wondered what new term she would learn that evening.

Marco was putting lamb shanks and shoulders in the pressure cooker, his favorite piece of kitchen equipment. Sometimes after payday instead of having beans and vegies for dinner they had Marceliano or Geronimo. All those vowels in one of her student's name, Marceliano, and the Spanish word for seafood, *mariscos*, had gotten slurred together in her mouth one too many times. So they called them Marcelianos – a man's name – and not shrimp. Marco's workmate Geronimo moved his mouth around just so while he placed a nail or cut a board, so his friends nicknamed him *Borrego* – sheep. It didn't take long before that became another familyism. Tonight they were having Geronimo, their delectable lamb dinner.

Any opportunity they came up with to be creative with their languages, they took. It wasn't the deep, intellectually stimulating conversation like she'd had with John on their hike, but she had also never had this type of fun. Marco and she were both natural hams, and having to use facial expressions and sign language to get across meaning was merely an excuse for what they both loved doing, seeing the humor in life and making others laugh.

"¿How was your day?" Marco asked her.

"*Bien*. Rosa is doing better after the hospital. She told me her story of crossing the border. ¿Do we have enough Geronimo for everyone?"

"¿Why didn't someone else take her? ¿One of the other teachers?"

"I speak better Spanish. And she's my friend."

"¿Can you bring me a little garlic?" Marco asked. Bette began to clean the husks off of the cloves, but Marco interrupted the process. "*No, están bien, como este.*" He tossed them in the pot with the meat, papery sheaths and all. "¿Why did you take time from work to help Rosa?"

"Marco, she was in pain. And *ademas*, besides," Bette loved being able to use a recently-acquired word, "I have vacation time I can take. It was only a few hours." She began to empty the dish drainer then turned and looked at Marco who was washing *tomatillos* in the sink. "¿Why are you mad that I helped Rosa?"

"She's not your friend. She's like other Mexicans who use you."

"No, she's not," Bette said. "¿How can you say that? We go to *yardas* on the weekends when you're working. She brought us flan. ¿Why is it okay to do things for you and not for my other friends?"

He clamped the lid on the pressure cooker, placed the wiggly thing on top, and turned the flame up high.

"Marco, you're different. You're my sweetheart." She wrapped her arms around him, pulling him close. His head rested on her chest. "I'm your *chaparita*," she said, using one of his favorite words for her, short one. "But I have other friends, too."

He pulled away and got up on his toes, tilted his head, and squinted at her out of one eye, still having to look up at her with the substantial difference in their heights.

"Oh, I'm afraid," Bette said, holding her hands in front of her mouth. "*Qué grandote.*" What a tall one.

Bette would have liked to confide in Marco that she, too, sometimes got tired of helping her friends and complete strangers, but she wasn't going to give him ammunition to use against her. Because of her knowledge of Spanish, however limited, she had found herself in uncomfortable situations more and more often such as talking to the deputy sheriff about an unlicensed driver, a pot-bellied, gruff, bearded man about a towed car, a used car dealer about exchanging two cars for one. In her own life she tried to keep away from such confrontations, but now was being forced to put aside her timidity to help where needed. Marco would think she wanted to quit doing it, but she didn't, she was just tired.

Even Tracy wanted her to slow down, back off. When she had called to see if acupuncture would help mediate the side-effects of Rosa's strong antibiotics, Tracy had asked Bette if she was doing too much. Where Marco was expressing jealousy, Tracy seemed to be analyzing Bette like a medical professional as much as a friend. But Bette had a lot of energy. Besides, thought Bette, *if not me, who?*

The next night she didn't last long at her margarita night with her friend Cat. The low-lighting of the wine bar wasn't helping with her sleepiness, but she loved the ambiance there. The dark paneling was accented by Mediterranean prints, each heavy oak table had its own small lamp, and overstuffed couches surrounded a cozy fireplace.

"I can't believe I'm eating this," Bette said. A piece of cheese stretched from the bowl of French onion soup to her mouth, and she bit into it trying to break the connection. "I needed a little comfort food after my time at the hospital."

"I can never turn down this gruyere either," Cat said. "I hate hospitals. Did you wash your hands after touching the doorknobs? There's no way I'd do what you do – going to hospitals to help people – even if I could speak Spanish."

"My sister the nurse turned me into a compulsive hand-washer. I think they should have sinks outside of hospitals so people can wash right away before getting into their cars."

"Yes. With one of those foot pedals."

"Exactly."

Their main courses arrived, and Bette tried not to think about the farmworkers bent over to weed and harvest the delicious mixed greens she was about to eat. The dried pear slices, feta cheese, and pecans atop the colorful lettuce made her mouth water.

"Did I tell you I only have periods every three months now? I'm on birth control pills that regulate it that way. Now I'll only have The Headache four times a year," Cat said.

"Aren't you worried about messing with your hormones?"

"No. I'll be able to re-regulate them if they get out of whack."

"I guess that if I had a headache every month that made me want to poke my eye out with a pencil, I'd do anything to get rid of it, too." Cat was the most kid-unfriendly person Bette had ever met. She hoped her friend went through menopause early so she could be on the other side of menstruation since she certainly wasn't going to use it to get pregnant.

Bette had never wanted to have children, either, but she was getting a big dose of them now with Rosa's extended family. Also Marco talked to his girls for at least an hour every Sunday and passed the phone to Bette if she was at home. Spanish was hard enough in person, but over the phone she was sure she sounded like the village idiot, saying *si* to everything like she understood. What a joke, but his daughters didn't seem to mind.

A busboy was clearing dishes from a table a little ways away. Bette caught his eye trying to see if he was one of her current or former students. Sure enough. They smiled and tilted their heads back at one another in greeting, but didn't speak.

"Do you want a piece of this pizza?"

"No, thanks. If there's extra, bring it back to Jeff. My salad's great, and I never get anything like this at home. One night a while back, Marco and Enrique and the guys were over, and we were thinking about what to have for dinner. Fernando, he's the fifteen-year-old, stood in front of the open fridge and said, 'We can't have dinner. We don't have any tortillas.'"

Cat stared at her. "No wonder you never want to eat Mexican food on margarita night anymore. You must be tired of it."

"Yup, even though I like cooking as a team with Marco and the guys."

"I like that Jeff likes to cook. I'm fine cleaning up."

"Even after years of it? You still don't mind?"

"He's a pretty tidy cook, and I hate it."

"Uh, I went hiking with a guy from work last weekend." Bette put a big forkful of salad in her mouth and waited. Sure enough, her friend knew right where the rub would be.

"What did Marco think?"

Bette shook her head.

"You didn't tell him?"

"No, why stress him? Why stress me?"

"I'm guessing that if you didn't say anything, there's something there."

"Uh-huh, unfortunately." Bette set her fork down and took a slow breath in and out. "He's the new guy in IT. I'm sure you've seen him."

"Definitely," Cat said, raising her eyebrows.

"I like him. A lot." Her hike up Spruce Mountain had been perfect. She told Cat how they'd hiked at the same pace, long legs working hard. The fabulous spontaneous picnic they created with her mushroom pâté, rice crackers, chocolate. His vegies and hummus and homemade rhubarb crisp.

"Sounds like something out of a Sunset Magazine."

"It was. And we talked the entire time. About the drought and plants and birds. He's a birdwatcher." Bette was quiet for a moment and then added, "He's done a lot of work with PETA. You know what that is, right, People for the Ethical Treatment of Animals?"

Cat rolled her eyes. She was as much pro-animal as she was anti-kid.

"Oh, yah, of course. What was I thinking? It was so comfortable. Kind of like talking to myself with the same values and interests. Oh, and he's nice to look at. You know." Tall, lanky, confident. "I thought he was a runner at first, but he's a vegan, that's what makes him so trim."

"Um, that feta in your salad sure looks tasty."

"I'm not dating the guy!" Bette heard herself and said more quietly, "I don't think he cares about me eating cheese, but I somehow failed to mention all the meat I eat with Marco."

Cat looked up and held her gaze.

"No, I did not forget to tell him about Marco. I said I was seeing someone."

"Seeing? Marco lives with you."

"Details, details," Bette said, shrugging. "I can't help it. I don't want to lie, but I guess I am by omission. But what if there's something there?" Marco was going to go back to Mexico one day, and he had two daughters. Maybe this was the guy. What if she missed him?

The waitress brought a box for Cat's pizza. "And what if Mr. Macho finds out?"

"He's not that macho."

"Ha."

"I'm not going to sleep with the guy," Bette added. "Just getting to know him."

Cat smiled. "I don't mean to be grilling you."

"No, it's okay. I have my doubts, too." Part of her wished she'd never met him. At other times she wondered how she could wait to see him again.

CHAPTER 5

YMCA Application for Scholarship Assistance

What benefits do you see in having this scholarship to join the YMCA as a member or participant? *Our family could learn to swim. Rosa needs to exercise more to help with her headaches. The young children need to learn good exercise habits.*

Why are you applying for scholarship assistance? *Because the family needs to relax and play together and for exercise. Also, we don't have enough money.*

That weekend Bette went to Rosa and Felipe's son's birthday party without Marco. She wished he was there to help her get more out of her conversations, but he was working. There were ten of them – Rosa and Felipe, Gerardo the birthday boy and his little sister, Isa, Catalina and Nemecio from the ESL class, and a family Bette had never met.

"Betty, *aqui esta mi cuñada*, Amaya," Rosa said, introducing her to a thin woman wearing tight pink sweatpants and a matching tee-shirt pulled tight over the soccer ball size of her pregnant belly. Her black hair was pulled back in a ponytail under her white N.Y. visor, and she looked to be in her early twenties. Bette looked over at Isa sitting at the shoreline of the lake with a little boy of about three.

Bette stepped near and shook her hand. "*Mucho gusto,*" she said, then asked Rosa, "¿What's a *cuñada*?"

"Umm. She's the wife of my brother."

"Ah, *si*." This must be the woman who crossed the desert with Rosa. The sister-in-law whose name Bette didn't catch was part of the family that lived next door to Rosa in the adjoining apartment. "*Lo siento, ¿*What is your name?"

"Amaya." She smiled with the most slanted eyes Bette had seen on a Mexican. She wondered if Amaya had it easier in the U.S. because folks must mistake her for Asian and not treat her as an unwanted immigrant.

"My brother, Carlos," Rosa said. Now there was a name Bette could remember. "And their son, Javier." The little boy was busy digging in the sand.

The party was just the right size to fit under a ramada beside the lake. It was hot, but Bette slathered on sunblock and went swimming with the kids when it got to be too much.

"Ouch!" Isa said, grimacing and freezing where she stood.

Bette understood that universal word. She picked Isa up and carried her to deeper water, the rocky lake bottom not bothering Bette through her water sandals. She helped Isa float and said, "Put your hands here," tapping her shoulders. "A pony ride." Bette smiled as the little fingers gripped her. She trailed Isa behind her, snaking a path back and forth. Gerardo joined them, and they practiced their Tootsie Rolls and spins. The water was a murky brown unlike the chlorine blue of the pool they were used to but, just like there, they kept their eyes closed.

Last month Bette had signed the kids up for swim lessons at the YMCA. Rosa's cleaning job conflicted with the class, so Bette used her lunch hour from work each day for two weeks to ferry them back and forth. It was the first time she had felt like a mother in her thirty-eight years. To her surprise, she had liked it. She'd sit on the bleachers with the other moms and yell, "Kick! Kick! Kick!" as Gerardo paddled away, clutching the pink kickboard. Occasionally his teacher would pull him by his board and Gerardo would look over at her and smile as he got a little ride.

She loved sitting there watching the Minnow kids on the other side of the pool act like chickens flapping their wings before their instructor would let them jump in the water. And jump they did. These little stick-thin children hopped right in, including Isa. There were only three students in Gerardo's Pollywog class, so with two teachers, he had his own instructor. Keith, a tall teenager with a broad swimmer's chest, cannon-balled into the pool every day, making a huge splash. Bette would catch Gerardo's eye as he sat on the edge of the pool, smile, and nod encouragingly – this was the first time he had ever been in a swimming pool. Keith talked almost non-stop in

English to Gerardo. She wasn't sure how much he was understanding, but Keith just kept talking. Maybe they were communicating in some universal guy language.

Off to the right of the Pollywogs were the Guppies, a group of about six eight-year-olds. Bette was fascinated by the two teachers. The lead instructor was about sixty-five, heavy-set, and balding, and his assistant looked to be around fifty with a long ponytail, Fu Manchu moustache, and a paunch. Would John be volunteering here one day? Besides being part of the solution to a better world, she could see him enjoying himself.

The older man held a Hula Hoop under the water and had a kid swim through it. When the child emerged, the younger guy turned the girl around, had her point her arms over her head, then shooshed her back toward the side of the pool. They had the system down and made it look like a choreographed ballet.

During the two weeks, Gerardo progressed from clinging to the side of the pool to being able to semi-crawl for twenty feet. She couldn't have been prouder. On the last day of class, Bette took them to a drive-in for a root beer float, their first. She shot Gerardo in the chest with the straw's paper covering, and he looked at her in amazement. Who would have thought a fifth-grader didn't know about shooting straw covers?

The three of them swam together most weekends at the YMCA, and Bette had gotten them so that they could jump in the deep end and even go down the tall, curlicue waterslide, *la toboggan*, without slowing down with their hands.

At the lake, the adults took turns paddling Bette's little plastic kayak, then with help, she managed to squeeze Gerardo in with her. He sat on the floor of the boat between her legs while she paddled wherever he wanted to go. "*A sus ordenes.*"

They were exploring a finger of the lake when they came upon a log cut to the size that would make a perfect seat for her back deck. After many tries, they lassoed the log with the line meant to secure her boat to a beach. Almost back to their end of the lake, the rope slipped, and the log floated free. They were in the process of re-capturing it when Bette heard, "Need some help with that?"

"Hey, John. What are you doing here?" Oh, that didn't come out right, she thought. "I mean, what a surprise."

"When you said you couldn't go hiking because you were going to the lake, it made me think it would be nice to take my boat out."

"This is my friend, Gerardo. Gerardo, this is my friend from work. John. Or Juan."

John zipped around in his red kayak and shook Gerardo's hand. "Nice to meet you."

"Nice meet you," Gerardo replied in English.

"¿You like his boat?" Bette asked. "*Demasiado flaco por dos personas.*"

Gerardo nodded and laughed.

"What'd you say?"

"He says he likes your boat."

"*Gracias,*" he said to Gerardo. "Tell him it's for running rivers. Used to do that in Colorado."

Running rivers? He's got to be kidding, Bette thought. She couldn't interpret that.

John helped maneuver the log between the kayaks and held it steady while Bette retied it. He didn't know much Spanish, but with her help, he did manage to communicate with Gerardo. They took turns teaching each other words as Bette towed their floating prize back to the boat ramp without tipping the kayak over.

"Come and meet my friends," she said as they approached the shore.

"I don't want to be a party crasher."

"It's okay. Besides, you've already made friends with the guest of honor."

When Gerardo said *come* in English, John agreed. He landed first and helped shuck Gerardo out of his tight fit. Bette pulled her eyes away from his straining muscles but then peeked again as he and Felipe heaved the waterlogged chunk of wood into her trunk. Later, when the stump was on her porch, Gerardo always sat on it.

Rosa, Amaya, and Catalina were busy cooking the meal, working together on barbecuing meat, shrimp, and vegetables on skewers, onions in foil with butter and *chiles*, and corn tortillas. John got pulled over to sit with the men. Amaya looked weary with her pregnancy and needed to put her feet up to lower the pressure in her legs, so Bette stepped in to help with the cooking.

The birthday party was different from those in the U.S. in that there was no special time set aside for Gerardo to open his presents. Watching all the participants give him a hug reminded Bette of seeing this at Marco and Enrique's birthdays. Aunts, uncles, and cousins were always holding babies and children, but Bette wondered at what age that touching stopped. Isa had rescued John, who had sat in silence among the men without a common language and was chatting away to him as he towed her back and forth along the shore in his boat.

Tracy had a canoe that she and Bette used to take out each summer, paddling to the end of their favorite mountain lake to camp in private. But Bette couldn't imagine Tracy here sharing boat rides with the kids with her limited knowledge of Spanish. Bette's two worlds almost never overlapped, except now a little with John.

They all ate together, squeezed at one table except for Catalina's husband, Nemecio. He was the shyest man Bette had ever met and rarely even made eye contact. It would have been easier if John sat with him so that she didn't have to interpret everything, but she could tell he was happy in the thick of things. His curly hair poked out under his hat and ringed his smiling face.

She was the only bilingual one of all her friends, semi-bilingual, and wasn't sure how to bridge the widening gap in her two worlds. Maybe if some of her friends learned the others' language, like John was trying to do with Gerardo and Isa, then she could pull the Anglo and Mexican halves of her life together.

After the meal, Gerardo went to one of the vacant picnic tables and opened Bette's present, a model car kit. It wasn't like the remote control cars he had at home, but she was hoping to instill in him a love of doing and creating to keep him from becoming a couch potato video game junky. She wasn't sure if he wanted company or help, but she went over and stood across from him.

"¿Is this your first car to build?" She had chosen one that didn't require glue or painting, thinking that she would try him out on something simpler first. If he liked it, they'd go from there.

"*Si*, I like this Mustang." He had all the pieces spread out around him. "Look at this flame." He held up one of the car's fenders. "And *mira*, such tiny taillights." Bette sat down beside him and started to look over the directions. They worked snapping pieces together with Bette trying to keep them proceeding in the right order. John sat on Gerardo's other side. He and Bette held down the box and instructions which were starting to lift and fly as the afternoon wind picked up. A raven cawed as Bette was reaching for the paper and while looking up to see the bird, her hand touched John's. Trills of energy ran up her fingers. She moved her hand away quickly.

Bette heard Marco's truck and her insides started vibrating. She wondered if she'd be able to keep her hands off of him, but when he spoke, everything chilled within her.

"¿What are you doing?" he asked.

"Building a car." He had been with Bette when she picked out the present.

"This is a friend from work, John."

John leaned back from the bench where he sat and stuck his hand out to Marco, who eyeballed him for a long awkward moment before giving him a brief shake.

"¿Do you want something to eat? There's lots of food," Bette said. She didn't want to get up and serve him and was glad when Rosa came over with a plate of meat and shrimp. She could tell he was mad because he walked to the table of adults to eat rather than sit beside her.

"Sorry," John said. "I'll go."

"No, it's okay. He gets like that. I think it's cultural."

"I don't want to mess up the party." He got up and headed toward his boat. "See you at work." He thanked the women for the food, then Isa gave him a little hug before he climbed in his boat and pushed off.

Maybe Marco was mad because she was sitting with a man he didn't know or playing with Gerardo. Too bad. Gerardo's car was going to be something to see.

***

That night she butted her head against grave communication problems when she tried to talk to Marco about John.

"Marco, people have friends of the..." How to say *opposite* sex? "...of the other sex."

He pushed his chair back from the kitchen table and stood up. Bette reached for his hand, but he pulled away. He was trapped by her legs in the small breakfast nook unless he wanted to walk around the wooden table. "I want to be with you, but I also have another friend," Bette said, looking up at him. She took his hand this time and pulled him back down into his chair. "I have enough room in my heart for more than one person," she said. "I have Cat and Tracy and Rosa."

Marco rattled off something in Spanish, but Bette could not catch it.

"I don't understand. Please talk slowly." He tried again, and she still didn't get it. Marco reached for a sheet from the pile of Bette's one-a-day Spanish word calendar pages. He wrote quickly in his tight, small print. Bette tried to read while he wrote but was missing a lot. She got up and retrieved one of the Spanish-English dictionaries she had scattered about the house. When he pushed the paper toward her, she flipped through the dictionary and filled in words she didn't understand. They argued in writing and conversation, passing the dictionary back and forth to find words to support their arguments. The difficulty of debating a topic that was controversial in the U.S., let alone in a Latino culture, without adequate language skills made Bette want to let loose a stream of swearwords. In English. She needed more Spanish to conduct such a soulful conversation, and she wanted to learn it with this man. She also wanted John's friendship and was loath to lie about it.

Marco was Bette's first Aries, and she had read about that sun sign in an astrology book of Tracy's. It said they were impulsive, impatient, bold, and confident and always ahead of others (and sometimes themselves). They were leaders with bubbly enthusiasm, not capable of going halfway. That didn't hold promise for what she was proposing. They were idealistic and natural rebels who thought they were smarter than everyone else. She was asking this Aries man, this Latino, to step into a role where his culture would see him as cuckold, one of their most powerful slurs.

"*Por favor*, Marco. My heart is big enough to love many people."

Marco spoke rapidly, but when Bette didn't respond he grabbed another word-a-day paper. He wrote, "When I am between two persons, the best is for me to withdraw and to suffer the loss. I don't like to share."

"¿What are my..." Bette grabbed the dictionary and looked up the missing word. "¿What are my choices?" The intensity of her desire to have this man in her life confused her. She felt present and alive with him, seeing everything with new eyes and a vibrating alertness she hadn't experienced in a very long time. How to say, *don't make me decide?* She settled for, "I do not want to decide."

The chair scraped on the linoleum as Marco pushed it back and stood. Bette reached toward him and put her long arms around his waist. She pulled him close to her as she sat on the edge of the hard oak chair. "Please, Marco. Don't go. I want you." She pressed the side of her face to his solid chest.

When the night had ended, and Marco wouldn't budge on his position, Bette had faced her own choice and decided to back away from John.

CHAPTER 6

Committment
Comitment
Commitment
Comittment

As autumn arrived, Bette re-centered her focus on Marco and their life together drifted into a routine. Marco bought an old Toyota pickup and started driving himself to work. Bette liked being able to walk and bike to her job again but missed those early morning conversations when she used to drive him to the pick-up spot at the grocery store. Once while she had been reviewing English words with him in her car she had said, "Neither is *tampoco.* Also is…"

"I know, I know." Marco interrupted her. "Also is like fucking also."

"No, Marco," Bette laughed. "¿Did you learn that at work? They're saying fucking asshole, not fucking also. It's like *pinche pendejo.* Also means *tambien.*" He leaned away from her, lowered his chin, scrunched his eyebrows, and said, "¿*Pinche pendejo?*"

"Hey, I learned those words from listening to you, *Señor.*"

He smiled and shook his head.

The patchy silver-and-gray truck came in handy, she had to admit, and they used it for carrying things they found at *yardas* and doing chores around her place, like hauling manure for the garden. Landlords tended to like Bette for her timely payments. After a childhood of being the new kid on the block, she had learned what it took to be liked. She also took care of the yard and had been able to talk most of the owners into letting her dig up part of it in order to put in a garden. It was only two sunken beds at this place, but it was enough to satisfy her craving to get dirt under her nails and be part of the miracle of growing food. It never failed to thrill her to see how a single seed would produce a huge plant covered with zucchinis or green beans or peppers. Something like being pregnant and giving birth, she imagined.

"Marco, ¿Do you have a garden in Mexico?" Bette asked one evening as he came in from emptying the compost bucket. She was glad he always volunteered for that job as she disliked the inconvenience of moving all the rocks which held the chicken wire over the pile to keep the javelinas out.

"I had a farm."

"¿A farm?" Bette scrunched her eyebrows and wiped her hands on a dishtowel. "¿I think you are a veterinarian in Mexico?" Somehow he was managing to turn her present tense Spanish into past tense, but he corrected that mangled word.

"*Sí*, v*e-ter-i-nArio.*"

She nodded instead of garbling it a second time.

"Yes, and I had a farm to raise forage for my animals. I had a big bull, *pero muy grande.*" He held his arms out wide. "And pigs and chickens."

"¿To eat?" Bette asked.

He nodded. "And to sell."

"¿Did you..." Bette drew her finger across her neck.

"No, a man came to the farm and did it."

"¿Then why come to Arizona? ¿Why not stay and be a...and have your business?"

"Because..." Marco picked up a pencil and began tapping it on the table. "People waited until their animals were very sick before calling me. They didn't have money and were hoping the animals would improve on their own. I'd come at the last minute when it was often too late. I couldn't stand to watch the animals suffer."

Bette took the pencil out of his hand and stroked his fingers. "They paid me with eggs and corn, which was not enough for my medicine."

Marco always changed the subject when she asked about his wife. Now Bette wondered if her death had been a deciding factor in his decision to come north.

"I was the only one of my eight siblings to go to university. I received scholarships for good grades and for being poor. I wanted to be a lawyer, but my father made me study to be a veterinarian." Bette knew Marco would have been an excellent lawyer with his intellect and confidence that he was always right. "He was wrong," Marco continued, "I couldn't make a living as a veterinarian." He picked up the pencil again. "*Aqui está mi finca.*" He drew a diagram of his land showing her where the corn was planted, the fruit trees, corral, pigsties, and his house.

Bette tried to picture herself there, creating a home in a rural setting. Would the satisfaction of leading a simple life be enough, or would she get bored when the newness wore off? It was impossible to visualize it, never having been to Mexico.

"When I return I'm going to buy more land for forage and have more animals." He continued drawing on his paper, trying to make it come alive for her. The man who had learned to save animals would earn his living killing them.

***

That Sunday morning they drove out of town to pick up her autumn's supply of manure. Bette drove Marco's truck when they were together since he did not have an Arizona license. She preferred the risk of her getting fined for transporting an undocumented immigrant to having him be racially profiled, pulled over, and deported.

What a choice, she thought, as she struggled to drive. The seat wouldn't go back to accommodate her long legs, and the steering wheel was almost in her chest. She pulled the truck through a gate and into the yard. A man working near the barn walked toward them. He wore faded jeans, a green tee-shirt under a blue chambray shirt, and a baseball cap. As he approached he reached in the window and first shook Bette's, then Marco's hand. His grip was firm and raspy with dry, calloused skin.

"Hi, I'm Bette. This is Marco."

"Bob," he said. "Did you have any trouble finding the place?"

"Nope, just like you said. First right after we crossed the fifth cattle guard."

"The pile's over there." He led them toward a mound of horse manure as large as a car. "Here's the most decomposed part." He dug around, flipping over a shovel-full for them to see the underside. His thumbs had deep cracks near the nails which made Bette wince. It had taken her over a month to heal her own when she had let them get that bad.

"This'll be great. Thanks so much for placing the ad."

"Not a problem. It works out for both of us. Go ahead and back your truck up and load from here."

Marco had wandered off and was stroking the neck of a brown horse, so Bette backed the truck up then joined the two men at the fence. They were managing to carry on a conversation in a language created out of a love of horses.

"He's trying to tell me something about my horse's feet," Bob said. "They've been bothering her, and he noticed it right off."

Bette interpreted that the horse's shoes were the wrong size and that by changing them, her feet would improve.

"Is he a farrier?" the man asked.

"No, he was a veterinarian in Mexico." She smiled at Marco standing in the sun, smiling himself and noticed something cloudy in his eye.

"Oh yah? My vet has more work than he can handle," Bob said. "Maybe he can work for him." Bette wrote down the vet's info then headed to the manure heap with Marco. She took Marco's chin in her hand and tilted his head. It was a pterygium growing on his right eye, the milky strands had crept from the white into the chocolate brown but were not yet in the iris. Too much time in the sun at nine thousand feet and close to the equator. Ah the things she'd learned over the years bookkeeping at various places.

"¿*Quál es*?" he asked.

"*Nada.*" Why tell him about something he wouldn't spend money to correct? Most likely he would be back in Mexico before it got bad enough for surgery.

She peeled off her long-sleeved shirt and started shoveling alongside Marco. The fall morning had started cool but was warming up quickly. Living in the high desert mountains taught a person to dress in layers. Taking a break, she noticed a big, dense alligator juniper amongst the smaller shaggy bark junipers. The tree must be at least a hundred years old, Bette thought, knowing how slowly they grew without much water.

***

Marco wheelbarrowed a load of manure from the truck to Bette's small garden, and together they tilted it up and dumped it on the soil. "Hey. ¿Do you want to go to a, to a..." Not a *fiesta*. Bette couldn't find an equivalent so retreated to English. "...*una* fair?"

"¿What is it?"

"*No se en español.*" Bette dug her beet fork through the manure and into the soil, working the two in together. "It happens every fall, and people bring their best vegetables and flowers and show their animals – cows, sheep, chickens, and rabbits. There's lots of food and rides like a carnival."

That was a word he knew. "Oh, *una feria.*"

She hated any Spanish word with more than two consecutive vowels and knew it would soon be garbled in her mouth to create another familyism. "*Sí.* One of those. We can invite Fernando and Mateo and Enrique. It's entertaining." She thought she would get to play tour guide again, showing him another aspect of North American culture, but Marco was the one who got to shine in a way she'd never seen.

***

At work the day of the fair, Bette turned to see her friend standing in the doorway holding a blue Nalgene bottle. "Hi, Cat." Bette twisted from side to side in her chair.

"I've been standing here awhile." Cat worked in payroll but dressed more like she was an executive secretary, always something attractive. Today it was a long, faux-suede tan skirt, a spaghetti-strap white tee under a lacy brown sweater, and cowboy boots. Cat loved living in the West and didn't give a rip if her outfits clashed with her New Jersey accent.

"Sorry. I'm so close to finishing this report. The more complex, the better but this one's a pain. I'm still hunting for a few errant entries."

"Let me guess. Probably someone not filling out their paperwork correctly," Cat said. "How many scientists does it take to change a light bulb?" They both smiled. "A Ph.D. doesn't make anyone smarter."

"That's for sure," Bette said. "I like your skirt. Aren't you going to be hot though?"

"No, they crank the air in the back of the building. Got time for a walk?"

"Yes, I need to clear my head. I'm going cross-eyed trying to figure this one out. How are things in payroll?"

"Oh, I'm fine, but Antoinette is freaking out over how many new subjects there are for the Walker samples." They walked out the back of the building and headed up a hilly, tree-lined street. Even though it was autumn it was still hot during the day, and Bette was glad for the shade of the pines and for her new dress she'd found at a second-hand store last weekend.

"Why doesn't she quit whining and just do her job?" Cat shared an office so couldn't get away from Antoinette's complaints. "They're not going to disappear just because she gripes all day."

"Maybe she needs a margarita night," Bette said.

"Or to get laid."

"Probably both. I set up the accounts for that trial," Bette said. "Why do people complain so much about their jobs? If they don't like 'em, find another."

"Spoken like a true rambling woman."

"Huh. I know. I've got it easy being kid-free, not owning a house. No debt. Not so hard to just quit. But that's by choice, not by chance. I like having options."

"And no commitments," Cat added.

"I'm committed to the ESL class. Try doing that twice a week. And I try to make it work with my sweethearts, but things seem to fall apart."

"A little touchy are we?" Cat looked over and waggled her head.

"Busted." Bette put her hands on her lower back and stretched her shoulders. "I've always been a good speller but don't ask me how to spell commitment. I get it wrong every time."

"Thank God for spell-check. And that you're done with your last boyfriend. There must have been something good there, but all I remember was you complaining."

"Did I? Things sort of fade in hindsight. I remember wanting a lot more of him, but sort of being put off a lot."

"It's not like that with Marco?"

"With Marco? Ha. He loves being with me. We argue sometimes, but he's always there for me. We cook together, go downtown to the square, sightsee." Everything. He was like a sponge, taking in his new world, and loving being beside Bette.

"What about John? Done, done?"

"Yes. There wasn't anything there, really. Just potential. I'm not ready to give up Marco, and he's not the type of guy who shares." Marco had made it blatantly clear at the picnic that John wasn't wanted in their life and both she and John saw that. Bette ran into John now and then at work, but they only said hi Just John, hi Just Bette, and gave each other a wide berth as they passed in the hallways.

"I'm glad you still make time for margarita night."

"Always. Marco never begrudges me time with my *gringa* girlfriends." Bette turned and smiled at Cat. "Nice boots." Her friend must have a dozen different styles of cowboy boots, one for every outfit. These were cinnamon brown with square toes. "Are you guys going to the fair this weekend?"

"We went to the rodeo Friday night, but we'll skip the fair."

"I thought you'd hate the rodeo because of how they treat the animals."

"I go for the cowboys. Those long legs in tight Wranglers…"

"What does Jeff think about that?"

"He doesn't care. He knows I'm going to want sex when I get home, so how can he complain?" Cat and Jeff had a great sex life for a couple married eight years. The longest relationship Bette had ever had was three years, and the sex had faded over time, but not Cat's. Maybe it helped that Jeff was five years younger or that they didn't have kids to stress them out. But still. Bette wondered how long it would last with her sensual Latin lover.

Marco was eager and passionate. He would parade past the bedroom door, completely naked, then strike a pose highlighting his butt, as firm as two coconuts. "You *tontito*," she'd say, sitting on the bed laughing with him. And always love notes. *Suit dreams*, on her pillow one night. Once a small white box that contained bird pins from the Goodwill. Bette interpreted the note as saying:

The most wonderful is freedom and to be together. You like nature and within nature are these beautiful birds that are going to like you a lot. Always wear them next to your heart. They signify that here we are together and within your heart. Bette this is that which you desire. With love, your Marquito. I need you by my side, my güerita.

As she and Cat reached the rear of the building, Bette pulled her thoughts back from her affectionate times with Marco and opened the heavy metal door for Cat. "Hopefully Antoinette has finished the Walker samples, and you can work in peace."

"Or I'm going to have to kill her and plead a hostile work environment."

"Ah, the things we learn in our sexual harassment training."

—

CHAPTER 7

Puercos	Vacas	Caballos	Geronimo
Jamshir	Herford—carne	Criollos/natives	Pelibuey—carne
Duroc	Angus—carne	Arabe	Merino
Landrac	Suizo—queso	Percheron	Jamshir
York	Holandesa—leche	¼Milla	Somali—black face

That evening Bette drove to the fair using four-sixty air conditioning – four windows down going sixty miles an hour. The county was large and mainly rural so there would be lots to see, and the 4-H kids would show their best. She had always wanted to be one of those farm kids, but her father had never lit in one place long enough for her to sink down roots. Even though the fair created an aching nostalgia in Bette for a past she never had, she could not keep herself from going every year. She was envisioning herself in an arena receiving a blue ribbon for her black sheep when she felt Marco's hand on her thigh.

"I want you bañina," he said in English.

"Marco," Bette whispered, tilting her head toward the backseat where Fernando and Mateo sat talking over the loud *Ranchera* music on the radio.

"They don't know what it means," he said.

Bette smiled. Even people who spoke English didn't know what it meant.

"This is a big place, but I'd rather park back here by the animals," Bette said as she maneuvered her car into a spot in the dirt field. The sun was low in the sky, and the empty fields around the fair were golden with autumn grasses gone to seed. "It'll be easier to get out tonight. We can walk up there later." She pointed toward the thrill rides which could be seen above the fence, spinning, rotating, and rolling. A low hubbub of noise punctuated by the occasional female scream flowed toward them from that direction.

Marco told her that the guys weren't interested in looking at the animals and would call later when they were ready to meet.

"Fernando, you're going to be cold when the sun goes down." Bette guessed he had chosen not to wear a coat so he could show off his clothes. "I have a coat in the car. ¿Do you want it?"

"No, *gracias*."

Teenagers, Bette thought. She and Marco went into the first building they came to, and she stopped and inhaled deeply. "*Me encanta este olor,*" she said.

"Me, too," Marco said. "It smells like my life in Mexico." They walked inside, holding hands and breathing in the odor of fresh straw and manure.

"Hampshires," Marco said as he leaned on the low metal pen looking at a mom with eight piglets suckling on her. Bette read the sign on the pen. Sure enough. "They're good for meat, and they grow fast."

"¿What are those?" She pointed to a different breed.

"Yorks. They have lots of babies." Ah, that would be an important thing to know when raising animals for meat. They moved to another pen, and a fine powdery dust settled on the tops of Bette's black shoes turning them tan. "Those are Durocs. They grow fast, too, but the *madres* only have a few *niños*."

"¿Did you have any of these?"

"Yes, and one race called eSpot. Hampshires and Durocs have fewer diseases. They have good resistance." Bette understood a lot of the diseases and problems Marco mentioned because the medical terms he used had Latin roots, and sometimes they sounded like an English word she knew. He called them *razas*, though. Maybe *race* meant *breed* in Spanish.

"In Mexico, many people will not pay as much for meat from pigs that are certain colors. They think the color makes a meat dirty."

Bette wrinkled her nose. "¿*En serio?*"

"They may only pay twelve *pesos* per kilo for a black pig but fifteen for a white one." Marco shook his head.

"¿And the taste is the same?"

"*Si.*"

"But you think people are better depending upon their color," Bette said. "*Los negros.*"

He looked at her but didn't reply. His racism was one of the things that bothered her the most about him.

"*Vámanos.* They're starting an auction over there." They sat in the metal bleachers and watched while Marco provided a running commentary until every sheep and cow was sold. By the time the hour was up, she knew more than she ever wanted to about complications of pregnancy, common diseases and ailments, and the type of food and care these animals needed. He spoke with admiration about the young girls and boys who stood with their animals in the ring.

"I bought a wheelbarrow for Maite so she could help me." He held his hands close together and drove the little imaginary wheelbarrow of his daughter around in front of them.

"*¿*How old was she?"

"Three. She came outside with me all the time to feed the animals." Marco said. "And a little pair of rubber boots." He held his hands one above the other about six inches.

"*Qué* cute. She must miss her papá," Bette said.

They breezed through the rabbits but spent more time with the chickens. "*Mira.* Look at the colors of these feathers. Each one is like a piece of art." Marco focused more on which were good layers while she marveled at how the yellow highlighted the maroon and red in the fluffy crests of some. There were a lot more people walking among these cages, so Bette led Marco outside. He was like a kid anyway. Where are the cows? Where are the horses? It was time to give him what he wanted.

A skinny little boy who looked to be about eight had climbed up the metal framework of the doorway to the cow barn and was hanging in the opening, talking to his brother. He was scooped up around the waist by a tall man in Wrangler jeans, cowboy boots, and a finely woven, but dirty western hat who nodded to Marco as they entered the next building.

Bette liked the animals at the fair but wasn't used to looking at every cow and learning which were good for meat and which for milk or cheese, but she was thrilled to hear Marco hold forth with such passion.

Outside the back door, a blond-haired family had their cow tied to a stanchion and were grooming it for judging. Standing a little ways off but still part of the group was a man who looked to be of Mexican descent. His skin was a lighter shade than Marco's, and he had a fluffy black Pancho Villa moustache, but he was built the same way. Bette considered what it would be like for Marco to live in the U.S. on a ranch, helping with the animals and farm maintenance, rather than having a job constructing McMansions. Heaven, she guessed.

As darkness fell, they walked past the last of the goat pens, peeking over the sides into the wooden stalls. Marco stood at the end of the white buildings and looked back and forth. "That's it, honey. Those are empty." He looked disappointed but then perked up when they climbed aboard a wagon pulled by a tractor and rode to the back entrance of the fair. The bright lights of the rides added to Bette's mood. "Look. There's the Kamikaze." The yellow and blue lights sparkled against the dark sky and peels of delight or fear shot out from it. "¿Do you like rides, Marco?"

"No."

"Me either, but I like to watch them." Her mouth started to water as she smelled fried food. "¿Do you want something to eat? There are all sorts of foods that are *el costumbre* at the fair." She'd learned that word recently, so similar to the English equivalent and was glad to have it. Cognates just might save her.

"¿Like what?"

"Well, hamburgers with...onions." She mimed slicing and sautéing. "¿Can you smell them? And curly fries." She wiggled her fingers together, not knowing the Spanish word for curly. "Elephant ears and caramel apples. I love those."

"¿Want one?"

"No, too messy. I want dinner. Kids love this..." She pointed at the cotton candy.

"We have that in Mexico, but it's too sweet for me."

"¿What? ¿Something too sweet for my Mexican?"

Marco rolled his eyes. "¿What else?"

"Every part of the country has food that is *raro*, strange. Big fried onions, like a flower." She demonstrated with her hands, opening them until they held the gigantic blooming onion. "And scones with jam, like *pan y mermelada*. Oh, here are the corn dogs. You have to try one of these." They were Bette's mom's favorite part of the fair, and the smell of them brought back fond memories of some of their times together as adults. They had reconnected when Bette was in her twenties, and she had enjoyed getting to know this almost-stranger.

She and Marco shared a big corn dog that was clearly hand-dipped in the cornbread coating, which was uneven and not made in some factory. It had just come out of the deep fryer.

"*Qué deliciosa*," Marco said, wiping mustard off the corner of Bette's mouth with a napkin. They walked through the aisles of games and watched people shoot rifles at stars, throw baseballs at milk bottles, and pick yellow duckies out of flowing water. People pressed on them from all sides, moving from the games to the rides.

Marco asked her how to get one of the huge stuffed animals some of the teenage girls were carrying, but after learning how much he would have to spend for a chance, he decided not to try to win one for his daughters. Better to wait for *una yarda*.

"If your girls come here to study English, we will bring them to the fair so they can go on these kiddy rides." Marco put his arm around her waist, and she, her arm around his shoulders and they watched children go around and up and down on miniature cars and motorcycles. Bette saw a few people staring at the tall blond with the short, muscular Mexican pulled close to her side and was glad to add to the ambiance of the fair amongst the carnies with their missing teeth in halos of smoke.

"You have to try a Navajo taco." They were happy to find a container of salsa on the table beside the stand and poured it on the lettuce which topped the fry bread, pinto beans, cheese, and onions. Marco tore off chunks and fed Bette while she leaned over the paper plate to catch falling goodies. They washed it down with fresh-squeezed lemonade purchased from a man inside a giant lemon on wheels.

"I'm full." To heck with Marco's rules about it being uneducated to use that term. "Let's walk to the other end and look at the arts and crafts and vegetables. *Mira.* There's Fernando and Mateo." She pointed to a booth down a row where young people were getting fake tattoos airbrushed onto their arms. Bette smiled and waved, but they only smiled, too cool to wave back.

Marco spent time at a booth displaying clear plastic cubes with three-dimensional holographic items floating in them – flowers and birds, cars and motorcycles. They were certainly made for pennies in a factory somewhere and served no purpose other than collecting dust. Just the type of thing Bette wasn't interested in, but Marco loved. She looked up and saw John walking by with a woman. They smiled and nodded at one another then Bette tried to push down the jolt of jealousy that had coursed through her.

She and Marco meandered through the commercial building, picking up free stickers and bags, paint stirrers and candy. Two gray-haired retirees were selling timeshares to a resort in Acapulco, Mexico. Bette felt like speaking Spanish to them to make a point, doubting that they or anyone else at the resort spoke Spanish except for the underpaid help. The pictures showed tall hotels lining beaches facing the aqua sea. From stories her students told about life in Mexico, she doubted that much of it looked like that. She turned her back on their spiel and walked away.

"Oh, I love this part – the vegetables. Look at these tomatoes."

"¿What are those?" Marco asked, pointing to paper plates, each holding six perfectly uniform okra.

She explained how it was a food from the southeastern part of the U.S., and when it was cut into rounds, coated in cornmeal, and fried it was *muy sabrosa*.

Slowly they made their way through Bette's favorite buildings, admiring the fine tailoring in a bridal dress, hand-stitched quilts, and knit socks. Marco liked the photography exhibit, especially the humorous shots of animals. Outside again, they rested on a set of metal bleachers which were almost empty, and they watched a group of eleven-year-olds on the stage in blue leotards and lavender skirts dance to Sting's *Heavy Clouds but No Rain*.

"They're good with their umbrellas," Marco said. "Their timing is great."

"The short girl on the right side is our daughter." A man sitting a few rows below them had turned and addressed them in Spanish.

"You must be very proud," Bette said. The woman sitting beside the man looked Hispanic, too, but replied in English. She must have heard how poor Bette's Spanish was. "She's always dancing around the house. She's in gymnastics, too." The song ended, and they clapped loudly and waved to the girl.

"I didn't think I'd get to watch her tonight," the man said, switching to English. "I was deported and just got back this week."

"What happened?" Bette wished that Marco could understand. This had happened once in Phoenix when Spanish-speakers at Ranch Market saw them together and spoke English so she would understand, not assuming that her Spanish was better than Marco's English, and he was being left out of the conversation. The man told her how he had been driving his car at night in a nearby town and was stopped for having a broken taillight. He was arrested for not having an Arizona driver's license and then deported.

"I came to Arizona from Mexico when I was five," he said. "I'd get a driver's license if I could, but I don't have papers."

"He was lost in Mexico," his wife said, chuckling a little. "He can't read Spanish."

"I never went to school in Mexico," he said. "When I got there I called my mom, and she asked, 'Where are you,' and I said, 'I don't know,' because I couldn't read the signs." His wife rubbed his shoulders.

"How'd you get home?" Bette asked though she was pretty sure she already knew the answer.

"I crossed the desert. I never want to do that again. My wife and daughter are legal. I'm glad they'll never have to do it. It's just me." Their daughter was coming around the back of the stage, and they rose to go get her.

"Good luck, *Señor*," Bette said and reached to shake both of their hands. "¿Did you understand any of that?" she asked Marco when they were gone. He just looked away. She started to explain when Fernando and Mateo showed up.

"¿What have you been doing?" Marco asked.

"Looking for you."

"¿Why didn't you call?"

"We did, but you never answered," Mateo said.

"It's right here." Bette took out her cell phone to make sure it wasn't turned off. "We never heard anything. Call me again." Mateo punched a few buttons, but nothing happened. She held out her hand. "*Dame.*" She looked at the number on the display. "You've been calling my home number, silly." It was 2008 and people still had landlines.

"¿*Vámanos?*" Marco asked.

"*Sí*, if you want to. It's late." The four of them waited a little while before the wagon showed up to take them back to the stables near the car. Fernando was shivering, and she hoped that looking stylish had been worth it. On the drive home she learned that they were famished. They hadn't gotten up the nerve to get food at any of the booths. Too unsure about their English. The next week she would create a lesson plan around ordering a meal in a fast-food restaurant. The question remained, however, how could she get her students, and Marco, to study?

That night at home she whipped up some scrambled eggs for Mateo and Fernando while Marco pulled out the makings for *huevitos*, egg tacos – chopped onions and cilantro, *tomatillo* and avocado salsa, and a block of cheese. Mateo was always willing to help and heated corn tortillas on the *comal*, the flat steel griddle. The three men were talking when Bette inadvertently interrupted the discussion.

"Oh, sorry. Sorry." She scrunched her brow. "Later." Spanish was still difficult enough for her that if she didn't concentrate on what was being said, it just sounded like noise or music in the background. She regularly forgot that it was an actual conversation, and she butted right in. Her friends probably called her *the interrupter* behind her back but were too polite to complain to her face.

When she brought the castiron skillet of eggs to the table, she saw that Marco had been making a list of farm animals on the back of a one-a-day calendar sheet, complete with what the animals were good for – meat, cheese, and milk.

"I talked to a man at the fair who has lived here since he was five but was deported this week," Bette said.

"*Hijole*." Mateo said. Bette told them the story while they ate dinner and she sipped mint tea.

"He was probably drunk, that's why he got pulled over."

"Marco, ¿How can you say that?"

"¿Why else?"

She tried to explain how it wasn't unusual to be pulled over for a broken light though normally you only got a warning.

"He must have been doing something wrong," Marco insisted. "¿Why'd he tell you?"

"I don't know," Bette said. "I guess he felt safe since we were together. It seemed like he wanted to share the... *que raro fue*...how weird it was."

"He wanted to *presumir* his English," Marco said.

"¿What's *presumir*?" Bette asked.

"Look at my shirt," Marco said. "Look at my shoes."

"Oh." Show off. "You're just mad because you couldn't understand. He wasn't *presumando*. He speaks English like a *gringo*. He is a *gringo*, almost. ¿Why would he need to show off?"

"You don't know Mexicans," Marco said, and the guys laughed.

What did those two know? Bette thought. They couldn't even order a hamburger. "I'm going to sleep."

Slipping into bed, Bette wished that her fun time at the fair could have ended cleanly, without complications. How dare he tell her she wasn't good enough, that she didn't know his culture. She'd never even been to his country, and she spoke better Spanish than he did English. Not fair, Marco, she thought. Not good enough? Don't know your culture? Just watch.

CHAPTER 8

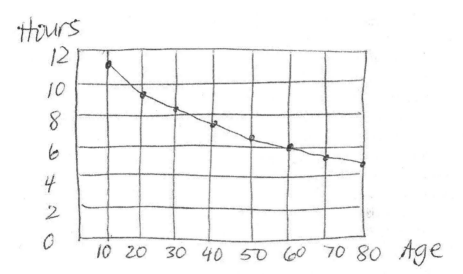

Bette had taught Rosa to drive, but she was still more nervous than confident, so when they headed out to her niece's three-year-old birthday party, Bette was the chauffer. Marco had picked up a weekend job so couldn't attend; it would be the five of them in her dark blue car. Felipe had been pulled over one too many times in his identifiable red Jetta and ultimately had to sell it to keep the situation from getting worse. The stops were always for minor infractions – a broken light, no seatbelt – but the police now recognized his car, and it was simply a matter of time before they hassled him more about his Mexican driver's license. His white van blended in better, but it was still safer for Bette to drive them in her car.

When they arrived at the party, Bette looked at the scratch paper where she'd scribbled the names of Rosa's family members and pushed her brain hard to remember some of the names.

"*Buenas tardes, buenas tardes,*" she said, smiling as she and Rosa walked through the hard-packed dirt backyard. The men were standing in the shade of a raggedy elm tree but reached out and shook her hand.

"My brothers," Rosa said. "Carlos, Ignacio, and Oscar. Over there is my nephew Rodrigo."

Inside the single-wide pink trailer were Rosa's sisters-in-law, Luna and Alma, plus Amaya whom Bette knew from Gerardo's lake-side birthday party. A bunch of children wove in and around everyone. Central Arizona was in the throes of an Indian summer, and it was hot inside the narrow trailer even with the front and back doors open. There wasn't much room in the kitchen to help, so Bette went out to the front yard and pushed the three three-year-olds, *los tres tres* as she liked to call them, on the swing hanging from a large tree. Isa had found her way outside and was helping Mariángela, nicknamed Mari, onto an orange tricycle.

Bette tried to think of a birthday party she'd had as a child but couldn't recall one. There was the time her sister received a cake in the shape of a doll's dress with a Barbie sticking out of the top. That was pretty cool. She remembered various Christmases and getting a big bike that her father had fixed up and painted red, but no parties specifically for her. And with all that moving, there were also no aunts, uncles, or grandparents, even for holidays. Bette's brother and sister had sunk down roots in the same city, but neither had kids yet. Would they have parties like these? Her reverie was interrupted by the women calling their kids inside.

She unstrapped Javier and lifted the giggling boy from the swing. Ushering them into the house, she pointed out the rotten front step, but they hopped over it like little lambs. *Brincan, brincan los borregos.* Even with the open format of the living/dining room/kitchen, the trailer was stuffed with people. A beige couch held three men. Gerardo was sitting on a purple couch with his ten-year-old cousin and Rodrigo was holding Amaya and Carlos's new baby boy. Some of the women were preparing plates of food in the kitchen while others settled the three-year-olds at the kitchen table. The sound of a TV came from a room down the hall.

Bette tried to help with the food but was shooed away. She found an empty armchair and sat as Luna placed a red plastic plate in her hands that held a mound of *ceviche de atun y camarones* with tostada shells and avocado slices on the side. Bette watched as people poured ketchup and *Valentina*, or *Calentina* as Enrique called the hot sauce, over a mixture of tuna, shrimp, onions, *chile*, and cilantro then squeezed lime juice over it all.

No forks were necessary as she learned to break off pieces of the tostada shells and scoop it up.

"¿*Te gusta*?" Amaya asked.

"*Sí*. It's very delicious. You are thin again." Amaya had given birth to Estevan only a month ago and was almost back to her tiny frame. Maybe that came with being a twenty-five-year-old.

The TV and radio were both going in the dark particle board entertainment unit beside her, and everyone was talking and laughing at once. Bette let her concentration drift and instead looked around at the furnishings and watched the moms and aunts, dads and uncles feed whichever child was near at hand, *los tres tres* having long ago left the table.

On top of the gold shelving unit in the corner between the two couches were the same type of porcelain dolls that Marco had purchased for his daughters. They stood stiffly in their fancy clothes, definitely not the type any child would cuddle. The other glass shelves held artificial flowers, two large white pottery cats, and glass knick-knacks. One shelf was full of framed pictures of Luna and Ignacio's twin teenage daughters who were living in Mexico with their grandparents. In one silver-framed photograph they stared solemnly at the camera, so beautiful in their pink *quincinera* dresses. Three-year-old Mariángela already had their serious looks. Maybe they used her nickname, Mari, to try and lighten her up. Bette was learning that many Mexican names had nicknames attached to them, such as Chuy or Chucho for Jesus, Paco for Francisco, Nacho for Ignacio. She had so much to learn.

Next to the couches were two wind-up baby swings, more artificial plants, and a tall lamp in the shape of a saguaro cactus. White lace curtains hung limply in the breeze-less room.

The women collected the red plates, then served white plastic cups filled with *gelatin*, a mixture of squares of orange Jell-O, pineapple chunks, mandarin orange slices, pecans, and raisins in a sauce of sour cream and sweetened condensed milk.

Before the cake was cut, they took dozens of pictures of family members in different groupings standing behind it. These were the days before everyone had cellphones, so they used actual cameras. Bette had never seen kids and men so accommodating. Later when she looked at the photos, the top of her head was cut off in most of them.

"Here's your *sombrero*," Alma said. She picked up a hand-knit pink skull cap which had fallen on the carpet and pulled it onto her niece's head. It seemed like such an odd word for the tiny hat, so delicate and made with small gauge needles. Bette followed Luna into the bedroom when it was time to change Anali's diapers, wanting to spend more time with the little girl, Mari's new sister. Luna chatted away while Bette made up the half of the conversation she didn't understand. When the new diaper was in place, Luna wrapped Anali tightly in a blanket then placed her in Bette's arms. She was surprised to feel that that was exactly what she had wanted without knowing it.

Bette walked into the living room grinning widely, carrying the child like a precious gift. She nestled in a little space on the purple couch beside Rosa's daughter Isa who leaned over to look at Anali and said in Spanish. "Oh, she's getting much bigger."

"*Sí*, she has little tires on her legs," Bette said, squeezing a leg through the blanket. "I love tires on babies' legs." There was silence for a moment and then smiles and laughter. Bette could hear Luna saying her name and the word *tires*, *llantas*, then more laughter from the kitchen.

Mari had received a make-up and jewelry kit for her birthday, and since Bette was the only woman in the room without make-up, she gave the baby up and sat on the floor to receive the treatment. While Isa applied polish to her nails (and fingers), Mari put stickers on her earlobes, sparkly blue eye shadow in her eyebrows, and pink and green clips in her hair. Later, Mari applied a second coat of polish to her nails (and fingers). Bette would be sure and show off her painted nails to Cat the next day at work. It might bring a smile, or at least a snort, to her un-kid-friendly girlfriend.

"Okay, Betty. Time to go," Rosa said.

"¿Already?"

"*Sí, mija*. It's almost ten."

"¿*En serio?*" Bette asked.

Rosa laughed. "*Sí*. Give Betty a kiss," she directed her niece.

Bette hadn't understood much that the three-year-old Mari had said to her that night and attributed it to the child's tiny voice and budding language skills. But when she put her arms around the thin girl, like holding a bouquet of delicate flowers, and received a tender kiss on her cheek along with a shy smile from the birthday girl, she remembered that words were only a small part of communicating.

***

When she got home, Marco was there, sleeping spread eagle on the bed. His beautiful brown skin so soft and almost hairless – she wanted to run her face along it. The foreskin on his penis scrunched down to make it look like a sea anemone. Come alive, little creature.

She ran her hand up his muscular thighs and cupped his warm balls.

He opened his eyes and said, "Come to bed, *chaparita*." He reached for her, and she leaned down to kiss him then stepped back to undress. "It's late. Why didn't you leave sooner?"

"The *fiesta* was…" How to say *still going*? She settled for rolling her hand forward.

"You spend too much time with others. You should be here."

You told me I didn't know your culture, so now I'm learning, she wanted to say, but held back and only replied, "No. I can have other friends." She wanted this wider world she was creating and wasn't going to give it up for something she could not understand.

"Tonight, Marco, in the kitchen with Rosa and her sisters-in-law, I say, *me duele mi culo*." As expected, Marco guffawed. "*Si*, I…" Bette rubbed her neck to demonstrate the missing word, "and tell them it hurt." She had been so proud of learning the complex way of saying something hurt in Spanish.

"No, *chaparita*," Marco said, "This is *cuello*." He stroked her neck. "*Culo* is asshole."

Bette was laughing with him. "That's what Rosa say." My asshole hurts. The four women had cracked up while correcting her, but refused to tell the men what they were laughing about. Bette guessed it would all come out later when they were alone.

As intended, she had managed to distract Marco from his insistence on monopolizing her life. Maybe with more Spanish, she would understand his reasoning, but right now it just sounded like selfishness. She loved the web of family she was creating that included Rosa's family as well as Marco and the guys. ESL and a few parties were nothing, really. Wait until he learned she was going to tutor Rosa's kids.

***

The next week, Bette started going to Rosa and Felipe's home at least once a week to help the kids have a better chance of being successful in U.S. schools.

"¡*Hola, Gerardo*! ¡*Hola, Isa*!" Bette hollered as she stepped through the door to their small triplex. Isa was first to greet her with a kiss on the cheek and a hug. Today she wore a salmon-colored spaghetti-strap top and matching shorts, the unseasonal heatwave still in full force. Her glossy black hair was pulled back in a series of intricate braids. Next came Gerardo, who had red, raw spots below each nostril.

"*¿Tienes una resfriada?*" she asked.

"*Sí, pero no mala.*"

The cold looked bad to Bette, but Gerardo was grinning at her. His broad, flat chest shook when he coughed, but he didn't seem to be running a fever. He had socks on and who wore those in this weather? A forest green Seattle Supersonics tee-shirt and long black shorts made him look elfish.

The two sections of the blue couch lined different walls. Almost every time Bette came over to visit, they were in a new arrangement. She opened her arms wide and said to Felipe, practicing her past tense, "You changed the sofas again."

Felipe, just back from work and grimy with dirt, smiled and shrugged. "Rosa keeps looking for the best *disposicion.*" Now there was a cognate she could figure out. Bette knew they slept on the floor of the living room, and the kids shared the one bedroom. Rosa had told her they were trying to come up with an arrangement where they didn't have to move so much furniture every night. Felipe worked in a metal fabrication shop and sometimes looked like a raccoon with his face completely black except around his eyes. A grinning raccoon.

Gerardo, Isa, and Bette crossed the living room into the kitchen where Rosa was preparing something delicious with which to stuff her. She wore her shoulder-length hair tied back in a ponytail but still managed to look stylish with white eyeliner accentuating her eyes.

The kids pulled their books from their backpacks, and Bette said, "*Ah, matimaticas,*" as Gerardo laid the inch thick textbook on the smoky glass kitchen table. "*Mi favorita.*" Gerardo sat to her left at the round table and Isa to the right as was their custom.

"What books do you have today?" she asked Isa in slow English. She was six, in first grade, and was learning English faster than Bette could imagine. Isa laid out three thin books – one about gorillas, the second featured *meanies*, and the third was from the Easy Reader series. Bette remembered a reading program in her second-grade classroom that consisted of a cardboard box with tiered shelves holding cards of many colors. Students got to read at their own pace and move up as their reading proficiency increased. It fit Bette perfectly with her love of bright colors, small things, and reading.

Rosa set a glass of iced water in front of Bette and broke her reverie. "*¿Tienes hambre,* Betty?"

"*No, gracias.*" The two-foot square fan whirred a few feet behind them in the open back door but didn't do much but blow around the hot air. Bette took a long drink.

Thus began the ritual of Rosa trying to feed Bette and Bette trying to decline. She didn't like taking her friends' food, knowing how little Felipe made from filling out the YMCA application, but she also didn't want to be rude. Rosa stood stirring something at the stove that smelled like chocolate. *Mole.* Behind her over the kitchen sink were four bags of corn tortillas, the size Bette had seen at Enrique's, each six inches high. Before the evening was over, she was sure she'd be pinching up chunks of chicken simmered in the thick *chile*-chocolate-sesame sauce with some of those tortillas.

"Okay ¿What do we start with tonight?" she asked Gerardo in Spanish. Then switching to English asked, "Charts? Graphs?" She couldn't remember learning about those in fifth grade. Had they given him the wrong textbook? But she was getting a handle on them with the help of her big, thick Spanish-English dictionary. She got Isa set up copying her spelling words then worked with Gerardo on scatterplots. That evening she learned she was going to sleep less and less as she aged. What a thing to learn in a math book.

Rosa placed three bowls of *mole* around their papers and notebooks along with a stack of tortillas and refilled Bette's water. "¿Will the cool weather ever return?" she asked.

"I hope so. *Gracias* for the food, Rosa." Around a mouthful of the rich food, Bette asked, "Isa, how to you spell cat?"

"That's easy," she said and wrote the word in little child big letters. "Now your turn. Girl."

Bette was impressed with how quickly Isa was mastering the difficult *ir* sound. When she wanted a chuckle, she had asked Marco to say bird. That or breast. His efforts were so endearing. She always ended up hugging him or running her hand through his hair. Today she wrote the word on the scratch paper she brought from work – one side printed with profit-and-loss statements or trial balances. She couldn't think without paper and pencil; also it helped her to explain things she had trouble with saying in Spanish, like rounding a number.

"Okay, boy," she said to Isa. Back and forth they went, giving each other words to spell. She had no experience helping with homework and was going by the belief that these kids would do as well as they could, having been in the U.S. less than a year. They certainly attended to their studies with enthusiasm.

"Ah metrics," she said to Gerardo. "You can teach me this."

"No, I no understand metrics," Gerardo replied in English. Every day he showed more willingness to use the language.

"What?" Bette asked. "It's your system. You're Mexican." She laughed with Gerardo. "Okay, let's learn this together."

"¿Do you want more?" Rosa asked her, gathering up the napkins laden with chicken bones from the table.

"*No, gracias. Estoy satisfecha.*"

"*Poquito más,*" Rosa insisted, furrowing her brow and looking pained that Bette was only eating one huge bowlful of *mole.*

"No. It's delicious but I can't."

"¿No, Betty? ¿*No poquito más?*"

Bette patted her stomach, "*No hay espacio.*" Finally, Rosa smiled and relented.

Felipe came in then, fresh from his shower. "Let's sing for Papi," Isa said, hopping up from her chair. Bette joined her, and they sang *I'm a Little Teapot* complete with one hand on their hips and one in the air for a spout. Singing and looking at Isa, Bette guessed she had a matching orange ring around her mouth from the *mole.* One large and one small teapot making all in the room laugh.

Bette's family had broken apart long before her mother finally left when she was Isa's age, and she relished reconnecting through this family with her playful childish side. Her brother, two years her junior, used to pull out his bag of tricks in the living room of one of their countless trailers and reach into a pillowcase then withdraw his hand, holding nothing but his imagination. Then he'd move his little body in hilarious ways. Reading was all she could remember doing as a child, and it had saved her from loneliness, so she was trying to pass that love and solace along to all of her new friends.

Isa and Bette read three books with Felipe looking on when they were interrupted by Amaya arriving from the apartment next door, carrying a pitcher of magenta liquid.

"Hi Amaya." It had taken her a while to master that name but was proud it now rolled off her tongue. "Hi Carlos," she said to Amaya's husband when he stepped through from the living room doorway, carrying his new son, Estevan. A little squeal preceded their son Javier as his cousin Gerardo pushed him through the kitchen on a yellow Tonka truck on their way to the bedroom.

"Betty ¿Do you think you could help me and Carlos with some measurements from work?" Felipe asked.

"¿Some what?"

After a bit of back and forth she figured out what they wanted. "Sure, sure." She drew a giant inch on a piece of paper and worked with that and an actual tape measure to help them understand feet and inches down to eighths and sixteenths. She'd gone over this in ESL class, but it was before Felipe and Rosa started attending. They were good students, and she gave them many practical examples and questions that they could use in their work.

The hibiscus drink Amaya brought was sweet and tart, sort of like Spanish and English getting mixed in her mouth at once. Their conversation drifted to Mexico, so Bette stayed to hear more.

"¿Do you want me to teach you to drive, too, Amaya?" Bette asked.

"No, no."

They smiled at her quick response.

"¿Why not?"

"None of our families in Mexico have cars. We walk or take a bus."

"Or a *combi* or taxi," Rosa piped in.

"I don't want to learn," Amaya said. "Carlos takes me to the store here."

"In Mexico, we can walk everywhere."

Bette yearned to see Mexico. When she arrived home late that night, Marco and Enrique were still on the back deck, drinking limeade that Enrique had made. Marco poured her a glass, and she joined them, sitting close to him and running her hand through his hair.

"¿Did you have cars in Mexico?"

"*Yo, no,*" Enrique said. "No one in my family has a car."

Bette shook her head.

"And we live a long way from town." He explained that they grew flowers in big greenhouses so they had to live where there was land.

"¿Is it beautiful?"

"*Muy,* that's where all the flowers in the stores here come from. And avocados. And maguey."

"I'd love to see it."

"I had a truck for my business," Marco chimed in, "but no one else in my family has one." One of his brothers drove a snack food delivery van for a living, and sometimes he would run the family to different places. Otherwise it was walking, buses, or taxis.

"*Y don Fausto con su bici.*" Enrique laughed along with Marco.

"¿Who's that with the bike?"

"*Mi papá.*"

"¿You call your dad by his first name?"

"Wait until you meet him," Enrique said. The two of them chuckled, but Bette couldn't figure out why.

"He has a knife sharpening stone on his bike that he operates with the pedals," Marco said. Thank goodness for Enrique helping to explain.

"¿That's his business?"

Marco nodded. The contrast in her nomadic father and Marco's who was tied to how far he could cycle made Bette shake her head. Unimaginable. She needed to get to Mexico to see for herself.

Bette kneeled beside the bed that night and slipped her hands under the covers and down Marco's body, headed toward his crotch where she found a large mound. He'd tucked her nightshirt in his underwear to pre-warm it. She slid her hand into his undies and gently held his testicles while pulling out the shirt so she wouldn't hurt him.

"Ooh. *Qué caliente. Gracias, Marquisimo.*" As she got into bed, they snuggled close to one another.

"Come with me to the farmers' market tomorrow." He'd been once before, and she'd seen her world through his eyes – the booth selling expensive dog treats, fresh eggs that cost more than he got paid in a day in Mexico, the ribbon tiaras he bought for his daughters, and the chair massage where Marco had said *relax* and his hand made a beeline toward her crotch before she knocked it away while giggling. The farmers' market would be a nice distraction, and maybe the El Salvadoran selling fair trade coffee would be there, and Marco could converse in his mother tongue.

"I can't. I'm working with *la esposa peligrosa.*" She heard the smile in his voice. After his five-day week with eScott building houses, Marco often got day jobs on Saturdays at the *desempleo*, the unemployment pick-up site. He worked regularly with Glen, an oral surgeon, and his wife, Rebecca, who were landscaping their new home. One day Rebecca had tossed one of the round river rocks poorly, and it bounced and hit Glen's finger, causing it to bleed. Marco had called her *la esposa peligrosa*, the dangerous wife, and the name had stuck.

"Okay, honey. Be careful around her," Bette said while scrunching her brow.

Marco drifted off with Bette's magic fingers running through his hair. At last she slept herself, looking forward to an outing at the farmers' market with her girlfriend Tracy, speaking nothing but English. They were on such a similar wavelength that they didn't even need words much of the time. That's the way it had always been – a natural bond.

CHAPTER 9

Marco		John	
Pro	Con	Pro	Con
Funny	Drinks w/ friends	Reads a lot	To be determined...
Good natured	Fiscally unequal	Environmentalist	Once I quit
Companionship	Different music	Hikes/Camps/Birds	Projecting
Helps my Spanish	Different food	Volunteers	
I feel I'm needed	Doesn't read	Deep connection	
Always something	Doesn't listen to	Shared values	
new	the news	Feminist	
	Stubborn	Is legal so can travel	
	Can't discuss		
	anything in depth		

Bette was getting canvas bags out of the back of her car the next day when she heard Don's animated voice. It had been months since she'd seen Tracy alone. She sighed then found a smile within, and turned and greeted them. They made a cute couple, both of them short, extroverted, and talkative. Don wore a Mandarin-collared burnt sienna shirt and a pair of cream-colored pants with elasticized ankles which looked like they were purchased off of an Arabian caravan. Tracy was holding off autumn as long as possible with her short, batik sundress topped by a kelly green sweater.

"Hi, Bette," Don said, hugging her tightly. He was about Marco's height, but thin and wiry. "Can you believe this is almost the last market of the season? How did it get to be October? I hope they have lots of tomatoes left. Maybe with that last heat spell we had. I want to try canning. Maybe salsa or just whole. And that goat cheese." He tilted his head back and closed his eyes. "Hey, maybe we should get their contact info so we can keep buying it throughout the winter."

"I have it," Tracy said while giving Bette a hug.

"I just need to get my egg carton, and then I'm ready," Bette said. She stuffed it into one of the beige cloth bags and noted how dirty they were. Holding one upside down to let the onion skins flutter to the ground, she saw where brown stains had crawled up the sides.

"Tracy says you've canned a lot. Tomatoes should be okay since they're naturally acidic, right?" Don continued his string-of-consciousness chatter, not waiting for responses while they walked across the parking lot to the two rows of white-topped booths. It was a small market with many vendors selling canned goods, cheese, homemade pasta, and soap with fewer offerings of fresh fruits and vegetables, but she was happy to have it. She loved buying her food locally and supporting growers who lived in the area.

"What are you guys up to today?" Bette asked Tracy as Don headed off on his quest for tomatoes.

"Maybe canning if Don finds anything. Birding this afternoon. The warblers are migrating through. I thought we'd go up to Wet Beaver Creek, have a picnic and go swimming. I heard a report of an orange-crowned warbler. We're on the hunt."

Bette paid for a beautiful garlic braid then let it drop heavily into her bag. "Sounds nice."

"How about you?"

Bette knew she would have been the one to be canning and birding with Tracy before Don entered their lives and wondered if Tracy thought about that, too. Her twinges of jealousy were less frequent these days with Marco around. At least she and Tracy were going to get away one time this fall like they used to when Don was headed to Colorado for yoga instructor training.

"Oh, I might go hiking. I'm not sure yet. The guys are coming over tonight."

They moved to the next booth, and Bette exchanged her empty egg carton for a full one then bought a treat of herbed goat cheese for Marco. She would have it prepared for him when he came home from work. The domestic picture made her smile.

"Aren't these beautiful?" Tracy had stopped at a booth selling stones with sayings painted on them. "They'd look so nice in the garden. How about this one?"

Bette picked up the smooth, heavy tan river rock and held it in her palms. *To love and be loved is to feel the sun from both sides.* Don came up behind them and said, "I saw those, too. That's the one I liked." Bette placed it gently in his hands and stepped back. While Tracy paid, Bette looked around her at the busy scene – a couple laughing while each carried one handle of their cloth bag loaded with small apples, a heavyset older man standing patiently while his young black-and-white Jack Russell terrier dashed back and forth around his feet, a small girl following behind her parents cradling a gourd birdhouse in her arms. What a treasure this market was to her town.

"Don got what he needed. We're headed home."

Bette turned to say goodbye and came face-to-face with John, who was passing behind her. He stepped back when he saw her, then a big grin lit up his face. A bunch of kale poked out of the top of his canvas bag over the eyes of a snowy owl. "Hi John. I have a bag just like that."

"Audubon, donation," he said. "Owls are some of my favorite birds."

"My friend Tracy's, too." Bette raised her chin, and John turned to look behind him. "These are my friends, Tracy and Don. John, a friend from work." They smiled and exchanged greetings, all hands too full to shake.

While Don started telling John about his canning project, Tracy caught Bette's eye and raised her eyebrows. Bette had to agree that John looked pretty good. Anyone shopping at the farmers' market was starting off on the right foot, but he also looked relaxed in a worn work shirt, faded jeans, and hiking boots. He must not have found a local barber yet since his hair reached his shoulders now, but it was the sparkle in his eyes that drew her in.

"We better head home and get started," Tracy said. "I'll call you later, B." They set their bags down and hugged then Bette turned back to John.

"I've finished my shopping and was thinking about getting a tamale. Join me?" he asked.

"Sure, that'd be nice."

They found a vacant table and sat in white plastic chairs. The mushroom, spinach, and corn vegan tamales were moist and flavorful.

"This is better than I imagined," Bette said. "Just lacking a little heat. Thanks for breakfast."

"You're welcome. You must be used to eating spicy foods?"

Bette nodded. She hadn't intended to bring up Marco, but now that it was there, she plunged in. "Sorry about the scene at the lake."

"No, no. I understand. I shouldn't have just dropped in."

"He doesn't understand about the American way of having friends of the opposite sex."

"Even people who live here don't get that." He smiled, and Bette stared into his green eyes a long moment before breaking away.

"It's not always safe. Things can start out so innocently and then…here come the complications."

He nodded. "People just have to go into it conscientiously, deliberately."

Bette smiled and took another bite. In theory, she thought. "Getting along in your new town?"

"Definitely. There are things I miss about Phoenix, but not many. It'd still be too hot there this time of year to eat outside in comfort." He told her about his work on the trails association, the criteria they used to prioritize the many projects they wanted to do. She could imagine the computer nerd in him, making a program to evaluate and weigh all the factors. Her inner bookkeeper smiled.

"The biologists up north are designing a wildlife corridor called the Y2Y – the Yukon to Yellowstone."

Bette nodded her head to encourage him to go on. He explained that it was designed to serve grizzlies, wolves, deer, wolverines, elk, and smaller animals, predator and prey, to move from one area to another to make the species population more robust. As he spoke his eyes glistened with excitement.

"If we can preserve and connect habitat, we'll facilitate the survival of all species."

Bette smiled at him, happy for his enthusiasm, but thinking about passageways and interconnectedness on a more human level.

"We've put up so many barriers with our roads and housing developments that wildlife are being isolated; they can't move between suitable habitats. We need to act fast to create the web of life before it's too late, and we can't reverse the fragmentation."

Bette hadn't had such an engaging conversation in a long time, but others were eyeballing their table, so they stood and went back through the booths again, slowly. They talked about organic farming, canning, flowers, favorite recipes, shade-grown coffee from El Salvador. Like on their first hike together, they bounced back and forth between topics, each of them taking turns going off on personal rants and passions, before reigning themselves in with a laugh. Bette learned that he'd converted an old diesel VW to use waste oil from fast-food restaurants.

"Oh, you're that French fry smell that keeps taunting me around town."

"Guilty," he said as they both laughed. "I've talked myself dry. Have time for an iced tea before you head home?"

They agreed to meet at an old multi-roomed home that had been converted into a coffeehouse. As they left the farmers' market, Bette splurged and bought a mason jar full of sweet peas. She loved the colors, pink, white, and purple, and they reminded her of Washington where they grew wild along the roadsides. Her disappointment at having only a brief, shared time with Tracy was fading fast as the sweet fragrance filled her.

***

That evening between coughs Marco asked, "¿Where's the cheese?" He was standing at their kitchen table surveying the items he and Bette had laid out for dinner. It was a typical cornucopia: a small plate held cut limes, cilantro, and chopped onion. An oval dish featured a ripe avocado, the leftover goat cheese from the market, and a paring knife. Pickled *jalapeños* and carrots in their vinegary broth were in a clear bowl next to a white one filled with thin pork chops that had been cooked in a mixture of *tomatillos* and onions. Mateo moved from the stove to the table, shuffling three hot corn tortillas from hand-to-hand before nestling them with others into the usual red-and-white checked hand-towel to keep them warm.

Enrique stood at the counter, pouring salsa from the blender into a bowl. It was the fumes from the *habañero chiles* he'd roasted on the *comal* that had all five of them coughing. The overhead fan was whirring at full speed, and the door and windows were open, but that still wasn't enough to combat the constrictors on their lungs.

Fernando complained about food that spicy, but he always spooned it on, soon to be blowing his nose and wiping his eyes. And Enrique's stomach must be feeling better. He'd been avoiding *habañeros* for a while and sticking to the milder green *jalapeños* when he made salsa.

"¿What cheese?" Bette asked.

"The orange cheese from yesterday." Marco loved to have the table covered with choices. Bette wondered if it was cultural or just Marco. Of all the people to get involved with a Mexican, it was ironic that she knew so little about his country.

"*Aqui,*" she said, pointing to her stomach. Mateo and Marco laughed. They'd seen her do this when she was pre-past tense in her Spanish grammar, and it had made its way into their family lexicon. No need to remember how to conjugate a verb to say, I ate it or I drank it. Now they all just said, "Here," with a finger on their stomachs.

The guys had been over so often that they now paused as Marco and Bette prayed before eating, each saying part of their regular *oracion*.

"*Gracias a Dios...*" Bette started.

"*...por todos los aliementos...*" Marco continued.

"*...que vamos a recibir. Y por...*"

There was a pause while Marco thought of what to add. It was their custom to always give thanks for something in addition to the food. "*...nuestros amigos.*"

Shy smiles lit up Fernando and Mateo's faces, but Enrique just reached for the pork chops. Throughout dinner Marco rolled various items into corn tortillas to make each individual taco unique. He'd lean over to Bette and say, "Try this one," holding the rolled taco up to her mouth as she bit through it to taste the mixture of flavors and heat explode in her mouth. It felt personal and tender, to be fed, not pushy or demanding. She was getting used to the intimate act of sharing taking place in front of the young men and Enrique.

After they had eaten and carried their dishes to the counter, Bette asked, "¿Okay, whose turn to do the dishes?" Silence. Was that another Mexico thing? Men never wash the dishes? Bette's friend Cat hated to cook, but her husband Jeff loved to so they had an agreement where he cooked, and she cleaned up. She bet John believed in a fair distribution of household maintenance.

"¿Why is it so difficult for you to wash the dishes?" Bette asked them all. It was her second favorite household chore, after sweeping, but that still didn't mean she was going to wash the dishes every time they ate together. When it was just the two of them, Marco helped without being asked. But when company was there, he reverted to what she could only imagine were the gender roles in Mexico. He would sit back and expect her to serve him, then wash the dishes. When would he get out of the 1950s? It all felt like too much at times.

Bette walked into the living room and over the sounds of *Los Tigres del Norte* on the boom box she heard Enrique order his nephew Fernando to wash. She had listened to that disc so many times she could belt out the choruses along with the guys. *No, no, no me peges papacito.* She missed her jazz, but the *Ranchera* music was helping her start to grasp the principles of Spanish commands. But why so many forms of ordering people around? Why? One of her Spanish teachers had told the class they could ask *how* to say something or *when* to use it but not to ask *why*. *Why* got you nowhere in learning a language and was a question for linguists, not language learners. Just accept the fact and get on with learning. ¡*Vámanos!*

Enrique, Marco, and Mateo came into the living room, and Enrique started to dance to the music. He held his shoulders up high with his arms bent at the elbows, making small, rocking movements to accompany his tiny steps. He laughed along with the guys watching him. Fernando finished washing the dishes and joined him, the tall, thin nephew with his pot-bellied uncle in his ever-present polyester sweaters. Bette wanted to dance with Marco, but he wasn't interested, and she was too self-conscious to dance without him.

She put her hands on her hips and surveyed the room. The lamp on the end table along with the floor lamp provided a warm, yellow glow and though the two big chairs and sofa were mismatched, they were clean and inviting, Mateo in one, Marco in the other. There wasn't much art in the room, only a print of the Grand Canyon and a west coast seascape.

Most of the walls were taken up by bookshelves or windows. She ran her hand along the top of a row of books instinctively bringing them all to the front of the shelf. First, she straightened the fiction books, then spirituality and psychology, knitting and crafts, birds, nature, and hiking. She pulled out a guide on where to find birds in Arizona and thought about a road trip with John. How would it be to be able to travel freely, without worrying where they couldn't go because of the border patrol? Not to mention, Marco wasn't interested in birds or nature for their own sake but mainly what animal produced what usable product.

She slapped the book shut and re-shelved it then squatted to the bottom shelf which was stuffed with thick Spanish textbooks and unruly notebooks, tall and short ESL books, bilingual kids' books, pictionaries, and boxes and baggies stuffed with homemade flashcards. The shelf resisted her efforts at orderliness. Mateo was sitting nearby, so Bette pulled a coffeetable book off the shelf titled, *Over Mexico*, and placed it in his hands.

"I think you will like this. It's your country from the air." He did like it, as well as Marco, who moved to sit beside him on the couch. Pretty soon they were all crowded around. Marco had only traveled through Mexico once with a friend who drove a tractor-trailer but he told stories about every place he'd seen on that trip. Then he and Enrique started telling stories about stories they had heard. Bette understood so much more now than when *Señor Cuentos* had been going on and on. Part was that she was used to how the guys spoke, but she hoped part was her improving Spanish. Now she cataloged places she wanted to visit, foods she must try. She had been collecting books on Mexico from the secondhand stores and pulled more out. She would be thrilled if one of these young men took up reading, even if they were books filled with photography about their own country.

When the guys left that evening, she asked Marco, "¿Are you ready for your interview Monday?"

"Yes. I have my university papers and my license."

"Okay. Let's practice your words some more tomorrow." Marco's foreman at the construction company was taking a long weekend to go to Nevada for a four-wheeler race, so he'd canceled work for the day. Marco was using the time to interview with the veterinarian they had heard about when they were getting manure for the garden. His sister had sent Marco's documents via FedEx, and Bette had gone with Marco after work that week to arrange for the interview. They were impressed with his credentials and happy that he spoke Spanish. Monday was to be his trial run. If it worked, he'd get away from the dangerous, physically taxing construction job he worked all week. Knowing Marco, he'd still try to get extra work on the weekends, but his vet job, even if it was simply a tech position, would pay more and he could put his years of schooling to work doing what he loved.

***

When the day came, she told him how handsome he looked in his dark blue jeans, white button-down shirt, and brown, rubber-soled shoes. "*¿Estás nervioso?*" she asked.

"A little."

"You will be fabulous. Come by my office when you're done and tell me…" She struggled with finding the words. Okay, maybe her Spanish hadn't improved that much. "Tell me how it was."

"*Bien.*"

But he didn't stop by, and she had to wait until she was home to learn what had happened. Though it was now almost freezing at night, the days were still warm, and hardy flowers clung to life. She loved experiencing the various seasons as she wound down from work on her walk home. "*¿How was it?*" she asked as she opened the door.

He shrugged and turned away.

"*Dígame,*" she ordered, using the formal command. It would be another year before she'd figure out the difference between formal and informal, positive and negative, and all the irregular commands there were in Spanish. She took his hand, and they sat on the couch.

"Tell me what happened," she said again, squeezing his fingers.

"They spoke English really fast and never took the time to explain anything. When I started with eScott, he always spoke slowly and explained something before I had to do it. Not here. They just put me in a room, showed me where things were, then left. *Chinga su madre*," he swore, throwing his arm in the air.

"¿What kinds of things did you do? ¿Did, you know how?"

"I gave injections and put in IVs. And cleaned a bunch of *pinches perros'* teeth." Bette smiled at that one. Her friends all assumed that Marco liked dogs and cats since he was a vet, but they made his skin crawl with all their fur. He'd been a large animal veterinarian working with cows, horses, pigs, goats, and sheep and didn't understand the North American obsession with house pets.

"I worked with the veterinarian to put medicine into a horse's vagina," he added, using the English word she'd taught him, pronouncing it *bañina*. Some of those lessons had paid off.

"¿What do you think?" Bette asked. "¿Will they call you...again?"

"*No se.* They didn't explain anything, and I couldn't understand."

"You've been here almost a year, Marco. ¿Why don't you speak more English?" Unable to stop herself, she added, "You never come to class anymore. ¿Why don't you use one of the millions of books I have?" She waved her arm across the room at the two tall bookshelves against the wall. "*Mira.* You could read the book from this weekend."

"They never helped me."

"It's hard to learn a language, Marquisimo," she said more gently, using one of her pet names for him. "You've got to spend time studying." Bette didn't understand how he could have spent years learning to be a veterinarian and yet not have developed better study habits. Maybe at heart, he didn't want to settle here. His life was in another culture, far away.

"You need to speak English with me, and then I'll learn. You only speak Spanish."

"That's because if I spoke English, you wouldn't understand me. And we'd never even be together." She glanced up from the couch and saw starlings sitting on the phone line. Starlings! That was the first time she had seen that invasive species in her yard and had to remind herself that they were just trying to survive, too. "We couldn't be having this argument if I didn't speak Spanish." Now there was a thought. "¿Why don't you come to class? Just come to class straight from work."

"It's disrespectful to go to school when you are dirty."

"It's okay here if you still have your work clothes on. It's different here." She would prefer her students came consistently and on time, rather than be late and clean, or worse, not even show up. But in her mind's eye, she could see her students – none in dusty, grubby clothes. They had all gone home, showered, and changed. Or skipped class if they couldn't.

Marco shook his head, emphatically. "In Mexico, students take school very seriously."

"This isn't Mexico, Marco. Students are serious here, too."

"I'm too tired. And I don't learn there." He took one of the calendar pages from her Spanish-word-a-day calendar and started practicing his signature.

"Rosa and her family come every week, and they're…learning. And Felipe works…forty hours a week." Missing words, bent sentences, flat concepts.

"Rosa, always Rosa." Marco underlined his name with sharp, black lines.

"This is not about Rosa. It's about you. You never study. I read my Spanish textbook and practice. ¿What do you do to learn English?"

"I speak English at work. Your Spanish is good because of me."

"My Spanish is better because I talk with you, but mostly it's because I study. You can't learn a language solely by hearing it. You have to help me, Marco." His signature was dramatic and angular, unlike her curvy, shortened one. He must have spent a lot of time practicing.

"You have to speak English."

She wanted to yank the pen out of his hand. "Only if you study. If not, it's going to frustrate me more." She already talked at half the speed her mind wanted to go, having to figure out everything in Spanish. She wasn't going to creep to the speed of a baby to accommodate his laziness. Bette sighed and looked out the window. She'd taken two semesters of Spanish at the community college but recently hadn't been able to find a night class to fit around teaching ESL. Still, she continued to meet once a week for lunch to practice her Spanish with two friends from those classes.

"You have to study, Marquisimo. I can't do this all on my own."

She scooted over and put her arm around him. "It's okay about the vet, Marco. You've got a great job with eScott." She pronounced it the same way he said it. "And if you want to be a veterinarian here, you just need to learn more English because your diploma is here now." Bette knew that if he learned the language, he might be able to get a veterinarian to sponsor him to be here legally. She hated to see him having made the treacherous desert crossing to be framing houses for nine dollars an hour rather than be a veterinarian, but she couldn't put the English words in his mouth.

CHAPTER 10

High-protein energy bars
Water in a Camelback
Water purifier
Electrolytes
First aid kit
Ace bandages
Compass
Maps
GPS
Cellphone
Lightweight, high-tech, water repellent, warm-when-wet, sun-blocking,
    quick-drying clothing
Headlamp
Journal/pens

The hills were covered with barrel cactus and saguaros of various sizes that looked plump from recent rain but still dangerous with their fishhook spines. There were bushy teddy bear *cholla* glowing golden in the sun and droopy green pencil *cholla*. The *palo verde* trees were in leaf, and there were masses of rabbitbrush and flat prickly pears. The lance-like branches of ocotillo plants were green from the rain, but Bette knew they had fierce spikes all the way up to their red-flowered tips. Black, dry mesquite trees lined the arroyos.

"Do you think this was the type of terrain Marco hiked through when he came over from Mexico?" Tracy asked Bette. They were backpacking in the Sonoran Desert near the Santa Maria River having gotten a full day together with Don out of town.

"I was just thinking about that." Bette looked around her and hoped that Marco had flowers to cheer him on since it was early spring when he crossed. "I think he was somewhere near Organ Pipe National Monument." It was hard to tell because of the language barrier, and Marco wasn't even sure where he had been. "I've heard his story in pieces and think I understand most of it."

"How long did it take?"

"Three days and nights. They walked a lot at night because it was cold and they couldn't keep warm without moving." Marco thought it would be hot in Arizona and had left his big coat behind. It rained one night, and he had wrapped himself in a black plastic bag he'd found and shivered for hours until they started moving again. "He'd been told it was only a day's walk, but when they arrived at the fence the guides had them sit on the ground and then gave them the real story. Marco said the coyote asked if they'd been told they'd be walking a day and a night." Tracy stopped hiking and turned to Bette as she continued the story.

"'Well, it's three days and three nights,' he'd said. Marco told me a lot of people dropped their eyes, and others stared hard at the coyote like he had something to do with the false information or the depth of the desert. 'Be careful with your water and food,' the guide said. Then he asked the group, 'Did they tell you you'd just be walking at night?' Marco definitely didn't want to hear what was coming. 'We have to get to the pickup point by Wednesday or the cars will leave us. You have to walk day and night.' So off they went over the fence which was only a wobbly three-strand thingy."

"I've seen that fence at Organ Pipe," Tracy said. "I stepped over it once and joked that I was visiting Mexico."

"That's the one. I saw it, too, when I went birding with Bonnie's class. Anyway, one coyote took the lead, then the few women, next the men, and at the end the second guide. Marco heard, 'Stay close,' and 'Be quiet,' and saw many people cross themselves and touch their *Virgen de Guadalupe* necklaces. Enrique still wears his."

"Is Marco religious?" Tracy asked.

"No. We always say a blessing before we eat, but that's my practice, not his. I don't know why he's not. Maybe all those years at the university or having his mom die when he was young. And now his wife." They stopped and drank from their Camelback water bags. "I bet it's because he can't stand the thought of something being more powerful than he is."

"Still struggling with Marco?"

"Now and then. For the most part, it's good. I want him to study more, drink less."

"How often does he get drunk?"

"Every couple of months. It would be nice if he could have gotten that vet tech job, too. Then he could go back and forth legally."

"I can't imagine people crossing the desert in the summer. Why aren't they told how dangerous it is?"

"Who knows? Money. Maybe the coyotes are trying to get more customers by telling them it takes less time on their route than on other guides' paths. How are you doing? Do you want to take a break?" Bette asked. She was carrying their tent and all of the cooking gear since she was a more frequent hiker than her friend and also had longer legs, but she still had to watch her pace.

"I'm good. Which way do we head from here?"

"Well, we can go up and over that mountain or rock hop down the arroyo and around to the right." They were hiking in an area without trails, setting their own direction. It was too rugged for ATVs which was one of the reasons Bette frequented the area. Without motorized vehicles, she could hike above beer-can-line, where the type of person who didn't carry out his empties wouldn't go without wheels.

"Let's go down the arroyo and see if there's any water in the river."

Bette led the way, paying closer attention to her speed. Marco, her hard-working burro of a boyfriend, had told her how he'd used his pride to keep him going when he was exhausted and didn't think he could take another step. He refused to believe that he couldn't make it, that others in the group might outwalk him. It made her own hiking, even if it was off-trail, seem frivolous. She could stop and rest any time she wanted and wasn't pursued by people in cars, four-wheelers, and helicopters.

"How much did Marco have to pay?"

"A thousand. It started out as eight hundred but increased once he got to Phoenix, which I think is usual. Enrique is the one who really had to pay a lot."

"What happened?" Tracy asked.

Bette told her how at the border in Nogales he had agreed to eight hundred, but when he arrived in Phoenix there were armed men at the doors of the house keeping people from leaving. "The main guy told the group, 'I bought you.' Can you imagine? I bought you. He'd purchased them from the coyotes and the new price was twenty-five hundred."

"Shit oh dear. What'd he do? Where'd he get the money?"

"He paid," Bette said. "Well, a friend paid. The way it works for the guys I know is that when you get to the U.S., they ask, 'Who's going to pay for you?' Then you call the person who's expecting you, talk for a minute, then hand the phone to the coyote who tells the sponsor where and when to meet. Sometimes they up the ante a little, or so Marco says." Bette explained how that time was different. They were locked up, and Enrique said there were people in the house who had been there over a month waiting for their friends and family to gather enough money for their release. "Since Enrique'd been here before, he had friends with money and they paid."

"Did they feed them?" Tracy asked.

"Yes, Enrique said they ate *frijoles y huevos, huevos y frijoles* – beans and eggs, eggs and beans. He can joke about it now, but he was scared. You know what he's like," she said to Tracy. "Mr. Cocky. Mr. I've-Been-in-the-U.S.-the-Longest and know everything. It frightened me to see how scared he was even retelling the story sitting at my kitchen table."

They walked in silence, concentrating on the shifting ground below their feet, taking turns leading. The rocks and boulders in the dry creek bed looked solid but often moved under their weight. They bent low to go under mesquite branches, but Bette still got caught on her backpack and had to tug herself through. It was shorts weather in the Sonoran Desert, but they both wore pants to protect their skin. Her well-loved hiking jeans had loose threads on them from being torn by spikes and thorns, and her arms looked like she had broken up a catfight.

Bette looked up and saw that Tracy was approaching an area of large boulders. "Hey, let me go first," she said. "I can use my stick to let snakes know we're coming." She tapped her walking stick in front of her before climbing up and over the boulders, singing out, "We're friendly and mean you no harm. Just passing through."

"Marco told me that during their hike, they came upon an area filled with abandoned backpacks from earlier crossers. The coyote was sticking his hand in them looking for loot and got bit by a snake. It was a little one, and Marco told me the venom is worse because young snakes don't know how to control it yet and often let out too much."

Tracy's face was scrunched into worry lines, and she looked around her feet while they stood talking. "Did he die?"

"No. He let Marco cut the wound open after he learned he was a vet, then he sucked the blood out. The guy, not Marco. Marco said the guy's hand grew as big as a melon and he carried it in the crook of his other arm all day."

"I never thought that bloodsucking thing was supposed to work."

"Me either, but I guess you'd try anything in that situation." Bette was used to hiking alone and getting bit by a snake was one of the things that worried her. That and breaking her leg, but they were risks she was willing to take for the pleasure of being outdoors. At least snakes gave her plenty of warning before she got too close. There was nothing in the world like that rattle to get a person's full attention.

"There were other problems along the way," she said. "One guy was very ill. He couldn't eat or drink and had a fever. They helped him walk for a bit, but he had to give up."

"Did they leave him?"

"Well, the guide told him which direction to go where he could find a path that would likely run him into the border patrol. The last time Marco saw him, he was lurching off in the direction of the trail."

"How could they just leave him?" Tracy took off her lime green baseball cap and rubbed her forehead.

"The guy was alone, just like Marco, and didn't have a friend or family member to go back with him. It's so creepy. Marco still brings it up every once in a while. So many people die out there each year."

"Does everyone come across that way?" Tracy asked.

"Well, the majority of undocumented people in the U.S. came across legally with visas but then overstayed their visas. My friends are all poor, and none would qualify for a visa. They all came across on foot. I wonder if it makes some kind of fraternity thing, like hazing but on a life-and-death level. Sometimes when I look around at my Mexican friends and students I think about the heavy price they paid to come here." They walked with heads bent low, watching their steps.

"The little kids come across differently. The parents pay a lot for them, maybe two thousand each, to have a Mexican-American woman drive them across in her car." Marco had told Bette about one of his co-worker's attempts to get his two girls here, and she relayed the story to Tracy. "The younger one, maybe three, thought she was being sold to the other woman and cried and wouldn't leave her mother. The mother had to spend more time at the border figuring out another way to get her daughter across."

"Great. Now we're creating PTSD in children," the healer in Tracy said. "Hey, here's a little pool of water." They bent down and gazed at the one-foot wide puddle.

"I bet there's still water in the river." Tracy cocked her head. "Do you hear that?" Behind the sound of a cactus wren droning like a car trying to start was the unmistakable swish of water flowing over rocks.

"Water," Bette whispered. She was sure that before the day was over, her water-loving friend would talk her into getting into that ice-cold river.

At the river's edge, Bette picked a sandy-grassy place under a mesquite tree, kicked away a few cow pies, then arranged a sheet on the ground. Using their backpacks as pillows, she and Tracy lay down and read their novels. They made perfect hiking and camping partners that way, both of them content to relax, talk, wait for birds to come to them, and read.

"How's Don's massage business going?"

"It's slow. He doesn't get many referrals. He's doing better with his yoga classes." Tracy explained how he was creating a niche with gentle yoga for older clients. "It's fun to see him associating with older people. Older, ha. People his own age." Tracy sat up. "Did you bring tea?"

"*Por supuesto.* Can it ever be too hot for tea?" Bette dug through her backpack and pulled out her camp stove and a dented pan. "I forget sometimes that he's that much older than you. He has so much energy that he doesn't seem to be in his fifties." Also he still dressed like a hippy, Bette thought. "Has the fifteen-year age difference affected your relationship much?"

"It's my expectation of where I think he should be professionally by this time in his life that bothers me. He's not doing much to push his business. Seems content to let it develop on its own meandering course. You'd think he'd be more together by this time."

Bette knew that Tracy was always figuring out ways to promote her acupuncture business, giving classes and workshops, displaying at local events.

"Don seems happy to let his professional life limp along. At least he pays his share of the household expenses." Bette handed a cup of tea to Tracy.

"You must pay more for Marco," Tracy said.

"Yes. It's better than it used to be but a long way from being equal. I quit paying for beer, thank goodness." She told Tracy how they split the food expenses and that he gave her a hundred dollars to help with the rent.

"He pays when we go out to dinner, kind of that I'm-the-man-of-the-family thing, and I pay when we go to the movies. The food costs are higher because of the meat. And the guys are over at our house a lot."

"But you like that."

"I do, most of the time. It's like the family I never had. I get to play auntie. Enrique comes over almost every night and Fernando and Mateo once or twice a week. I like sharing what I have and doing special things for them."

A bird flew by and landed in an acacia tree. They both grabbed for their binoculars.

"Think it's a black-throated sparrow?"

"Yes, that's it. I haven't seen one of those in a while. Did I tell you that John's a birder?"

"You did mention that once or twice."

"Oops. Sorry."

"Still managing to keep it friendly with him?"

"Yes. Sort of. I think so. Geez. We had a great day at the farmers' market, but I think he's still sobered by the black cloud over Marco at the lake party."

"I've never seen that side of him."

"Lucky you. He can be so intense, and no amount of talking will get through to him."

"Just a language thing?"

"No. He shuts down so I can't talk to him. I don't know if it's cultural. He's intolerant of anything that's not as it *should be*. Kind of like how I can get on my high horse about politics."

"Don't we all."

Bette nodded and sipped her tea. "I'm used to being able to talk about things that bother me. It's kind of what modern couples do."

"Where do you get these notions? Can't you remember back to Mike and how he took what you said differently than how you intended it?"

"Yes, but at least we tried. Marco's like, this is right, this is wrong. I'm wondering if it's wise to be involved with a guy who's so rigid in how things should be. And yet I'm happy. I love coming home and knowing that Marco will be there after he gets off work. I like grocery shopping together, cooking, going to the laundry mat, sightseeing." Bette looked at her friend, who was smiling at her. "You must feel the same way with Don."

Tracy nodded.

"But should I be seeing John, even as a friend?"

"*Should.* Now you sound like Marco."

"I just want to do the right thing and not hurt anyone."

"As if. How many years have we known each other?"

"Ten?"

"I can't imagine you *not* moving toward John. But how about slowing it down a bit. See how things go with Marco before you complicate the issue with John."

Yes, slower, wiser, safer, Bette thought. All good in theory. She looked up through the tiny mesquite leaves to the blue sky. "Let's just be out here and not think. Especially about my thorny life."

"You'll survive this and whatever comes next," Tracy said. "I've seen you go through lots of men over the years." Bette opened a package of lemon cookies and bit into one, the tartness making her saliva run.

Tracy picked up a can of mushroom pâté and popped the lid. "What'd Marco eat on his crossing?"

"The coyotes gave them two plastic bags that contained a gallon of water, about three cans of tuna, two cans of beans, a can of *chiles*, a can of juice, and about a two-inch stack of flour tortillas. Marco never eats flour tortillas."

"That's not much food for three days," Tracy said as she smeared the beige spread on a rice cracker.

"Or water. Marco said they ran out, but found more at a little pond for cattle."

"Ick. That's pretty desperate."

"It had rained the night before and the water was all murky and stirred up. A couple of the people got diarrhea on the last day." Bette popped a few almonds and raisins in her mouth then said, "You know, I think if a *gringo* made that crossing, like you or me, we'd be all decked out. High energy food, lots of water and electrolytes, medicine, and first aid for injuries..."

"A water purifier," Tracy added, "and a compass. Lightweight gear for all weather conditions. And a headlamp so we could write in our journals at night."

"Sometimes I bring maps of Mexico and Central America to my ESL class to get the guys to talk about where they're from, and many of them have never seen one before. They tell me where they lived, and then I show them on the map. These guys have traveled all the way from Guatemala to Arizona, crossing two borders illegally, and have never seen a map." Having been raised in the backseat of a car, Bette had spent an eternity studying them, tracking their progress, figuring estimated times of arrival, playing find-the-city with her siblings. She doubted she could let go of that much control, to travel without a map, even with the natural one she felt was implanted in her brain. "I can't imagine going through life with that much faith."

"It sounds like they don't have much of an option," Tracy said.

"I want to go to Mexico to see what their life was like. Marco told me that when they got to the drop house in Phoenix, he spoke with a man who had finally made it on his fifth try."

"Fifth!"

"That's what Marco said. The man must have really wanted to be here. He was planning on bronzing his shoes and putting them on his mantle as a reminder of his final trip across the desert." Marco said it was his good luck, of course, that had rubbed off on the man. "Most of the people with Marco had blisters and swollen feet. One guy had a cane he'd made from a stick after twisting his ankle on a rock." Bette remembered Marco telling her that when he arrived in Warren, he bought some cheap shoes two sizes too big, knowing that he'd have to give them away when his feet shrank back to normal size.

"How far'd they walk?"

"I think it was just south of Tucson. How many miles is that? Fifty? A hundred? They hid in a ditch beside a freeway until cars came and picked them up. Marco said at the end of the journey, the coyote sounded like a broken record, 'Only half an hour more,' then later, 'Only half an hour more.' Over and over." Marco had thought the guy was lost for part of the trip. It all looked the same, one pokey thing after another, rocks that rolled under his feet, up one draw and down another. "The guides had made them throw away the last of their food and most of their water in the morning, saying they were close and wouldn't need it. They didn't want all that trash at their pick up spot for future runs. It'd been dark for at least two hours when they got to the freeway, and they hadn't eaten since morning. When they got to Phoenix someone made them egg tacos."

Bette peeled an orange and tucked the rinds into her pack. "The next day, Enrique drove to Phoenix and waited in a Food City parking lot. A car pulled up beside him, and he handed the money through the window. After they counted it, Marco hopped out and got in with Enrique. That was it."

"Wow, and this happens all the time."

"All the time. Enrique told us that there were about thirty people in the house with the guys with the guns. Twenty-five hundred times thirty. Someone's making a lot of money." Bette knew the crossing used to be easier, and they didn't have to hike so far to get beyond the border patrol checkpoints.

"It does sound like the crossing creates a bonding of sorts. Kind of like those of us who have hiked in and out of the Grand Canyon. It's an accomplishment of endurance that connects people."

"Except not so many die in the Canyon," Bette said, "and it's an adventure by choice, not necessity."

"Right," Tracy said. "Are you ready for your dip in the river?"

"Okay, my little fish of a friend."

They left their clothes on the shore and rock-hopped out toward the center of the water. It was only about two feet deep, and Tracy slid in first and dog-paddled upstream. Bette squatted on a rock and watched the river flow toward her, enjoying the sound of the burbling water blocking out all other noise. Slowly she placed her feet and legs in the water then rolled in onto her back. She held onto the rock with one hand and let her head sink back until she saw nothing but azure sky.

***

Marco wasn't back from work when she returned home the next day, so she decided to take a shower and start dinner. In their bedroom she saw a small teddy bear propped up against her pillow holding a book as if reading, its legs under the covers. It was adorable and made her smile with joy.

When he arrived home, he asked, "¿How was your *viaje* with *la chicis*?" Besides Bette's friend Tracy, she had a German colleague with the same name. To differentiate the two she had referred to her office mate as the *alemaña*, the German, but in her poorly-accented Spanish it came out with all those vowels like *la animal*, the animal. That's all it took for Marco's sense of humor to latch on to a new family word, not English, not Spanish, not even Spanglish. Their private family vocabulary grew daily. So her friend Tracy was referred to as *la chicis*, the small one, while her German co-worker was fondly referred to as *la animal*.

"It was good. We saw lots of birds. ¿How was it here?" she asked him. "¿What did you do last night? ¿Did you and the bear have a nice time together?"

He laughed and kissed her, then said, "*Puis*, Enrique, and Fernando came over."

She was quiet for a minute staring at the ground then looked into his eyes. "¿For dinner or drinking?"

"We just drank a little." Bette had never known them to be able to stop until they couldn't hold any more.

"Marco, he's only fifteen." Bette drew in a big sigh. "¿Did they drive home?"

"No, they slept here."

"¿*De veras?*" Really?

"*Si. De veras.* I want to cook tongue on Sunday," he said to change the subject. "Let's pick the last onions from the garden for the top." He mimed chopping and sprinkling and smiled at Bette while licking his lips.

She remembered the gray-pink four-inch wide cow's tongue, plastic-wrapped on its white tray, so long that it was doubled back on itself. Ick. And yet she'd had to admit that it was her favorite of all the strange meats she'd eaten since she'd been involved with Marco. It was firm but not chewy or stringy and tasted somewhere between prime rib and bacon – *muy sabrosa.* She'd confessed this love of a food most Americans found gross to *la animal* thinking she could relate since they ate odd foods in Germany, too. Bette had watched her shiver involuntarily and try to smile through a grimace. Oh well.

She and Marco had had tongue only in the Mexican restaurant one town over or brought it home pre-cooked in a white, foil-lined deli bag from Garcia's Market. Marco had never cooked it in Mexico, so this would be his first try.

"¿Where are you going to buy it?" she asked, letting him off the hook about his drinking with a minor. Garcia's was forty minutes away, round trip, and she couldn't imagine him driving all that way. He was still a cautious driver in the U.S. and usually stayed in town.

"It's very cheap at...at the store whose name cannot be said." They laughed, and Bette thought: Walmart. Before he had his truck, she would sometimes drive him there and wait outside in the car, reading a book, but she'd never go in. She hated how towns paid millions of dollars to such a rich corporation to draw them to their towns and then Walmart ran smaller local companies out of business and underpaid their employees. "¿Remember it was really expensive at Safeway, maybe fifteen dollars?" Marco said.

She saw the tongue again in the meat cooler and wondered how it could fit in a cow's mouth. If Marco ever went back into veterinary work, she was going to have a look.

"At Voldemort, it's only seven," he said.

"Voldemort!" she blurted. "The store whose name cannot be said." She leaned down and kissed him. "Help me unload the car, *tontito.*"

CHAPTER 11

Pasilla
Chipotle
Guajillo
Pequin
Habañero
Chile de Arbol
Serrano
Jalapeño
Thai
Cayenne

"Tom, how are your boys doing?" Bette asked.

Her friend worked every summer in the U.S. to build up his finances for the rest of the year when he lived in Bolivia. The money he could make guiding river trips for four months was worth a year's living expenses in Latin America's second poorest country. He often stayed with Bette before returning home. This fall he had come up to be part of a conference and had made an effort to visit and try to talk Bette into living in Bolivia for a while. They had met when he was a student at the school where she had done billing, and they'd remained friends over the years. He stood in the doorway twisting his torso from right to left, working the car kinks out of his back.

"The boys are great. Memo is reading now and Paco's turning into a little jock, just like his dad." He grinned at Bette.

"Oh, I bet that makes you happy." Tom wasn't like one of those guests who hung around all the time waiting to be entertained. Bette had plenty of alone time each morning as he did his stretching, practiced Tai Chi, and went running.

They were in her spare room that had easily converted from her office into a guest room by the addition of a thick foam pad and bedding. The room was a mishmash of furniture from second-hand stores and yard sales. The particleboard desk had been found beside the road with a "free" sign on it though its previous owner had once liked it enough to stencil climbing ivy in green and brown up its sides. Her silver laptop sat on the desk, the only new item in the room, in sharp contrast with the two mismatched file cabinets, a glass-fronted china hutch filled with yarn and dyed wool, and a wall full of bookshelves crammed to the gills. Tom would be cozy here as soon as his laptop replaced hers.

"When are they going to start coming with you for the summers?"

"That's a hard one. Candelaria will have to come, too, to watch them while I'm working and she still doesn't like it here."

"I can understand that." Tom and Candelaria's marriage had been dubious from the start. Tom hadn't wanted to have children and only agreed on the condition that they raise them in the U.S. After their sons were born, Candelaria changed her mind and Tom had to move to Bolivia to be with them. Watching his sons' health deteriorate in the polluted country had been one of the factors in his pursuit of a graduate degree.

He and Bette had met when he had been working toward his master's degree, focusing on how to educate the citizenry of his adopted country about the ills associated with burning garbage, including plastic, which was the accepted mode of disposal. One of the results of this practice included sick children as they breathed the noxious fumes. His passionate mix of love for the environment and social justice was enough for her to seek him out as a friend. His knowledge of Latino culture through marriage to a Bolivian had become an unexpected bonus.

"I thought she might like seeing a new place, especially knowing it's just for a few months."

He shook his head. "I hate not seeing my boys for four months, especially when they're growing so fast right now."

"At least the money will go a long way down there. Hey," Bette said, switching to cheer him up, "I brought you a treat from the *panadaria*. *Churros*. And they're filled with *cajeta*."

"Yum." They moved into the kitchen and Tom reached for the plastic bag containing the long donuts covered with cinnamon sugar and stuffed with caramel. As he bit into one, his eyes closed, and a smile came to his face.

"Here, have a seat," she said, pulling a chair out for him at the table in the breakfast nook. She'd lined the walls with maps of the world, the U.S., and Mexico. Her "South Is Up" map was Tom's favorite, so she positioned him so he could see it from his chair. "Let me put some water on for tea to go with our *churros*. These caused a fight last night, so I want to thoroughly enjoy them after what I had to go through to get them."

"Let me guess," Tom said. "Marco."

"Yup." As she moved about her small kitchen filling the teakettle with water and lighting the stove, the day before haunted her. There was just one Mexican food store in the area, so when she and Marco had gone out to dinner in that town, they had swung by to pick up a few things. Standing at the pastry case she had asked Marco to get six *churros*, two for each of them and two for Tom who was expected the next day. Marco had thrown the bag of *churros* onto the bakery shelf and stomped out. They had Marco's favorite that day – pineapple cake – so she added a slice to the bag of *churros*, paid for their groceries, and headed out to the car.

Marco sat in the back seat of her car, as silent and impenetrable as a barrel cactus. He'd gained weight in the U.S. and now presented a formidable, solid presence. She used to feel intimidated by his strength. As a veterinarian, he could man-handle a three-hundred-pound pig, but once she'd learned how ticklish he was, that took the edge off. Now, however, she wasn't about to touch the prickly mass in the back seat.

She knew why he was mad…*churros* for another man. Just let him sulk, she thought. But no, not this time. She was tired of him still not understanding that her relationship with him wasn't in jeopardy if she had other friends.

"Marco, I know why you're mad. Because I bought something for Tom. *¿Estás loco?* This is the way I am – *generosa*. *¡Por Dios*, it's a good quality!" She flipped back and forth between Spanish and English, unable to quickly find the words she needed and frustrated at still having to be the one to do the work to communicate. Besides, she didn't care anymore if he was getting it or not. "I was buying a thirty-five cent sweet for a friend. *¿Quál es tu* fucking *problema?*" English for that word as she rarely used it and knew it would jolt him. "*Acéptame como soy.* It's the kind of person I am. Get used to it. It's a good thing, and I'm not going to change that because your ego can't take it." What was *ego* in Spanish? "Marco, *Me gusta como soy. ¿Entiendes?* I like who I am. If you don't, too bad. *¿Qué te importa?* I'm not going to change to be a person I don't like so you feel better. You and your rules." Even as she said it she could see all of the changes she'd made to accommodate this machismo's view of life including doing more than her share of the cooking and cleaning and wearing more shapely clothes. No more. "*Madura*, Marco. Grow up."

"Tom," she said to her friend as the teakettle began to whistle, "I keep waiting for him to change, but he never does."

"I hate to talk in generalities," Tom said, "but it's likely more than just Marco's personality. I've learned a lot about the Latino culture from my years living with them. They have no tolerance. Not even of their own culture, let alone ours."

"What do you mean?" She poured the boiling water into a blue and white Chinese-patterned teapot, and Tom got up to bring the mugs. The teapot, like a few of her dishes, had rice kernels baked into the clay. Marco had refused to believe it was rice even though he'd never seen those types of dishes before.

"Marco," she had said, "Look, you can see they're rice. Look how beautiful they are." She held up a cup so he could see the light through them. He hadn't bothered to look, and she had dropped the subject rather than have an argument. With the current rice shortage, Marco would never believe they would use their food staple for art.

Now Tom answered Bette. "They come up here and live in our culture but don't have any interest in learning about us. There is no cultural tolerance."

Bette sighed. "And from what I've seen, no cultural curiosity. He just wants his life, customs, and food transplanted up here." Bette had already given up trying to introduce him to foods of different cultures – Thai, Japanese, Greek – because he'd just pour *salsa* on it until it all tasted like the food he was used to. Looking over at her spice rack, she saw that all of her herb and spice jars were dust-covered from lack of use. Their basket of *chiles*, however, contained at least six varieties which were always fresh.

Turning back to Tom she said, "The Mexican guys I hang out with are always complaining about the U.S. I thought they were just spouting off because they feel impotent in this culture and wanted to show how much better Mexico and its customs are. You're saying they actually feel this way because they're intolerant as a whole?"

"Yes."

"Wow. That's a lot to take in." Bette thought about the tirades her new students spewed forth when they found a North American who could speak their language. They'd go on and on about how bad everything was in the U.S., the legal system, food, and how we treat our pets better than our children until they slowly petered out. Bette had learned to let it wash over her, partly because she couldn't understand most of it, partly because she thought she recognized their need to express simmering pent-up anger. They'd been voiceless for so long, unable to communicate, and often poorly treated by clerks in stores and those who hired them for day labor. Her students reported feeling unwanted, unintelligent, and invisible. She had tried her best to listen and see them.

"I threw a birthday party for myself, and invited my former Spanish teacher and Marco and three guys who always hang out at our house."

Tom nodded.

"Everything went pretty well for a while and then Marco, two shots of tequila in him, went off on something. He brought the liquor to my party, by the way. I couldn't catch what he was saying because he was talking fast, something about soccer or history, but whatever it was it upset my teacher, and she said, 'I don't have to listen to this,' and got up and left." After seeing her out, Bette had asked Marco what they were talking about, and he said she acted like she knew Mexico just because she'd lived there for a while. He'd been setting her straight.

"I was furious at Marco for ruining my birthday. I told him it was rude to hold forth with a monologue, especially one I couldn't understand, and to drive away my friend. But he's never apologized. He always goes back to her being at fault."

"I rest my case," Tom said.

"I'm afraid to let my mind go to stereotypes. It's safer to think that it's just Marco, the bull-headed Aries. I can't tell you how much time I spend explaining and defending immigrants to the *gringo* world. It's such a hot topic in Arizona. I feel like I'm bottling up the other half of every conversation."

"Give me an example."

"Oh, like I'll talk about how English is such a difficult language to learn, especially on top of full-time work, but inside I'm thinking, Why don't my students try harder? Why am I the only one who carries around a Spanish dictionary? They're in an English-speaking country. I wonder why they don't use flashcards. They come to class, and I have to teach them the same things over and over. They don't do their homework, don't practice. My dad was such a task-master. I worked hard in school and out." A bird flew to the white oak tree outside the window distracting her from her diatribe. It was a spotted towhee which landed near a squawking scrub jay. What was a ground-feeder doing up so high? The scrub jay harassed it until it flew away.

"I can't believe I'm saying these things out loud. I sound just like one of those close-minded people I rail against."

"Don't be so hard on yourself, Bette." Tom poured the Afternoon Darjeeling tea. The aroma rose and made her smile. "Do you want milk with your tea?" he asked.

"Yes." Bette rose to get it.

"No, it's okay," he said, putting his hand on her shoulder, encouraging her back into her seat.

She'd forgotten what it was like to be waited on.

"And the way they treat women," she said. "*Hijole.*" Tom laughed. "When I was hanging out with only the guys, I could get them to serve themselves and wash the dishes, but it was a struggle with lots of nagging and cajoling. Now that I have women friends in my Mexican world, I have to sit by and watch them wait on the men and children who are old enough to be helping out. I want to yell, Get out of the fifties, but it's not my place."

"I know. I hate to see it. Their roles are set, and they're rigid about change."

"So, how's it with you and Candelaria? She's got to be a little more liberal after her time in the U.S., no?" Tom ran his finger around the plate, then put his sugar-coated finger into his mouth. When he looked at her, she could see the answer.

"We struggle all the time, and she won't ever consider counseling. She's a product of her culture and doesn't want to change. Family. It's their most important value. But it's a larger family, not just us. So we spend a lot of time at her parents' house." Bette poured him another cup of tea and added a little milk. "Thanks. Except for the environment and our kids, Candelaria isn't interested. She refuses to exercise, won't try Tai Chi, doesn't value personal growth, and hates new things. I'm not so sure this mixing of cultures is such a good idea."

He and Bette gazed at one another for a long moment before simultaneously breaking contact. She wondered if he was sharing the same thought, that it would be so much easier if they switched partners. She ran her hand up the thick square glass vase of bamboo in the center of the table, one of her gifts for Marco.

Bette nibbled on her *churro* then took a sip of her tea. Again, movement out the window caught her eye, and she turned to see an acorn woodpecker land on a ponderosa pine and start pounding away. Birds had no weekends. No time off in which to enjoy themselves. Birds just mated, and that was it.

"If their ways around women don't hurt them, who are we to say they should be like us? It's their culture, and we just happen to be involved in it. Maybe the women are happy that way."

"Yes, but they're here. They don't want to assimilate, Bette."

"Do you think that's it? I try to believe they stay separate because of fear of not knowing the language. And to keep from being vulnerable. Maybe you're right. I don't know if I'd want to assimilate either. I like my ways." Marco often complained about something she did or wore, or how she acted, who she talked to. Women don't talk to men by themselves, he'd said to her more than once. He wanted her to fit into his world, even here.

"Candelaria says it's a different way of life, and you bring it with you wherever you go."

Bette had to admit that some of their ways were so tender, like how they treat their children. She smiled at Tom. "Can we pick and choose? How are we ever going to solve this whole mess?"

"This way," he said. "Have another *churro*." And as she bit through the brown crust, the sweetness flooded her mouth, turning bitter on her tongue.

When Marco came home, he instantly hit it off with Tom and insisted on making him a special meal of broccoli and egg patties in *tomatillo* salsa. It was as if nothing had happened the night before. Bette watched the two of them talk and work together in the kitchen and wondered why she wasn't able to let things go as easily. Didn't Marco want to improve his life? Where was his willingness to see how things operated in a different culture? It was like he didn't care about figuring out who he was and didn't have any interest in improving their relationship if it meant he had to change.

She cleared the teacups off of the table and stood beside Marco at the counter. She loved his short, muscular body, his skin now fading from the dark chocolate of summer, returning to mocha. Tom cracked up about something Marco said, but Bette missed it. She'd try to rein in her need to make things be a certain way – her way – and just be with the Marco she had. Humor, sex, free language lessons. She didn't want to be unwilling to compromise, too. If she could keep things relatively static, they'd be fine.

CHAPTER 12

Que quires decir con esto?
What do you mean by that?

Lo digo en serio.
I mean it.

Tomar en cuentra
To consider

Pensar + infinitive = to intend + infinitive
Repensar = to think over (again)

A veces, creo que este demasiado por mi.
At times, I think this is too much for me.

The next Monday, Bette's ESL student Catalina showed up at her office looking very serious. She said her car wouldn't start, and she didn't know what to do. Then out tumbled the story that her husband Nemecio had been arrested and her car was dead at Fry's Market. Bette called Enrique, but he said he didn't have time to look at the car.

"Why not? It won't take long."

He rattled off something in Spanish, and Bette knew he was trying to push her off.

"Please, Enrique. Just stop by after work. It's probably something minor." She stuck to English.

She hung up, shaking her head, no. Pinche Enrique, she said to herself, sounding just like Marco.

"Can I help with something?"

"Oh hi, John."

"I was passing by and overheard your phone call."

"Know anything about cars?"

"I converted my diesel VW to run on French fry oil. Does that count?"

A big smile spread across Bette's face. "Oh, I forgot about that. That's so great." They set a time to meet after work. Then Bette started in on their next priority of finding Nemecio.

"He was with four others on their way to work and was arrested," Catalina said. For falsifying documents, though all he had on him at the time of arrest was his Mexican driver's license and his identification card from the consulate. "He always keeps his forged social security card and green card at home."

Bette called the jail and was told that he was released at 11:54 so she took off from work, and they went looking for him thinking he might be walking home. Catalina sat in the passenger seat, tears streaming down her face, while Bette drove around and made phone calls. She offered Catalina water to replenish some of what she was losing. A slow shake of her head no.

They went back to Catalina's trailer, over to the jail, drove by their friends' homes. Back and forth. How could she doubt the jail when they had given her an exact time, but where was he? After searching futilely for three hours, she called back to learn that he had been transferred to a jail in Camp Verde. Didn't these people have computers?

Bette called that jail and was told he was being held for six weeks for a trial date.

"¿Can I stay with you tonight?" Catalina asked. "I'm scared staying alone. ¿What if *la migra* come for me?"

They met John in the grocery store parking lot, and he was able to diagnose and fix the problem within a few minutes, a broken battery cable connector. While he was monkeying with the part he asked Bette, "What did her husband do to get put into jail?"

"Doesn't sound like anything." She explained about the charges of falsified documents. "I'm guessing they were profiled because there were five Mexicans in one car."

"He must have done something. Did they find drugs on them?"

"He's one of my ESL students. Always comes to class. Hard working, shy. I can't imagine him selling drugs." Bette was glad when the repair was complete since she wanted his help but was confused by his assumption.

"Thank you so much, Sir," Catalina said in slow, precise English. She held his hand in hers, then dropped her eyes and stepped back.

Bette stepped closer to squeeze his hand then felt his arm snake around her, pulling her into a hug. A woozy sensation took over as she melted into full body-to-body contact. Separating and stepping back, she said, "I really appreciate this." Appreciate the hug? her mind yelled at her. "I mean, thank you so much." That wasn't any better, she thought. "For fixing the car, I mean." She knew she sounded like a fool. "I owe you."

"I'll find a way for you to repay me," he said grinning. "Call me if you need anything else."

"Thanks," she said but wondered why he was rushing to convict someone he had never met. Did everyone fall back on stereotypes? She gave an involuntary shudder against the instinctive rise of inner heat that had surged through her as she was held tightly by this tall man, their bodies meshing so seamlessly.

Marco wasn't making her confused emotions any less muddled. He wasn't happy about Bette's helping, but she silenced his complaints by telling him it was the loving thing to do. "¿No, tienes compasión?" She settled Catalina in the spare room.

The next day on her lunch hour, Bette and Catalina went to her trailer to pick up a few things. A neighbor came over and told her he had spoken with her husband. Nemecio had been deported the day before and had called from Mexico. Bette wondered what the jail would say this time if she called back. Thus began a trying two weeks, but she finally managed to help get Catalina reunited with her husband in Nogales, Mexico.

***

After she returned from her first visit to Mexico, she went to Tracy and Don's for dinner, and to decompress. The driveway leading to their house was so steep that it required Bette to downshift into first gear. She was glad it was short and paved since it felt like she was heading straight up to the stars. Bette let herself in the back door and called a greeting to her friend. A big, healthy Boston fern was in the kitchen sink with a trail of leaves leading across the floor from where it normally hung in the corner of the room. Tracy appeared from the living room with a large green watering can.

"Hi, Trace. I'll take care of the fern. Is it ready to be re-hung?"

"Yes, thanks. I just have a few more to water."

Bette placed the lush plant back on its hook in the ceiling then found the broom in the hall closet. "I had a come-apart last night. I'm embarrassed to talk about it but need to."

Tracy turned down the Krishna Das music and asked, "Was it about Marco?"

Bette pictured herself in a dark driveway with Marco, reaching toward him and poking at the lit numbers on his cell phone as he was dialing to speak with someone else in the middle of their argument. She heard her voice turn into a screech and watched the phone go flying as her hands slapped it away from him. It had lasted only moments but was enough to shred any final belief that her circumstances weren't having an effect on her.

She quit sweeping and said. "I just lost it. I was screaming at him, 'You don't think I'm stressed? You don't think I'm stressed?' Really screaming. I was so mad. I thought I was going to have a heart attack. It was like in *Aliens* when that creature ripped through the guy's chest. I had no idea that was inside of me." Bette's eyes lost their focus. The pressure in her chest ached all the way through to her back. She had thought she was handling things well enough but now realized she was only calm on the surface.

"I would have jumped on his phone and crushed it into tiny bits if I could've found it in the dark."

"What were you fighting about? Is he still mad that you helped Catalina?" Tracy put the watering can down beside the refrigerator then took the dustpan from Bette and emptied it in the garbage under the sink.

"Yes, he wanted me to call about weekend jobs for him. I told him I'd do it the next day since I was too tired and he started going off on how I always find time to help others but not him. As if. He thinks he has priority because he's my sweetheart. Yes, of course, he does, but he's always harassing me about helping others. It's relentless."

"I'm afraid to even say it, but help me with dinner, and then you can tell me more," Tracy said. "Don's going out to play music tonight, so it's just the two of us. The artichokes and quinoa are almost done. I thought I'd sauté some red peppers and onions. What's that sauce you make with the capers? Can you mix up some of that?"

Bette was gathering the balsamic vinegar, olive oil, capers, and garlic for the sauce when Don entered the room looking like a sprite. He wore wide-legged, moss green linen pants, and a purple long-sleeved shirt topped by a bright, patterned vest. Under his black beret, gray hairs poked out around aquamarine earrings. He greeted her then flitted from the living room to the kitchen and back again, gathering his drums and snacking out of the refrigerator.

"Hey, hand me that container of feta," Bette said. "That will go great with the peppers."

"How are things going?" he asked.

"Oh, they're a little rough right now. Marco believes he's doing me a favor by pointing out what he sees as errors in my ways, but he's just adding to the stress. We're still arguing on paper, try that in a heated argument, but things'll get better with time."

They talked about Don's business for a bit. Yes, he was still eeking out a living. "*Poco a poco*, eh?" He smiled at Bette. "Hey, T, do we have any avocado left?" He grabbed the half shell, salted it, kissed his sweetheart, and then hauled his drums out to his truck.

"And off the little whirling dervish spins," Bette laughed.

"Here, I've got the mayo and artichokes," Tracy said as she headed toward the back door to the table on the porch. "Bring the peppers and sauce?"

Bette carried her items outside, making sure to keep her foot between the orange cat and freedom. There'd be no bird-eating for him today. Tracy still had hollyhocks in bloom and baskets of petunias, and sweet Williams added color to the corners of the porch. A few small tomatoes dangled from vines but it wouldn't be many more nights before they needed to be harvested, ripe or not.

"Marco won't change his mind. About anything. He has these rules. Things are right or wrong, and he, by God, knows the difference and is going to inform everybody. I'm sick of his teach and preach kind of communication."

"You've said that before," her friend said.

Bette dropped her head on her chest. "I'm so exhausted with trying to get through to him. Part of it's the Spanish, part of it's cultural. But I think most is Marco's stubbornness. It's hard to sort out, and right now, it's just not worth the effort."

"Tell me what happened with Catalina. I never did get the full story."

"I don't think there is one," Bette said. "I'm not sure if the sheriff's office is doing things on purpose to confuse the public or if they're simply incompetent." As they ate their meal, Bette told of the runaround she'd received trying to locate Catalina's husband after he'd been arrested.

Tracy scraped a mayonnaise-tipped artichoke leaf across her bottom teeth then tossed it into the sage green ceramic bowl on the table between them. "She must have been so anxious to join her husband."

"That first day with her was pretty rough, but she pulled herself together amazingly well. I gave her advice and had to drive around a bit, but she took responsibility and figured it all out. She had to vacate their trailer and get all their furniture and clothes and other stuff moved to my garage, arrange to get her deposit back, shut off the power and gas and get those deposits back."

"Not easy even for those of us who speak English."

Bette told Tracy about the funky law Mexico has about the age of a car that can be imported into their country. It can't be newer than ten years, but if it's too old, the cost of legalizing it is so high that it isn't worth it. Even the used car dealers in Arizona knew about it.

"What's the purpose of that?"

"Who knows? Anyway, she had to sell the one car because it was too old to take into Mexico, but the title was in her husband's name. We figured out a way to get the titles notarized. I can't tell you how or I'll have to kill you."

"Ha ha." Tracy smiled.

"Finally she made the arrangements to have all of her things hauled over the border where she met her husband. She did it all."

"Pretty impressive. Her husband better watch out. He's getting an Americanized wife back," Tracy said.

"Exactly. I don't think that Rosa would come close to being able to do what Catalina did. It might have something to do with their ages. I'm guessing Catalina is about twenty-three and Rosa is in her early thirties. Nemecio wanted her to drop everything and join him in Mexico, immediately. I think he's in his mid-thirties and very similar to Marco in his attitude. But Catalina's been working hard and didn't want to leave everything behind. Oh, and she had to get all of their money out of banks here. Guess how much they'd saved? Don't even try. You'll never guess. Twenty-three thousand. In two years." Bette's mind went back to Catalina and her stuffing money down their socks, in their undies, in their bras so they could carry it into Mexico.

"That's a lot of money. Why can't I save that much? What did they do for work?"

"Nemecio worked in construction and Catalina at Taco Bell six days a week for a year, then she added on ironing at a dry cleaners. She'd also been buying clothes at thrift stores and K-Mart and is planning on selling them in Mexico. I guess clothes are expensive there so she can make some money."

"Is that where you got your sweater?" Tracy asked.

"Yes, Catalina gave it to me as a gift, one of many, for helping her. Isn't it great?" Bette held out the sides of the cotton periwinkle blue cardigan. "And this shirt, too. She spent a lot of time sorting through and repacking all of her stuff that we hurriedly crammed into my garage when she was afraid the border patrol would come for her. I knew the immigration wasn't in town and wanted to assure her that the sheriff wouldn't just deport her, but even I was wondering after I got such a runaround from them."

"Do you want tea? I'll put water on." They got up, cleared the table, and put the leftovers away.

"The whole time Catalina was with me, Marco harped at me about all the help I was offering her. He was nice to her but kept saying to me things like she should live somewhere else for the two weeks it took her to get everything ready. As if I'd kick her out. I don't understand why he couldn't step up and help her himself." Bette stood at the kitchen sink washing plates and remembered when she was sixteen and didn't have a place to go.

"I don't care where you go," her father had said. "I'm not going to have a liar in my house." She had gone camping with friends and hadn't told her father that boys were there, too. When he found out, he made her leave. How could Bette not share her two-bedroom house with a woman in need?

"Do you want green or Bancha?" her friend asked, pulling tea tins out of the cupboard.

"Bancha sounds good. Marco did give us the contact of the guy who hauled all of her furniture and stuff across the border, but he wouldn't even tell Catalina directly. He kept saying that *she* needed to ask *him* for his help, but she didn't feel comfortable speaking to him first because that isn't done in their culture." Bette mocked pulling her hair out, and droplets of dishwater flew about the kitchen. "I was stuck between Marco's demanding standards and the inefficiency of their cultural morays. Who gives a shit about propriety in an emergency?"

"Obviously they do."

"She had to sell her van because it was a 2001 and they have those ridiculous laws. The other car has a manual transmission which she doesn't know how to drive, so I agreed to drive her across the border. I wanted to see Mexico and who else could do it?"

"She could have paid someone," Tracy said. "I can see Marco's point on this one. You're wound up and have been talking nonstop since you got here. You don't have to save the entire Mexican population of Warren single-handedly."

Is that what it looked like, she wondered. "It's been a rough few months."

"Don made some No Pudge Fudge brownies from Trader Joe's, but I don't know if I should give you the caffeine."

"I. Must. Have. One." They took their goodies and tea back outside and sat in the twilight.

"What was your trip across the border like?" Tracy asked.

An Anna's hummingbird sipped at the feeder, his hot pink head catching the day's last light. Awfully late in the year for it to be here. "I think I could like it there." Bette had been enchanted by it. The mishmash of architecture with different building materials, styles, and sizes set cheek-to-jowl along the street – stucco, brick, wood, metal. There were dissimilar heights as sections had been added onto roofs. Old adobe walls had been stuccoed over, but the plaster was coming off to reveal the thick solid bricks behind. Most of the buildings had their electrical wiring on the outside, running up the walls and then looping to another building. It looked a little dangerous and patched-together, yet workable.

"The colors were wild. The buildings were turquoise and pink, lime green and bright orange. Marco's favorite was there, too. One day when we were walking in my neighborhood, we passed a lemon yellow house, and Marco said, 'What a beautiful home.' When I asked him what he liked about it he said that it stood up and said, look at me. I'm sure the neighbors didn't see it that way."

"Not likely, but what a nice image," Tracy said. "It's fun to see inside his head to understand why they like those bright colors."

"It was great that I was in Nogales on November first which is All Saints' Day, the day before the Day of the Dead. There were flower vendors lining the streets, and their carts were overflowing with marigolds and gladiolas and wreaths." At one of the flower stands Bette had watched a man whack off the stems with a machete, something she had never seen in the U.S.

"It sounds beautiful, even for a border town."

"It was. And along the wall between the U.S. and Mexico, which is this great big, tall, steel monstrosity, there were groups of school kids in their uniforms building altars. *Ofrendas*. They were lined up one after the other, and they got more and more elaborate as the day went on. There was one of Frida Kahlo."

"That sounds pretty cool."

Bette nodded. They'd left at three in the morning so they could get there by eight so it was a bit of a surreal day, especially by the end. The town felt full of life and energy. "There were also long lines at the bank and people sitting alongside the road, maybe waiting for buses, so it wasn't all wonderful, but the overall sense was of vibrant life."

"Yes, I can see how you'd like that," Tracy said. "You love intensity."

"And the cars...people drove kind of crazy, a little outside of the rules. A lot more than us. At first, I was behind Sergio, the guy driving the big pickup towing the trailer with all of Catalina's goods inside. It helped me to get my bearings as far as how fast to drive, how narrow a place to squeeze through, where to park." Bette held an imaginary steering wheel and maneuvered with her elbows close to her sides. "Then Catalina and I drove around for another two hours doing paperwork to get her car legalized while the others moved things from Sergio's trailer to another truck and trailer." The drivers in Nogales had been considerate, waving her into traffic when there were long lines. Once she crossed in front of a bunch of cars, making a semi-illegal left turn and no one honked or did the *chinga su madre* raising of their arm. There's no way she could have pulled that off without getting the North American equivalent of being flipped off. "It was kind of like a choreographed dance at times. More like driving in Boston than anywhere else I've been."

"I forgot you lived back East," Tracy said.

"Yes, though it was sometimes nerve-wracking in Massachusetts, I think they were better drivers than we are out here. Maybe it's from living closer together. You begin to think and drive like part of a unified field in order to keep things flowing."

"We're too independent out here to give way to others. The Wild West."

"Mexico is sure behind on child safety, though. There were lots of little kids standing up in front seats."

"Just like we used to do before seatbelts."

"And the roads are beat up, same as the cars."

"Probably related."

"It was all so relaxed and loose. I wonder what it would actually be like if I lived there. Most likely it would drive me, Ms. Efficiency Expert, crazy. We had to drive to three different places to get Catalina's car legalized, and the directions on what to do next were atrocious. Could I handle the convoluted bureaucracy?"

"I think your bookkeeping nature might have a few issues."

"Yeah, me trying to organize the entire country. You'd do much better. Most could benefit from your acupuncture."

"We've been considering moving to Mexico."

Bette didn't want that added to her plate right then so slipped it into a corner of her mind for later. "Do you have time for an owl walk?"

"Yes. You can use Don's binos," Tracy said.

"Great. Marco was in my head the entire time I was in Mexico. I soaked up everything, trying to see what it was that made him who he is."

"Good luck with that."

"Maybe the owls will impart some wisdom tonight on how it all fits together."

CHAPTER 13

Employer Sanction Law – 2008

"Under state law, if an employer knowingly hires an illegal worker, the business can be fined for the first offense, and a second offense can mean you lose the right to do business in the state."

Bette headed into work earlier than usual so she could check the election results on the internet. She'd listened to NPR and gotten the good news about the national elections – Obama had won – but didn't know how Arizona had fared. She loved her state but hated its right-leaning politics. She walked in and heard Cindy and Antoinette hooting from down the hall.

"Finally the Mexicans are going to have to learn English," Cindy said.

"Yah, just like my grandpa did when he came over from France," Antoinette said. "Why should we spend money on services for them? They're just lazy."

Bette walked toward her office, and they stopped talking. They'd seen Marco visiting Bette. She jabbed the on button on her computer and tossed her backpack beside her desk. She was looking at the election results on the screen when she heard a tapping at her door.

"Did you see that all three environmental issues got voted down?" John stood with his hiking boots firmly planted on the gray carpeted floor, his arms crossed over his sage chambray shirt. "I don't know if I can stand by and watch them give rights to corporations and developers to completely destroy what's left of our state."

Bette nodded. "It makes me embarrassed to be an Arizonan."

"We're living in the Dark Ages with a bunch of Plebes." John shook his head.

Bette had to agree. "Last year, when our fellow citizens voted to require documentation of citizenship to attend community college, the public-funded English as a Second Language program collapsed. Ours tripled."

"Right. Yours is volunteer-run."

"We don't require proof of anything. Now I wonder if it's going to fold, with the employer sanction law. If no one will hire them for fear of losing their business license, who will stay around?"

"You think the illegals are going to leave the state?"

Bette could feel her shoulders tighten and made herself speak calmly. "They're undocumented, not illegal."

"Right. Sorry. But they did break the law."

"They committed a misdemeanor to enter without documentation. They're not illegal." Bette forced a weak smile. "Sorry. Personal sore spot. Too many years being the outsider." She shrugged in a make-peace effort.

"You'll have more time for other things," he said.

"You sound like Marco." She watched him stiffen at the mention of her lover's name, part of her intention.

"Better get back to work," John said, and turned and left.

Bette opened her account file and watched the numbers line up. It was all right there on the screen. Why couldn't the politicians and voters see that? You lined the credits up on one side and the debits on the other and tried to make it balance at the end of the day. It was logical, not emotional. Couldn't they see the benefit of preserving the environment for the long haul? What about the value of allowing immigrant workers to go to school to learn the language or get a driver's license, so they understood the laws in their adopted country? It was a matter of black and white, of assets and liabilities, and with careful attention to a complex situation Bette thought they could come up with laws that benefited them all. She got out her ruler, straightened her printout, and began her work.

***

Bette's canvas bag was stretched wide to hold all of her ESL materials and felt heavier than usual that night. She plunked it on the coffee table in the classroom and started unloading paper, pens, Spanish-English dictionaries, and copies of *Ingles para Latinos*. Marco showed up that night, and she gave him a hug and a kiss before the others arrived. He'd brought her favorite energy bar, and she gave him another kiss.

"Hey *chaparita*." he said. "¿How was your day?"

"*No bueno*," she said, but more students walked in, so she didn't elaborate. Marco took a seat but kept his eyes on her.

"Good evening," she said in English to each new person. "How are you?"

"Fine," was the answer of choice that week.

She chatted with those with better English, waiting for the stragglers to arrive. "Sergio, how is your cold? Do you feel better?"

"*Si*, um yes. I feel good today. Less cough."

There were eighteen that night, including three women and two children. Isa and Gerardo were with Rosa and Felipe. Gretchen, the head teacher was already there and soon another volunteer, Robin, would be arriving when she got off work. Gretchen started the class with an exercise to loosen them up and review what they'd done on Monday.

"Okay, when someone throws you the bear," she said, tossing the black-and-red checked teddy bear to Rosa, "say something about a person like tall, short, and happy. Remember?"

Rosa giggled, looked at her son Gerardo and said, "Tall," and tossed it to him. Around it went. "Young." "Hard worker." "Thin." That student received extra praise from Gretchen because of the way he mastered the *th* sound. Robin arrived and entered the circle beside Bette. "Can you believe the elections?" she whispered. "Is Gretchen going to tell them the news tonight?"

"She's waiting until the end, so we don't ruin the class."

Bette's Spanish was better than the other teachers', so after an hour of class she agreed to speak to them. "We have bad news." She rarely spoke complete sentences in Spanish during class so knew she had their attention. "There was an election in the United States yesterday. In Arizona, they voted for a few bad things for immigrants without papers. If employers are..." How to say *found?* Start again. "If employers have undocumented workers, they..." Could? Can? Are they the same? "...can lose their license to do business in the state. This means that some, or many, employers, it's possible..." Hmm...How to say, *may let go?* "Marco, *¿sabes la plabra por* fire?"

Robin had been flipping through a dictionary and provided the word.

"I don't know, but I think many will get fired."

The classroom was deathly quiet.

Bette forced herself to go on. "There are other new laws coming, too." Gretchen and Robin helped her try to explain the propositions and their consequences. Marco provided them with a word when he knew it.

"I didn't vote for these," Bette said, shaking her head.

"Me either," Robin and Gretchen said in unison.

Ricardo asked what the other propositions were. Bette tried to explain the one that was going to take away their right for recourse against disreputable employers. She saw blank looks around the room, so she tried again with an example.

"Three friends of mine were working for a *gringo* who had a landscaping company. He said he was going to pay them four hundred dollars a week but only gave them two hundred and sixty, week after week. My friends went to the court." She said the last word in English while looking at Marco, who wasn't any help.

She turned to Jesus. "*Tribunal,*" he provided.

"And the judge," she looked over at Jesus again.

"*Juez,*" he filled in.

"The judge made the boss pay them all their money. Now you don't have this right."

A few students nodded. She wanted to know what was in their heads and hearts but didn't push them. "There are going to be articles in *La Prensa* about the changes coming to the state. It's a newspaper in Spanish. I'll bring some back the next time I go to Phoenix."

Her students filed out quietly without saying, Have...a...good...week, carefully enunciating each word. She wished Marco could speak more English so she could gain some insights into their reactions. Even he wasn't aware of the extent of the changes that were about to come to the state and his fellow students. He had always just kept his head down, worked hard, and sent money back to Mexico.

***

When Bette arrived at Rosa's house for dinner that weekend, Rosa placed a cobalt blue bowl filled with steaming burgundy liquid in front of her on the beige floral oilcloth table covering. The white hominy floating in the soup was tinged orange by the spicy broth. Rosa piled shredded iceberg lettuce on the soup, sprinkled a spoonful of chopped onions over it, and layered on several thin slices of avocado. Between two-tone nails painted white and sparkly pink, she squeezed two lime halves then crushed oregano between her palms and let it rain down on the heaping bowl. Bette picked up her spoon, her mouth already watering.

"*Momento. Momento,*" Rosa said. She reached into a bag of tostada shells and spread sour cream over one and handed it to Bette. "*Ahora.*"

Bette smiled across the table at her friend. "¿This is the custom?" she asked in Spanish. Rosa nodded. Bette slurped a spoonful, and the aroma filled her head and delighted her taste buds. It was incredibly delicious, and she wished Marco was there to appreciate food from his homeland. Once again he had a weekend job.

As Bette ate, she asked Rosa where Amaya was. She could see a baby's bassinet on the floor by the microwave stand.

"She's next door bathing Estevan," Rosa said.

"¿How dirty can a little baby get?" Bette asked. They laughed, and Bette thought, why bother when you were just going to get dirty again. Besides, this was a desert and water was in short supply.

Rosa told her that Amaya and her family were going to move in with Luna and Ignacio, another of Rosa's brothers where they'd had the birthday party for Mariángela. Their plan was to save more money so they could return home to Mexico sooner. Bette tried to visualize the rooms in the pink trailer but couldn't figure out where this family of now five with baby Estevan and Amaya's fourteen-year-old sister Valery living with them was going to squeeze in amongst the five that already lived there.

"Betty," Rosa asked, bringing her attention back, "¿Does Estevan need a passport to fly to Mexico?"

Bette knew nothing about babies and passports but said she would look it up. When Rosa asked her to also find out how much it would cost for her, Gerardo, and Isa to fly to Mexico, Bette set her spoon down. Rosa talked on, but Bette stopped trying to understand what she didn't want to hear.

"No, no, Betty" Rosa said, moving around the table and hugging her to her chest. She held Bette and patted her back as tears squeezed out of Bette's eyes. "You can come and visit." As Rosa went back to her chair, Bette wiped her eyes.

"It's not the same if you're in Mexico and I'm here." She fiddled with her spoon. "¿Who's going to take Gerardo and Isa swimming?" Bette wasn't ready for this to end. Rosa gave her a sad smile.

Amaya walked in the kitchen nudging Bette out of her sorrow by placing Estevan in her arms. He was small for his three months but had a head full of fine black hair. Bette turned him around so he could see his mom and aunt then leaned over and inhaled deeply. Breast-fed babies smelled like caramel. He was wearing a fleece suit to keep him warm on this cool autumn night, and Bette wrapped her forearms around him and played with his hands.

"¿Te gusta mi posole?" Amaya asked.

"¿You made the *posole*?"

Amaya nodded and grinned, which almost completely closed her almond eyes. She looked like a porcelain doll in her black stretch pants and hot pink sweater embossed with gold flowers. Like Rosa, she had her hair in a ponytail pulled through the top of a visor.

"*Tu posole es delicioso.*"

"*¿Picosa?*"

"No, it's not too spicy. It's perfect."

Amaya started talking with Rosa about moving, but Bette lost track of the conversation and let her mind wander, enjoying the little being leaning against her chest.

When Amaya addressed her directly with a question, Bette said, "¿What?" and then Rosa stepped in to repeat it. Bette had gotten used to how Rosa spoke, her accent, and could understand most of what she said. She also thought Rosa knew by now which words Bette understood, so she made the effort to stick with those.

"¿Can you talk with the landlady about getting the deposit back?"

"*Si.*" As the two women rose from their chairs, Bette asked, "¿*Ahora?*" They nodded, and Bette gave Estevan a little nuzzle on his neck before handing him back to Amaya. Her heart was beating fast, and her arms were twitchy thinking about the possibility of Isa, Gerardo, baby Estevan, Javier, and Luna's daughters leaving her life. She knew how a life in constant motion could affect children with new schools, streets, customs, weather, and no friends, but right now she was only thinking about herself. She wanted to be in the center of the larger family she had never had.

"Okay," Bette said, standing up and pushing the chair in. The cinder block house where Rosa and Amaya lived was divided into three apartments, two down and one up, and was located in the alley behind the main house. The walk to the owner's place was short, but the path was unlit.

The landlady opened the front door, and warm air floated out toward them. Bette had forgotten that the owner's home would have central heating, not just a space heater like in Rosa's home. She told the owner what they were there for and they were invited inside. Another woman turned to look at them from the leather sofa that Bette could smell clear across the room. Amaya's son Javier piped up, "Mama, I smell saddles. ¿Where are the horsies?"

"Shush, *mi amor.*"

"They're supposed to give thirty days' notice," the landlady said.

They wouldn't have to move if the legislature hadn't passed that law, Bette wanted to say, but she feared identifying her friends as being here without documentation. Surely the landlady must know because who else would rent such a rat hole with mold crawling down the bathroom walls and a heater that didn't work, but Bette couldn't trust someone she didn't know. She let the landlady's comment go un-translated.

"Can they get their deposit back at the end of the month?"

"They didn't give me a deposit."

Bette struggled translating to see what the story was. She asked Amaya about the deposit and learned they paid the money to the person who lived in the apartment before them.

"They paid Julio the deposit when they moved in," Bette told the landlady.

"Well, he didn't pay the deposit, either. It was Carlita who was there before him."

While Bette was explaining this to Amaya and Rosa, the owner said to her friend on the couch, "Look at how lush his hair is. And his eyes look Asian. What a beautiful baby."

Rosa told Bette that she knew Carlita.

"If they want their deposit back," the owner said, "they need to find Carlita, then I'll give it to her, and she can give it to them."

They walked back to the apartments through the black night. Bette had also learned that the electricity was in Amaya's husband's name and the tenants split the water bill four ways between the three tiny apartments and the two-story house. They had had to trust the owner to make the correct calculations.

"¿Do you have a contract?"

"*Sí, esta en la casa*. But we can't read it," Amaya replied.

Of course, Bette thought, and remembered helping Rosa and Felipe fill out an application for reduced-price membership at the YMCA. She'd had to ask how much Felipe made per hour and the invasion of privacy made her squirm. That night she had managed to move things along between Amaya and the landlady all without screaming at her for her ridiculous rental practices, but she didn't know at the time that this was only the beginning of the exodus.

***

The next weekend Bette went bird watching with Tracy. It was at the tail end of the autumn migration, but they hoped to see some unusual birds still making the journey. Hiking up a dry creek bed under cottonwoods was something Bette loved, and the weather was perfect. She was in an old pair of jeans and a flannel shirt. Tracy wore her well-loved faded baby-blue cotton pants, a fleece jacket, and an Indian print scarf around her neck to keep her warm until the November day heated up.

"Ready for Thanksgiving?" Bette asked.

"Almost. You've got the pies covered, right?"

"Yup. Pumpkin and pecan." Tracy always had a big spread at her place, coordinating her friends to bring different dishes while she focused on the turkey, stuffing, and gravy. This would be Marco's first Thanksgiving, but they planned to have a Mexican version the Saturday after.

"I'd love to see a western tanager today. I wonder if there're any left or if they've all migrated away?" Bette said. "Remember when we saw that one up by Walnut Creek?"

"It looked like a Rocket Pop." Bette pictured Popsicles with the yellow, orange, and red stripes from her childhood. "Don and I are going camping up there next weekend."

"Going to be cold at night. That was where those javelinas came snuffling around our sleeping bags. Remember that?" Bette had figured out what they were by their musky smell.

"Yes, that was the same trip we both saw our first blue grosbeak."

"Wow, look how high the water was this year." Twigs, leaves, and branches had piled up on the trunks of the cottonwoods and willows that lined the creek and hung from the branches as high as their heads.

"It's hard to imagine that much water."

"And force," Bette said. They walked next to the creek bed between clumps of dry grass. Occasionally the arroyo narrowed, and they made their way through the gray boulders in the center of the dry creek. "Did I tell you that one of Rosa's brothers left?"

"The one with the two little girls?" Tracy asked.

"No, they're going to leave, too, but I don't think it'll be as soon. They're all leaving." Bette made herself slow down. "This is the family with the two boys, kindergarten and fourth grade."

"Did they go back to Mexico because of the new law?"

"Because of the law, yes, but they went back East where they know some people who will help them find work in a factory." Bette had helped them sell all of their belongings then watched them drive off to New York City.

"The Bronx. We practiced saying that. The Bronx. All four of them squeezed into a Ford Escort. I hope they don't get pulled over. Sometimes I don't know how my heart can take this." Bette's eyes teared up, and Tracy stopped walking and hugged her.

"I made little travel bags for the boys with gum and honey sticks and beef jerky. I put in coloring books and crayons, those find-the-hidden-object activity books, matchbox cars. I found comic books in Spanish for Vicente. I tried to put in non-messy treats to eat and things to entertain them."

"You're good at that."

"I can't tell you how many times I made cross-country trips with my dad. My Mexican friends are amazed at how good I am at shuffling cards. All that time in the backseat of a car had a few advantages. It helped me plan Oscar's trip. He's the dad. We marked up one of those big fifty-state map books and put numbered sticky notes on the pages. He'd been told which states to avoid because of *la migra* being there. That's the border patrol. That's something I never would have factored in." Bette had printed out maps of New York City, highlighting the route to where they were going to live in The Bronx.

Tracy stopped and leaned against a large granite boulder covered with green, rust, and beige lichens. "What about Rosa's family?" she asked.

Bette told her that the owner of the plant where Felipe and his brothers-in-law worked was planning to move his business to Kansas where immigration laws were less strict. He wasn't able to run his business for enough of a profit in Arizona without undocumented workers. But Rosa was afraid of tornados and missed her home, so she and the kids were returning to Mexico while Felipe would follow the company and work for a few more years.

"So much for our family-values government," Tracy said.

"Rosa hates that scenario. I've never seen a more loving couple." A yank-yank sound caught her attention, and she looked past her friend and watched a bird climbing down the trunk of a ponderosa pine. It had adapted to its home and developed its own niche for finding food, looking down rather than up like other birds. "White-breasted nuthatch." She and Tracy had been bird watching together since their friendship started and were accustomed to a conversation dotted with sightings. "Rosa and Felipe are so sweet together, and they've been married for fifteen years. I don't know how they're going to live apart." Rosa had told Bette they'd tried to do that when Felipe first came to the U.S., but it hadn't worked for long. That's when Rosa, Gerardo, and Isa made their way north. "I feel an ache in my heart when I think about it, so I try not to." She rubbed her chest with her open palm. "I can see why people have children."

"I never thought I'd hear you say that," Tracy said.

"I didn't say I wanted my own. But you should see these kids. They're so smiley, and we have such fun. Isa is learning English, and it's like having a front-row seat to a miracle. Now she says sentences like, But she no can see. Soon that's going to flip to how we say negatives. And Gerardo, he comes out with these amazing lines like, Oh my goodness, when he makes a mistake in math. It's so cute."

"You've got Marco and the guys. And the rest of Rosa's big clan. They're like your family," Tracy said. "You're over there all the time."

"A couple times a week," Bette said. Marco didn't like it, but he was working a lot of long days finishing up the interior of another massive house.

"They've transformed you. You never used to like kids, and now you're cheery whenever you talk about them."

"I know." Isa's first-grade enthusiasm was contagious. Gerardo was on the brink of discovering the magic of math. And then there was Rosa's extended family. She remembered gazing into the dark depths of baby Estevan's slanted eyes and nuzzling his caramel skin. And would she ever again lose hours sitting on the floor building Lego cities with a ten-year-old? "I hate to let them go. Let them all go." It was like she was getting the chance to experience parts of motherhood and reclaim a small part of the childhood she had missed. "I like sharing my evenings doing homework and singing songs."

"And having dinner made for you."

"Yes, that too, even though I'm chubbing up," Bette said. "Part of me will be happy to have more nights at home. Between helping Gerardo and Isa with their homework and teaching ESL, I'm home less and less."

They started hiking again, walking around the larger boulders and peeking to see if they could locate any water. Bette pictured Isa sitting side-by-side with her at the kitchen table, alternately reading pages from her books. Her little feet, so soft and warm, would dangle down and rest on top of Bette's cold ones. How was she going to live without that?

"Do you think they'd be better off in their own culture?"

"That's a hard one. I talked to Oscar and Alma before they took off and they had plenty of bad things to say about Mexico. That's why they went to New York." She told Tracy about the public education, which in reality was expensive for poor people, the corrupt police, and the unhealthy hospitals.

"And Alma said everyone has bars on their windows. And no one has money so they mistrust whoever comes to visit thinking they're looking for what they can steal later."

"I can't imagine."

"Me either. Oscar said they couldn't make a living. No matter how hard he worked, they could never get ahead."

Bette had students who'd worked back East cutting up chickens for seven dollars an hour, six days a week, with no overtime and horrible conditions, yet swore it was preferable to living in Mexico. She had never seen that side of their country, nor her own.

"What about Marco?" Tracy asked. "What's he going to do?"

"Not sure. He'd like to go back to Mexico now because he misses his daughters so much, but he needs more money." He wasn't sure yet where he was going, maybe with Felipe to Kansas so he wouldn't have to travel alone.

Marco planned on buying land and a few animals to fatten up then sell – pigs, cows, rabbits, chickens. The land was fertile where he was from, and before she had realized how seriously they butted heads, she'd imagined herself down there ringing the property with fruit trees and planting a big garden. There'd be flowers everywhere, too. Before she'd fallen in love with kids, she couldn't picture what to do with Marco's daughters. Now she could see how it might work, except that the other side of the equation had fallen apart. She couldn't see any way she could live with macho Marco in his own culture.

"Will you go down and visit?" Tracy's question brought her back to the trail.

"Definitely. To see his daughters. To them, I'm just *la maestra*, Marco's teacher, not girlfriend. They're who I want to see. I've talked to them both many a Sunday. I want to meet his family, too, his dad, his sister Perla, Martin and Chay and his other brothers, and his nephew Scooby-doo. That's a nickname."

"I hope so."

Thinking about going to Mexico was the only thing that made these changes even slightly bearable. And from years of experience, she knew that no matter how strong the desire to keep in contact with someone, it always faded and they drifted apart.

Tracy stopped hiking and turned and looked at Bette. "You're not considering moving to Mexico, are you?"

Bette looked over at her friend whom she'd virtually lost the first year she was getting together with Don. Now she and Don were talking about moving to an intentional community to be with people who had shared spiritual principles. Bette had thought of joining them, but what if it was in a remote area where she couldn't find work or didn't like it, or them? "No. It's not my world, but I have toyed with the idea. And with you thinking about leaving..."

"We're not sure we're moving."

"I know, but I don't think I can just sit here and wait for you to leave me, too." At first Bette's own moving hadn't been her choice but her parents' faltering marriage and then her father's wanderlust that had disrupted her life. After that, no matter how strongly she resisted being compared to her dad, she had shown signs of his influence. Her own moves began innocently enough, as a young woman finding her way in the workforce, from Oregon to Florida where she studied horticulture, supporting herself as a waitress. Then she followed a boyfriend to L.A. When that fell through, she went to Massachusetts to experience New England. She had loved the stone fences, saltbox houses, and how old everything was but had always felt like an outsider among the easterners.

When her siblings settled in the same area in the northwest, Bette had joined them, too. She left her portable job of waitressing and studied accounting which proved to be equally as flexible. But she had suffered under the gray, rainy skies of western Oregon and moved to Arizona which now felt like home. With Alma and Oscar and their kids now in New York and Rosa, Isa, and Gerardo about to leave, she wasn't so sure she wanted to stay.

"Why do I have to be here without them? Is it payment for always being the one to leave?"

"Payment? No, sweetie," Tracy said, "but you might want to look at why it's so hard sitting with the pain of losing your friends."

"Because it hurts," Bette said and smiled. "Why stay when everyone is leaving? Is there growth in waiting to have my heart get ripped apart, family-by-family?" Was she expected to just sit under the pressure as one loss after another was piled on top of her heart? Her mom used to take Bette and her siblings to the Three Corner's Tavern, where she spent time with a man who truly cherished her. He would soon rescue her from Bette's father's abuse, moving her far away. Bette liked sitting in the maroon vinyl booth sipping her Coke through two thin red straws watching the Hamm's Beer sign with the turquoise and white waterfall flowing around and around behind the bear in the canoe. Sometimes she played pool with her sister and brother, always with Frank Sinatra singing *Strangers in the Night* in the background.

Her mother must have had the number-letter combo to that song memorized on the jukebox. Bette's mom had started the towering tier of loss when she left.

These new losses were about to do Bette in. Years of therapy had helped her to see the real cost of being left, but she still rarely let those feelings loose. "I'm having abandonment issues, I guess."

"What's that term your sister uses about you moving all the time?" Tracy asked.

"Doing a geographical. It's an Alcoholics Anonymous term. Instead of dealing with your problems where you are, you move but end up bringing those same problems with you to the new location. Do you think problems are bilingual and can follow me to Mexico?"

Tracy smiled and squeezed Bette's arm. "Did you bring your thermos?"

"*Claro que sí.*"

"At least your Spanish is good now."

"Even though I'm sure my friends are inwardly cringing at my bad grammar, they love me in spite of it."

"I'm sure they do. Let's take a break by this little pool. The warblers have probably all passed by in the heart of their migration, but maybe we can spot a few stragglers as they fly south."

CHAPTER 14

Guests	Menu
Marco	Turkey, stuffing
Bette	Smashed potatoes and gravy
Enrique	Yams
Enrique's 3 friends from Phx	Green beans w/crunchy onions
Fernando	Tortillas
Mateo	Salsa verde con aguacate
Rosa	Pumpkin pie and whipped cream
Felipe	Pecan pie
Gerardo	Martinelli's Sparkling Cider, pop
Isa	

On Saturday after Thanksgiving, a small gray-and-white older model Ford pulled up to Bette's house. Marco met Enrique with his three friends from Phoenix at the door and welcomed them in.

"*Bienvenidos. Bienvenidos.*"

"*Mi casa es su casa,*" Bette added while wondering if it was a corny thing to say, maybe too old fashioned for these men.

Convivio was the oldest, about fifty, and was short compared to Marco so he must have been about five-foot, if that. His apricot-colored ostrich cowboy boots matched his belt, and he wore Wrangler's, a jean jacket, and a tall white cowboy hat. His mouth had a natural downturn to it, even when he smiled, which he did often. Convivio's nephew, José, looked about twenty-five and had his hair shaved close to his skull. The haircut accentuated his ears which stuck out a good ways. His wide pants hung down over big white tennis shoes, and he wore an oversized jacket and a crisply pressed, untucked shirt.

He didn't smile but said in perfect English, "Thank you for the invitation."

"Welcome to our home," Bette replied, switching to English.

At the end of the line came Lalo, who was all smiles. He looked to be about thirty and wore new baggy jeans, a black leather jacket, and had a gold earring in his left ear. She shook hands with each of them and watched them follow Enrique out back to the deck, carrying bottles of tequila and cases of Negro Modelo, Budweiser, and Squirt.

As she was about to close the door, Mateo and Fernando pulled into the driveway in Fernando's blotchy maroon boat of a Buick. She was glad to see them pile out. Her patchy Spanish was nothing unusual to them, and they'd help her feel less awkward around the new men in her home. Mateo and Fernando were like nephews now, having eaten at her house at least once a week for the past six months. They had heated tortillas on her *comal*, gone to movies together, and asked her questions about American girls, customs, and phrases. "Hi, Mateo. Hi, Fernando." Bette said. "Happy Thanksgiving."

"Hi Betty," they chorused.

"Mateo ¿Would you help me carry the appetizers?"

"*Claro que si.*" He, too, had dressed up for the occasion and wore black jeans pressed with a sharp crease down each leg, a turquoise button-down shirt, and his hair was gelled with its usual curl in the front.

She handed him a tray loaded with an assortment of bowls and plates, all gems found at *yardas*, and held the kitchen door open for him. They headed outside to the others sitting in the sun on the back porch where it was still fairly warm. Enrique was pouring drinks.

"There are *cokas* and pop in the cooler," Bette said. "Here are the November 15ths," she said to Enrique.

"Ah, *si*," he replied. "The November 15ths."

The others looked their way.

"*Entremeses*," Enrique said the Spanish word for appetizers. "*Entre mes*. In the middle of the month. ¿Get it?" A little head shaking followed their weak joke.

While the men drank, Bette stayed inside and basted the turkey. There wasn't enough room in her small oven for anything else, so the rest of the food sat on the counters, waiting. Her solar oven had done a good job on the sweet potatoes, but soon the sun would set on these short winter days, and she would have to put them in the oven, too.

"¿How do they like the November 15ths?" she asked Marco when he came in for more limes. She'd prepared a spinach and jalapeño dip with carrots, mushrooms, and red peppers on the side, the traditional cheese ball and crackers, and of course, a bowl of olives even though there weren't any kids around yet to stick their fingers in them.

"*Bueno*. They've never eaten raw vegetables before, and they liked them."

She studied his lips to see how much alcohol he'd had. "*Cariño*, please don't get drunk. I need your help tonight."

"No, I'm not drunk."

"Please, don't drink too much." She held onto his hand.

"I'm only drinking beer, not tequila."

"Thanks," Bette said. A few Friday nights of seeing him sitting in the garage on a lawn chair with Enrique and Fernando, totally blotto, made her realize she wasn't safe even if he was merely drinking beer. They'd talk up a storm, drink beer, and listen to *Ranchera* music on her tinny radio with the space heater blasting away. It couldn't put a dent in the cold winter, and the guys would sit huddled up with their coats and hats on. They never accepted her invitation to come inside and drink. Somewhere along in the night, Marco would ask her to go get them some food.

"No. You knew you were going to get drunk and then hungry. ¿Why didn't you get food first?"

"Enrique will pay for it," Marco said.

"It's not the money. I worked hard all week and just want to stay home."

"Me, too. My work is harder than yours."

Bette exhaled a puff of air. "No, it's not. You do my job just one week, then we'll talk. ¿And when you went to the store to buy beer, why didn't you buy a roasted chicken, too?"

Half the time she ended up going to get them food. The other half, she said no and suffered the feeling of being a bad "Mexican" girlfriend in front of their friends.

When Marco left with the limes, Bette pulled the shelf out and basted the turkey again, kneeling at the oven. It was starting to brown and was filling the house with a delicious holiday aroma. She took a bag of yellow Finn potatoes outside along with a bowl, knife, and the compost pail, and sat beside Marco and started peeling.

"Let me help you," Enrique said.

"No, it's okay. I just wanted to be outside with you all for a while." Bette noticed that the three rectangular planters still had a few straggly snapdragons holding on which added a bit of color to the deck. The sage plant looked good and would make it through the winter. She'd pinched off a few leaves that morning and added them to the stuffing, glad part of this meal was from her yard.

"¿Aren't you cold?" Mateo asked. "¿Do you want to sit in the sun?" The guys had their coats pulled up around their ears and looked like birds with their feathers puffed up against the cold.

"No, I've been next to an oven for hours. I'm hot." Bette heard a muffled snort and saw eyes meeting and smiles spreading. What had she said? She'd come outside to make them feel welcome in her home, but they were quiet with her there, and she was searching for her Spanish to put them at ease. Did she dare speak again? Every time she was in the presence of a native Spanish speaker new to her, it was like all of the words she knew holed up. Her words must be as shy as she was.

**

When Rosa arrived with Felipe, Gerardo, and Isa, Bette realized what a help it was to have another woman in the house. She set the kids up in the breakfast nook with a coloring book for Isa and a Spanish comic book for Gerardo and a plate of appetizers.

Finally, the turkey was done, and they stacked the waiting casserole dishes in the oven.

"¿Have you made the filling yet?" Rosa asked in Spanish. Her English was still basic and difficult for her, and the two always spoke in Spanish. Always would, Bette imagined.

"¿The what?"

"The bread you put in the turkey."

"Oh, yes. It goes in before the bird is put in the oven." Rosa looked disappointed. "It's easy. I can show you with a chicken one day."

Bette scooped the stuffing out of the cavities and mounded it in a bowl. She gave Rosa a taste the way Rosa had done at her house, by placing a small amount on the heel of Rosa's palm. She licked it off.

"*Qué deliciosa*," she said.

"It's my favorite. We'll put this dish on our, um, our part of the table," Bette said. As she'd taught her ESL students, if you don't know a word, find a workaround. Who needed *end* when *part* would work?

This was the first time she'd cooked a turkey and struggled a little with cutting into its breast. Thankfully the legs sort of fell off on their own. Bette wondered if John would relax his vegan stance enough to cook meat for friends. Doubtful. He'd told her he always had Thanksgiving with his brother's family. Did they make him a stuffed acorn squash like she used to make for herself and her guests?

While Rosa mashed the potatoes, Bette switched to making the gravy which came easier to her – could hardly tell it came from an animal. She called Mateo in to heat the tortillas, and soon he had four going at once on the *comal*, creating a large stack. She, Rosa, and Gerardo set the food on the two long tables strung together in the living room and called the back-porch guests. Felipe came in, and Bette directed him and the kids into the living room.

"Marco," she called outside again. "The food's ready."

"*Momento, momento*," came back.

Finally, Enrique came in guiding Convivio who stood in the kitchen doorway with his head leaning back, inhaling deeply. He wavered a bit and took a few little steps forward and back, stabilizing himself. Enrique put his arm around his shoulders. Convivio smiled so wide his eyes looked like slits. "What a delicious smell," he said.

"Come this way," Bette said, and took his arm and ushered him into the living room. She helped him to a chair at the end of the table away from Rosa and her family. Lalo and José sauntered in glassy-eyed and sat next to Convivio. Bette looked at Rosa and Felipe and shrugged. "I'm sorry. They brought the tequila. I didn't hope for this," she said, thinking she'd said expect this. Bette had oh-so-briefly thought about inviting Cat and Jeff. What a disaster that would have been. How could she interpret for them when she barely spoke the language herself?

Fernando stood bent over in front of her little boom box, one hand on his knee, the other steadying himself on the bookshelf holding Marco's selection of music. She'd anticipated needing to play something and had the least raucous Mexican CD he owned queued up. It was more love songs than *Rancheros*, but was in Spanish and would do. She walked up behind him and put her hand on his shoulder. "Hey, Fernando, here's something," she said and pushed the play button. "¿Why don't you sit here by me?" She guided him over to a seat at the table. She and Marco had hauled the couch onto the front porch the night before to make room for the tables, but it was still tight in her small living room with the twelve of them.

"Stand up, stand up," Marco said. He motioned with his hands. "*Levántense. Levántense.*" Marco and Bette had been to a Thanksgiving celebration at Tracy's on the actual day earlier that week, and the group there had begun their meal holding hands and each giving thanks for something in their lives. Marco now took hold of Bette's hand, and Felipe's on the other side. Bette managed to get Fernando's hand, but he was too drunk to stand, so he sat with both arms up, Bette on one side and Mateo on his other. This wasn't exactly how it had happened at Tracy and Don's, but Bette was touched by Marco's attempt to give his friends a more authentic Thanksgiving experience. She had invited Tracy and Don to share this meal with her and Marco, but they'd said they had plans to go to a nature preserve. It wouldn't have been much fun for them anyway, she guessed, and now with the drinking she was glad they had declined.

Enrique smiled at her. "*Gracias a Dios por esta familia*," he began. Though he could speak English, he continued on in Spanish. "Thank you for inviting us into your home. It's an honor to be invited into a *gringa's* home for this special American holiday." Bette looked down at her empty plate. He continued on, thanking her again for the gift of opening her home, giving thanks for the food, saying things she couldn't understand. She didn't know if this was normal at a fiesta or if it was the alcohol talking. She looked at Marco then at Rosa and Felipe. Finally, Enrique paused and Bette sat quickly to staunch the flow of thanks and to try to get the others to begin eating while the food was still hot.

Bette and Rosa tried to serve the meal, but the guys continued to stand and give thanks. She saw that José was holding his uncle Convivio on one side while Enrique was on the other, their heads bent together. Maybe he was getting sick. She met Enrique's eye and said in English, "He can lie down on the bed if he needs to."

"No, him's happy. Him's crying because his nephew say he love him."

Bette could tell that Enrique was drunk when he messed up his pronouns. He usually caught those these days.

"Let me tell you," Enrique said. "Because of this," he spread his arms out to indicate the food on the table and all of them gathered around it, "for a *gringa* inviting them into her home for a Thanksgiving meal, him open his heart to his uncle and tell him he love him and want to live a different life."

Bette was relieved he had switched to English. She was embarrassed to think that such a simple act had affected them so much and didn't want the others to hear it. Even though she lived frugally compared to her North American friends, her life was luxurious in contrast to her Mexican immigrant friends. She had an entire house to herself, heat, plumbing that worked, a car, and a well-paying, full-time job. How easy it was to open her home for a holiday meal and share the good traditions of her country.

Convivio stopped crying and smiled down the table at her. Marco started passing bowls his way.

"Do you know what a gang banger is?" José asked her in English.

She said yes, but wasn't exactly sure and didn't want to get the full description at the dinner table.

"I used to be a gang banger, but tonight I asked my uncle for help in changing."

"Why do you want to change?" she asked.

"I've lived in the U.S. for six years and have never been in a white person's house."

Bette scrunched her face up. "Really? Never?"

"No," he said, shaking his head. "I didn't feel like I belonged in the U.S. or even like I wanted to."

"It's so interesting getting to know other people," Bette said, smiling.

"Yah, maybe there's a different life for me here."

Lalo was sitting beside José, but Bette didn't know how much English he understood. He smiled and rolled one taco after another filling the corn tortillas with mashed potatoes, stuffing, *tomatillo* salsa, and turkey.

Enrique stood up and started to give thanks again, but Bette said, "Please, no more thanks. I'm embarrassed." The others laughed, and the food continued being passed around.

"Betty" Enrique said from the other end of the table. "We need bowls."

"¿Bowls? ¿What for?"

"For the salsa."

Salsa? Since when did salsa go in bowls and not on food? She stood up and looked down toward Enrique. He had ladled gravy directly onto his plate, and it spread out in a brown puddle.

"No." Bette said. "That's gravy." She had to use English for that word. "You need to make a mountain out of potatoes. Here, like this." She plopped a nice mound on her plate. "Then put a lake of gravy at the top." She deftly made the depression and filled it with gravy. "It's the tradition." She looked over at Gerardo, who was watching her. "Here, you try it. Make a volcano." He grinned then and moved another notch deeper into her life and heart.

The rest of the meal went smoothly until it was time for the men to leave. Bette knew that Mateo hadn't drunk any alcohol so could drive Fernando home, but she was worried about Enrique driving the others.

"Enrique, I'll drive you home, and Marco can follow and drive me back here."

"No, I can drive. I'm not drunk."

"Yes, you are," she said.

"No, I'm not. I can drive."

She gave up after talking with him some more. She had known him for almost a year, and he seemed sober enough to drive; also she wasn't getting anywhere convincing him. And she knew she wouldn't in front of his friends. They would all be staying at Enrique's since the three visitors lived two hours away in Phoenix, so Marco invited them back for breakfast the next day. There would be eight of them sleeping in the one-bedroom house. If they snored like Marco when he was drunk, they were going to keep the entire *barrio* awake.

***

Bette got up early the next morning and put the huge stack of clean dishes away tucking the red plastic plates in the back of the cupboard for summer barbecues. While sweeping the back deck, she found about an inch of Tequila left in a bottle and brought it into the house along with a few glasses she and Rosa had missed the night before. Marco held the kitchen door open and had Convivio's hat perched on top of his head. Bette had forgotten to bring it with them when she had guided him to the car the night before.

"His *sombrecito* for his *botitas*," Marco said, holding his hands about four inches apart. Marco and Bette were chuckling at the cuteness of the little boots and hat when a car pulled up.

"They're here," he said.

"*Buenos dias,*" Convivio said coming up the porch steps. He smiled extra wide when Marco handed him his *sombrero.*

"¿How are your heads?" Bette asked. "It doesn't look like it's *buenos dias* to you."

"Sit. Sit," Marco said, pointing to the table in the living room.

"¿Do you want coffee? ¿Juice? ¿*Cokas*?" Bette asked.

"¿Tequila?" Marco offered holding up the bottle. A chorus of groans met him.

Bette pulled the leftovers from the fridge and began heating them in the microwave while Marco made coffee and brought out cans of Squirt and Coke. There were going to be eight of them that morning, so they had folded up one of the tables in the living room. Her own stomach gave a lurch as she watched Lalo pour the last of the tequila in a glass. He sat and sipped and ate one plateful of food after another. The crescent rolls she made from one of those whack-on-the-counter pop-open tubes were a hit. They wolfed down at least two dozen of them, stuffed with green salsa and turkey. Fernando was ill and wouldn't eat.

"You'll feel better if you eat something," came advice from a more experienced drinker. Where was the parental advice the teenager needed last night, Bette thought.

"No." He barely shook his head, looking miserable at having to move.

Lalo smiled and ate methodically just like the night before and offered his glass of tequila to the others, holding it up to their noses. They shrunk back from it like it was poison, grimacing and frowning.

"¿Why do you drink so much when you know you'll feel terrible the next day?" Bette asked.

"It's the custom at fiestas," Enrique said.

"The drinking is more important than the food," Marco added.

She'd tried to offer them a different experience and hadn't provided any alcohol for this Thanksgiving meal, but realized that this wasn't only her party. Though she didn't like the drinking, she was part of a broader world now, and alcohol flowed through it.

After clearing the table, she went outside to look for Fernando to see how he was faring. She found him and José sitting in the comfy deck chairs facing the sun and dozing.

"¿Do, you need anything, Fernando?" she asked.

"No, *gracias*. Marco gave me an Alka Seltzer."

"José, can I talk to you a little?" she asked in English.

"Sure," he said and straightened in his chair.

She pulled up a lounge chair. "You've been in the U.S. six years, right?"

"Uh-huh."

"Did you come here for work?"

"Yah, for the money," he said, smiling.

"What kind of work do you do?"

"Landscaping."

"Your English is really good. Where did you learn?"

"I took classes at a college."

"Do you know about the anti-immigrant propositions that were passed this month?"

"A little. I know that we can't go to school now. It's what the marches were about."

"They're also changing the law so you can't go to court if your employer treats you badly."

"That's okay. I work with my friend. It's his business."

"Did you ever do day labor before you got that job?"

"Lots of times," he said.

"It's the mistreatment there and other places that workers now can't do anything about," Bette said.

"I got that a lot. They'd tell us they'd pay us a hundred bucks then after working all day they'd give us fifty. They'd say, 'It's better than you'd get in Mexico.' *Chinga su madre,*" he said, flipping his hand up beside his head. "Once I got totally stiffed. Lots of times they wouldn't give us lunch, and we'd be out where there weren't any stores. Sometimes there wasn't even water. In Phoenix." He looked over at her. "I needed the money, but I hated the insults and shit."

"They were looking to make more money, too, I guess." She decided not to tell him about the other propositions. Maybe it was better that he continued living his life unaware of his loss of civil rights.

"Does Marco have papers?" he asked.

Her stomach clenched when she heard this question. She had never heard Mexicans ask it of one another, but they would ask her about someone else. Some of her students had volunteered the information.

"¿For how many months you live in the U.S.?" she had asked one of her new students in Spanish, trying to assess how much English he might have.

"Three months."

"¿Do you have any family here?"

"No."

"¿No uncle, brother, cousins?" That was quite rare.

"No, no one."

"¿Why did you pick this town?"

"The coyote said it was a good place to come."

Bette had been taken aback. She said, "I am your teacher, so you can tell me you came here illegally and were guided across the desert, but do not tell strangers, okay?" She had looked in his smiling young face and said, "Not everyone likes immigrants here." Their town was about six hours from *la frontera,* and there weren't any border patrol stations near, but it still wasn't safe. She'd heard about past raids at Walmart, restaurant chains, and on a large development site. Look what had happened to Nemecio simply riding to work in a crowded car. Marco and Enrique had asked if some of their fellow students in the English class had papers, but she had always told them to go ask the person themselves. They never did.

Her town was growing rapidly with an influx of retirees, and now, she realized, undocumented immigrants encouraged by guides. She doubted the coyotes knew how many men were already looking for work. Most of the images the public had of immigrants came from day laborer locations. She had heard and read more grumbling as the numbers grew in recent years, but she also knew many in that mass of workers as individuals. They were married men who had children, went to church, played on soccer teams, and had been here for many years. They came to her class after a long day of physical labor to work on their English.

Now, responding to José's question about Marco's legal status, she said. "No, he doesn't have papers." He was undocumented.

"Do you love him?"

"Yes."

"Why don't you marry him?"

"It won't automatically make him legal, and it's a long process. He'd have to go back to Mexico for years." She pictured his two daughters back in Mexico but didn't say anything about that complication.

"You love him very much."

"Yes."

"How old are you?"

There was another of those questions. She had told her students that this was not a polite question in *los estados* especially directed toward women. They'd been confused by that and Bette didn't relish having to give an explanation for her culture's obsession with youth.

"Thirty-eight. You?"

"Twenty-one."

She had thought he was older. "You were fifteen when you came to the U.S.?"

He nodded.

"Do you ever want to go back?"

"I don't know. Sometimes. I haven't been back since I came here. I don't know what it's like anymore." José may have wanted to get out of gangs but Bette wondered if it was going to be possible.

"Do you have a girlfriend?"

"Yes."

Bette knew it must be easier to find girlfriends in Phoenix, where the Hispanic population was higher. She felt for the teenagers and young men in her town of forty thousand where the ratio of Hispanic men to women was severely lopsided.

By now, most of the others had made their way outside and were sitting in the sun. "Where's Marco?" she asked Enrique.

"On the front porch."

"It's got to be cold there," she said, and headed around the house. Marco was lying on the couch with his sweater pulled up over his nose. Bette nudged him over with her hip so she could fit beside him and tucked her hands into his jeans, feeling the warmth of his firm butt. "Umm. How delicious. ¿Why are you here in the cold?"

"I don't know."

She bent to kiss him, and he didn't respond. "¿What's wrong? ¿Are you mad that I was talking with José?"

"No," he said and leaned up to kiss her. "¿What were you talking about?"

Even though the night before she had heard him telling Rosa and Felipe about how *gringos* are different in that they have friendships with people of the opposite sex, he still hadn't processed that through his own emotions. She sat with her arms around him and relayed all that she had talked about with José, especially his questions about how much she loved Marco.

"Marco, you know how I feel about you." He nodded. "¿And you know that *gringas* talk with men and it is just friendship?" He nodded again. "I just wanted to talk with someone who spoke English so I could learn more about what's going on in your culture."

"I know that, but he doesn't. Maybe he thinks you want to be with him. He doesn't know the way *gringos* have friendships here."

"He knows how I feel about you."

Marco sat up and put his arms around Bette.

"Go around back where it's sunny," she said. "I'm going to go inside and clean up a little."

"Okay, *güerita*," he said, using one of her pet names. At first, hearing the translation, something like little pale woman, it had sounded racist. Now, she had come to enjoy the endearment. Slowly, they were moving toward a place between their two cultures.

CHAPTER 15

Rosa's U.S. family

Rosa & Felipe with Gerardo & Isa
Alma & Oscar with Alan & Vicente (Now in The Bronx)
Amaya & Carlos with Javier & baby Estevan & now Valery (Amaya's younger sister)
Luna & Ignacio with Mari & baby Anali, Rodrigo, and *Las Gemelas* (in Mexico)

Bette had planned on having her typical tree her first Christmas with Marco, an agave stalk, which had lots of branches for hanging lights and decorations and didn't need water because the plant was already dead. She loved the ritual of going out to find one, sawing it down, and toting it home tied to the top of her car. She got all the joy without having to kill a living tree simply for three weeks of pleasure. Marco and Enrique wouldn't hear anything of it, however, and she came home from work one day in early December to see a Charlie Brown Christmas tree on her front porch.

"I got it at work," Enrique said that evening. "We were cleaning a yard, and they asked me to get rid of it." Bette didn't even think about asking him why he chose not to set it up at his place. Where would they find space in a one-bedroom house with five roommates?

They propped it in a five-gallon bucket in the corner of the living room, poured in water, then piled rocks and small boulders found outside the house to hold it straight. Slowly Bette's yard was being made over, maybe not exactly to the landlady's liking, but certainly more livable, as far as Bette was concerned. There was a small garden, a compost bin, bird feeders on each tree, a clothesline, and now fewer rocks to have to weed around. The scraggly lopsided juniper tree was definitely not cultivated for a role as a Christmas tree, but with lights and decorations, it would do fine. Bette was happy to be sharing this holiday with her growing family.

Marco made thin pork chops cooked in tart *tomatillo* salsa for dinner while Enrique helped Bette with her Spanish at the table. She was trying to figure out when to use the *preterito* versus the *imperfecto* in past tenses but Enrique wasn't able to explain it to her.

"You only need to hear more Spanish," he said.

"That doesn't work for me. I need both. You remember how much school helped you."

"I learn more by myself."

Bette let out a sigh then pushed her textbook away. Maybe it wasn't Marco's stubbornness that she butted heads with, but this same cultural pride. She got up and stood by Marco, who was slicing avocados at the counter.

"My stomach hurts," Bette said.

"¿Did you eat lunch at *La Casita*?"

"*Si*," Bette said. She rubbed her stomach and chided herself for eating beans again. Nine times out of ten, this happened when she ate them, but she couldn't resist. Besides, what else was there for a still-trying-to-be vegetarian who couldn't tolerate a lot of cheese to eat at a Mexican restaurant?

She'd been meeting two former classmates from her Spanish class at *La Casita* once a week for over a year, and they'd been chipping away at the language they were trying to master. Occasionally she'd invite Rosa to join them which pushed them to speak Spanish the entire hour rather than reverting to English when their brains got tired. The restaurant had plenty of tables, they weren't too busy, and it was an easy ten-minute walk from her job. The waitress also let them practice their Spanish with her and didn't make fun of them. Or at least not to their faces. One of Bette's ESL students cooked there, so Bette always stuck her head in the kitchen and encouraged Heredia to practice a little English.

"Hi, Heredia. What is the special today?"

"Hi, Betty." She smiled, then dropped her eyes. "*Gorditas*. Bery good."

"Okay, see you in class tomorrow."

Bette was glad there wasn't class tonight. "It's like I have little men in my stomach wearing big boots and they're playing soccer." To demonstrate she kicked her foot out, jabbed her elbow behind her, and thrust her head up to the left. Marco snorted and kept laughing as he headed to the bathroom.

"*Hombrecitos*," he said. Little men. "¿Want a half or whole Alka?" He loved American medicines. Her once pure bathroom cabinet now housed Alka Seltzer, antibiotic ointment, and Nyquil next to arnica gel, slippery elm throat lozenges, and milk thistle extract. She had to admit though, that at least the Alka Seltzer made the little men in her stomach take off their big boots even if the soccer game continued.

*** *

That weekend, she showed Marco how to string popcorn and cranberries. He showed her the glittery cuteness a few dollars at Voldemort could buy.

"Look at the work these Germans do," she said as she pulled out a wooden candle set that her friend had brought back from a trip home. Bette lit the candles, and the angels swung around, dinging little bells. Marco watched them fly and then dug through the box and hung more ornaments on the tree. She found two felted stockings she'd made several years earlier and hooked them on a cabinet next to the tree. Where had the red one with her name on it in white letters gone? Her childhood possessions consisted of the contents in a single wooden jewelry box which held an odds-and-ends assortment of mementos including an eraser with a tiger on it, a flattened penny, Continental Airline wings. Bette was drawn to small things because they were portable.

She arranged her nativity scene on the soil in a cactus plant sitting on the end table then hung her wreath on the front door. The forest green artificial wreath was a gift from her sister and had brightly colored birds on it. It was a not-so-subtle message on her sister's part to get Bette to settle down, get a permanent address. She loved it anyway and wondered if her sister missed the symbolism of the flight of birds, always seeking new horizons.

When the tree and house were decorated, she made hot chocolate, brought it into the living room, and sat with Marco on the couch admiring their work. He turned and said to her, "Tell me about the boots." Bette searched for what he was referring to as he pointed to the Christmas stockings. Now's my chance, she thought, to get a bunch of goodies for Christmas, but she restrained herself and told him about the U.S. custom of kids believing Santa comes down the chimney to fill their stockings with presents if they are good.

The next week when they were in the bank, she pointed out a long row of tiny red and white stockings with the employees' names written on them in sparkly ink. "The boots," he said.

Tracy called that Saturday and asked if they could meet at her house rather than Bette's. "We're leaving on Wednesday, and I'm still finishing up a few presents and packing."

Bette made the long drive to her house and wondered how her friend tolerated commuting four days a week to her acupuncture business and what she sacrificed for using the time that way. New Age music was playing in the background when Bette entered the kitchen, a mixture of synthesizers, harps, and guitars. Bette much preferred the artistry of jazz but was beginning to appreciate this semi-elevator music as well as Marco's Mexican version of country.

Tracy called from upstairs, so Bette made a cup of tea then found her friend in her sewing room which smelled of incense from its double duty as a meditation area. She sat at a white-tiled dining room table-turned workbench, gripping a lavender and green paisley penguin in one hand and a hot glue gun in the other.

"That's cute. Who's it for?" Bette stood beside the ironing board, which was draped with pieces of fabric and ribbon and ran her fingers through a pile of buttons.

"My mom. I need to get it to the post office before we leave."

"Are you making presents for Don's family?" Bette glanced over the sewing machine and saw three home-made stuffed cats lined up on a bookshelf, peering at her with their button eyes.

"No. He has to buy them something himself. There." She put the hot glue gun down. "I can take a break now. Aren't these adorable?" She took each cat off the shelf and told Bette which of her nieces it was for, pointing out its special features. Downstairs they sat together on the couch so they could look out the picture window.

Bette broke off a chunk of chocolate from the bar on the coffee table and let it melt on her tongue. "Are you nervous about meeting Don's family?"

"His kids more than his parents since we'll be staying with them, but we have other things to do while we're there so that'll break up our time. We're driving over to Seattle to see my sister and will spend a few days there." She explained that there was snow in the Cascade Mountains and they planned on going cross-country skiing. "Hey," she said and pointed out the window at a pygmy nuthatch eating at the suet feeder. "There it is."

"There're two of them. Look how adorable." Bette watched as the second one climbed down the trunk of the Arizona oak to join its partner at the feeder.

"I was hoping they'd show up for you today. They've been coming around for about a week."

"I didn't realize how small they were. I think I've only seen one before," Bette said. "When do you come back?"

Tracy told her a neighbor was going to feed and comfort Baba their cat and they'd be back by New Year's Eve giving her time enough to prepare for resuming work.

"You haven't changed your mind about visiting your family?"

"No," Bette said. She saw herself at her sister's house with her family gathered around, laughing and eating. It looked okay, but it was the days surrounding it that seemed flat. Her siblings had families and in-laws to occupy their time and Bette pictured herself walking around, twiddling her thumbs, and not fitting in. "I don't know. I like the idea of opening presents with Marco, having the guys over for meals and games, and Rosa's invited me over to make *tamales*. That'll be fun if I can understand what anyone's saying." Bette watched a spotted towhee do its two-footed shuffle under the tree, searching for a treat. "I couldn't imagine leaving right now. I guess my sense of family is shifting." She smiled at the little bird's hopping antics.

***

Bette found herself in the middle of her two worlds and two languages again in an unlikely setting the next week.

"We're invited to dinner at Robert's house on Saturday," Marco said.

"¿Robert? ¿eScott's boss?" He was the owner of the construction company – the man who signed the checks.

Marco nodded. "It's a big party for all the workers and their wives and children."

"¿Why didn't you tell me sooner? Today's Thursday." A party this big took planning, and they didn't invite guests just two days before. "I have plans."

"¿To meet your boyfriend?"

"I don't have a boyfriend. Only you, Marquisimo." She ran her hands down his sides and dug her thumbs in at his hips, making him snort and laugh.

Then he pulled away. "You don't have to go. Everyone will be there with their wives. I'll go alone."

Of course, she'd go. She'd make her apologies to Cat and reschedule their margarita night and would go with Marco, but was there no planning in the Mexican culture? It wasn't like she didn't see him every day so that he couldn't have told her sooner. Or was it that he knew she would do whatever he asked? She wouldn't, would she? But for this, yes.

It was a formal sit-down dinner for eighteen at the big boss's house. The crystal water goblets glittered under the chandelier along with the silverware and china plates. Robert's wife served them pork tenderloin, rice pilaf, green beans with almond slivers, and hot rolls and butter. No tortillas. Amazing. For dessert, she had made raspberry parfaits and offered brewed coffee.

After dinner, Robert gave all the men new heavy work coats, utility knives, and an envelope containing a cash bonus. There was a lot of laughter over the fact that they'd had to buy *Borrego's* coat in the kid's section since he was so small. The children got gifts as well as the wives – an assortment of lotions, salves, and bath products. Robert's parents were there, too, and it had felt like a big family. Bette would have liked to ask him his plans for the business when the new law took effect in January but didn't want to let on she knew his employees were undocumented. Maybe he would defy the law and keep them on.

***

A few weeks later on *Noche Buena,* Bette arrived at Rosa's home at two in the afternoon, hoping that was the time Rosa had said on the phone. *Dos, Dose,* Two, Twelve? She stood in the small living room, her Nalgene water bottle dangling off the fingers of one hand and a box of *applets and cotlets* held in the other, and looked around.

In addition to the two-part sectional blue couch, there was a black, glass-fronted cabinet that held delicate crystal statues including a vase with pink silk flowers, a swan figurine, and a heart paperweight. The cabinet was topped with two remote control cars the size of shoeboxes with their antenna extended. A white three-drawer dresser housed Felipe and Rosa's clothes and held a color television. In front of the couches was a square wooden coffee table, matching the one in the corner which held the phone and framed pictures of Rosa's two somber-looking nieces at their *quinciñera*, surrounded by uncles and cousins, all in tuxedos. Gerardo's turtle was perched on a rock above a few inches of blue stones in a little aquarium beside the photos. The newest addition to the room was an artificial Christmas tree decorated with maroon and beige bows.

Bette handed Rosa the sweets and was whisked off into the kitchen and put to work.

Amaya was at the stove stirring a frying pan bulging with tomatoes, jalapeños, and onions – the *rajas* filling. Bette stepped over and gave her a cheek kiss on her way to the sink to wash her hands.

Rosa was busy preparing two huge pots for the *tamales*. Bette tried to take note of the *masa* preparation so she could make *tamales* in the future, but it was one of those a-pinch-of-this, a-handful-of-that type of recipes. She watched as Rosa rolled a bit of dough in her fingers, then placed it in a glass of water. Whatever it did, the women seemed satisfied, so the three of them began working together at the kitchen table. Bette got the hang of smearing *masa* on the softened corn husks, adding a spoonful of the *rajas* mixture and a slice of crumbly white cheese, wrapping and folding the end, then placing it in the pot. When they'd used all of the *chile* and tomato mixture, they made dozens more *tamales* with pork and onions simmered in green *tomatillo* sauce, including the bones.

Bette didn't even try to understand what the two women were talking about unless they addressed her directly. She concentrated on watching their *tamale* technique to see if she was doing it right. Too much *masa*? Not enough? Two chunks of pork? One? She had yet to learn how forgiving *tamales* were.

"*Hola*, Betty," Rosa's husband Felipe said as he came into the kitchen. "¿Do you want *una Coka*?" he asked as he maneuvered past the women and opened the refrigerator. The entire front of the fridge was covered with magnets, but he managed to squeeze through the small space without knocking one off.

"No, thank you."

"¿Esprite?"

"No, *gracias*."

"She doesn't drink soda," Rosa explained.

"I'm content with water, thank you."

When it came time to put the pots of *tamales* on the stove, they wouldn't hear of Bette lifting them but called Felipe back in. He was a welder, so was undoubtably quite strong, but she was a good four inches taller which would have helped with maneuvering them onto the stove. She let it go.

Next came *ponche*, the traditional drink of Christmas, at least in central Mexico where Rosa and Felipe were from. Into another huge pot went water, sugar, lots of sugar, sticks of cinnamon and spears of sugar cane, sliced apples and pears, a bag of prunes with the pits in them, a handful of dark pink hibiscus petals, and jars of mystery fruit. They put this to simmering then Amaya went into the bathroom to take a shower.

Later, Rosa asked, "¿Can I bathe?"

"¿Excuse me?"

"¿Can I bathe?" she repeated.

Then Bette got it. "*Sí, sí.* I'll sit with Felipe" She had wondered if the women were going to be dressed that casually, with sweats, but now worried that she was going to be underdressed in her nicest jeans and long-sleeved purple shirt. When Rosa entered the living room a while later, she relaxed. This was the first time Bette had seen Rosa's hair down, and it fell to her shoulders in newly dyed streaks of blond and auburn. Her eyebrows had been plucked into thin lines, and her eyes stood out with eyeliner. A series of gold hoop earrings traced both ears, and she wore black stretch pants, a low-cut red shirt, and a short black jacket. Rosa had a roll of fat around her middle, but it didn't seem to bother her into hiding it. It was so...un-American and refreshing. Felipe didn't give the impression that he was concerned by it in the least, never harping on it as Bette's father had done to her various step-mothers. They were a happy couple.

"Let's go," Rosa said, waving Bette back into the kitchen. "*Hay más.*"

Rising, Bette asked, "¿More?" which made Felipe and Carlos laugh.

"*Sí, mija,*" Rosa said using an endearment. "There's a lot more."

Earlier in the day, Rosa had prepared *ensalada de manzana*, a salad in the loosest terms, made of apples, raisins, pecans, sour cream, and sweetened condensed milk. Now Rosa and Bette put pans of water on to boil for spaghetti which they would serve with butter, sour cream, and a little *chipotle chile* to add spice. Rosa checked the water level in the *tamale* pots occasionally, and as the hour grew later, she pulled one out, and they picked at it to see if it was done. Bette couldn't tell the difference and enjoyed nibbling at the trial ones with Rosa and Amaya.

"Hi Valery," Bette said. She licked a bit of *tamale* off her fingers, wiped them on a napkin, then took Valery's hand and leaned in for a cheek kiss.

"What are you doing?" Valery asked in English. She was one of Bette's newest and most advanced students. She was in seventh grade and spoke English all day long, but had also lived in the U.S. for several years with her mother in New York, and now her sister Amaya in Arizona.

"I'm learning to make *tamales*. Here, try one."

Valery picked up a plastic spoon and scraped out a bite of firm *masa*. "Bery good. You like cook?"

"Yes, I like to cook," Bette replied. She could see that Valery would be a distraction tonight, just like in class. She had her sister's thin frame and angled eyes, but unlike Amaya's shyness, Valery was an extroverted teenager, smiling and engaging with everyone in the room. She wore tight bell-bottom jeans, a midriff-length tee-shirt, and big tennis shoes. Poor Mateo with his broken-heart necklace, Bette thought. He's going to be tortured. There wasn't time to dwell on that as folks started arriving and Bette was caught up trying to remember names and who belonged to whom. Brothers, another sister-in-law, nieces, and nephews were introduced then rattled Spanish at her.

Luna was all smiles. Did that personality come with the name – moon? She held a hefty bundle and a dark face emerged from a furry yellow blanket with zoo animals on it.

"*Mira*," Bette said. "Look at those beautiful eyes." She leaned over the mom and gazed into the big, bottomless brown eyes of the child she had held at her sister's birthday party.

Luna smiled wide and tucked the blanket around her daughter's face. She spoke rapidly about something, but Bette's complete attention was focused on baby Anali.

Rosa set a paper plate in front of Luna that contained a *tamale,* and a little mound of spaghetti tinted a light orange from *chipotle chiles*. Luna placed Anali on her lap and started pulling the corn husk off the *tamale* while Bette stepped over to the stove to help Rosa serve. With two plates in her hands she parted the curtains into the living room and immediately stopped in her tracks. How could so many people squeeze into one small room? Marco had arrived with Enrique, Fernando, Luis, and Mateo and they were packed together on one part of the sectional couches lining the walls of the room. Felipe and more men sat on another part of the blue sofa and on white plastic chairs. Bette regained her forward motion and handed her plates to Felipe and another man.

"¿Betty, you remember my *cuñado,* Ignacio?"

Ah, the brother-in-law from the pink trailer. Anali and Mari's dad. He was also the father of twin girls who remained in Mexico and Rodrigo his firstborn who was standing quietly in the corner. Ignacio was holding the delicate Mari on his lap who smiled up at Bette. She was the birthday girl who had painted Bette's nails (and fingers). "How good to see you again," she said.

Bette wondered if the others were thinking about Oscar and Alma and their family, now living in The Bronx. Had they found a welcome there? Jobs? Community?

The front door opened, and Gerardo entered carrying Javier while on the other side of the room Valery stepped through the kitchen doorway carrying more plates of food. She held one out to Mateo. "¿Would you like something to eat?" she asked.

"*No, gracias*," Mateo said. He dropped his eyes, but Valery didn't give up.

"Betty made these," she said, leaning over and holding the plate at eye level.

He looked over at Bette and shrugged. "I'm not hungry. I just ate."

Enrique and Marco reached up at the same time and took the plates from Valery, giving Mateo a little nudge. Bette continued bringing in plates and plastic cups filled with *ponche* which had sticks of sugar cane and cinnamon emerging from the rims.

The *tamales de rajas* were her favorite, and at a certain point in the evening she decided it was better to stop counting how many she had eaten. There was a knock on the kitchen door around ten, and two men from the apartment upstairs asked if they could have some *tamales*. Bette had accompanied Marco one Friday afternoon to buy *tamales* from a woman in her apartment. They had waited in line with Mexican men, slowly making their way upstairs into the woman's kitchen. This was a traditional food from home that not many men could make themselves and yet craved on this holiday. Rosa piled two paper plates high with them and received many thank yous for the gift.

***

It wasn't until after midnight that Bette's head finally hit the pillow and a small groan of pleasure escaped her.

"You tire," Marco said in English.

"*Si, estoy llanta.* I was on my feet for many hours."

Marco rolled Bette over and lifted her tee-shirt to give her a back massage. His hands were small and unskilled at this new task, but he was strong and learning quickly. He was still inconsistent, spending too much time on one part and skipping over others, but that was something most of her other boyfriends had done, too. Bette wondered if John, who was more connected to the physical world, would have the same disconnect between his hands and brain. She told her mind to quit it, stop thinking about John. "Thanks, Marco." Bette turned on her side and gave him a kiss.

"You can tosh my hair," Marco said in English

Bette smiled as she brought her hand over to Marco's hair and started running her fingers through it. "Oh, *si Señor*? ¿It's okay if I tosh your hair? Thank you, Marco." Her hand was like a magic sleeping pill for him. He would arrange himself in bed so that his head was the perfect distance from her arm and hand. Then after just a short time of stroking through his lush black hair, he'd be asleep. Waiting at traffic lights, she'd often reach over and run her hand through his hair and once he had let his head drop like a rock to his chest, feigning sleep.

"Ha, ha. Very funny, you nut."

Tonight he moaned a little, too, then said, "It's an art, this hand, just like your *tamales*."

"*Gracias, novio*," she said, then drifted off herself.

***

The house was filled with the smell of cinnamon and chocolate when the guys arrived on Christmas morning, the day Bette was used to celebrating. She'd awoken early and made an apricot-almond coffee cake with yeasted dough, topped by a lemony-sweet glaze. Marco had joined her in the kitchen as she ground the Trader Joe's fair trade coffee beans he had grown used to and was stirring the hot chocolate. They'd given each other their gifts earlier, a porcelain heart-shaped jewelry box for her and a folding utility knife-pliers set for him.

"*Qué romantica*," he had said, smiling. He was right. They should have kept their presents for themselves instead of exchanging them. She would have much preferred the practical gift and he the romantic heart.

Enrique, Mateo, and Fernando arrived, and they sat around the kitchen table, pulling apart the cake Bette had made and dunking it into the hot chocolate.

"How delicious," Mateo said. "I didn't know you could cook."

"*Qué chistoso*. I can cook a lot of things but you guys only like Mexican food." Bette loved cooking and baking but had gotten out of the habit since Marco's palette was so limited. If cooking hadn't been expected of her, she might even have done more of it, especially baking. Part of her balked at the way the Mexican men she knew took women for granted, expecting and assuming that Rosa and Bette would always prepare and serve the food. Another part of her, however, secretly wondered how it would be to have the opportunity to stay home and be the homemaker, with the emphasis on home. She just might enjoy waking up early, her favorite time of the day, to make waffles, a fruit salad, even homemade tortillas. Bette pictured herself standing on the cold linoleum floor, smashing the masa in the press, then gently laying it on the hot *comal*. The meditative, repetitive task centering and calming her while allowing her to contribute to a happy family.

"¿Are you ready for your presents? In my family, it was the custom to open them early. It's already late for you." She had chosen a remote-control truck for Fernando, a puzzle of a Mediterranean coastal scene that she thought might look like Mexico for Mateo, and a photo album for Enrique. They spent the bulk of the day alternately working on the puzzle which they had set up on the kitchen table, then going outside to watch Fernando play with his truck. It had snowed recently, and the icy patches around the edge of the driveway gave his truck an extra challenge.

Bette brought out push pins and electrical tape and demonstrated how she thought he could attach them to the wheels to create more traction. He sat on the sidewalk and fiddled with them until he turned the wheels into studded snow tires. With a few chunky rocks piled in the bed of the truck for weight, he could maneuver the thing across the street and up the neighbor's steep driveway.

"Let's make a..." Bette's arm went up, indicating a jump. She found a partial sheet of quarter-inch plywood behind the garage and worked with Mateo to create a ramp. Maybe she'd buy herself one of these motorized toys.

When Rosa and Felipe and their children showed up in the afternoon, Bette taught the kids how to make a rocket while the adults talked. They worked together on taping the construction paper guides and cone-shaped head to the thirty-five-millimeter film canister. Bette didn't even attempt to explain what that was to the kids in her faulty Spanish. Then she gathered her friends outside.

"¿*Listos*?" She placed an Alka Seltzer in the canister, added a little water, snapped on the bottom, and then quickly set it on the sidewalk. Poof! It shot straight up in the air as the bubbles expanded and pushed off the lid. They all laughed, and Bette went to find more film containers as now Fernando wanted to make one. As she lifted her head from rummaging through the junk drawer she saw the framed print John had given her for Christmas – a

Haida image of a woman and a bear. She pulled the card from her desk drawer.

Hi Just Bette,

When I saw this print, I thought of you. A strong woman, a part of nature, not apart from it. Know that I will be thinking of you this holiday and always.

Just John

She hadn't thought to get him a gift. When she'd walked by his office and peeked in, she hadn't seen any decorations and thought he didn't celebrate the Christian holiday. Now Bette put the card away and picked up the print. The bold red, black, and white shapes appeared simple at first glance but were complex on closer inspection, flowing in their rounded shapes, developing new relationships and connections. Bette had looked up the legend of the Haida mother bear after receiving the beautiful, unexpected gift. Did John know that the woman had become involved with the bear through foolishness on her part? Had he read that she will be the cause of the death not only of the bear but many others to come?

Bette set the print down, positioning it carefully under a lamp where the woman and bear seemed to lift up off of the paper. She looked out the window at her friends standing in the halo of light on the front porch. All this would be over if she decided to be with John. It was no longer simply between Marco and John. The choice was now complicated with her expanding family to add into the equation.

CHAPTER 16

Driving While Mexican
– *pero está bien en* Washington, New Mexico, Utah *y más*?

In January Bette came home from a margarita night with Cat to find the house dark.

"¡Marco!" Why holler when she knew he wasn't there, but she couldn't stop herself. She looked in the bedroom at Marco's dresser which was topped with stacks of clothes, bottles of eyewash, Vicks, and rubbing alcohol. Scattered about were bundles of wires, horse supply catalogs, and paystubs but no keys or cell phone. When the phone rang she picked it up gingerly.

Marco, sounding very somber, said, "You have to come here."

"¿Where? ¿What's happening?"

"The sheriff stopped me. They think I stole your truck. I told them it was yours and I was driving it to see if I wanted to buy it." She realized he was telling her the story he'd made up so she would be prepared when she got there. What if the deputy understood Spanish and figured out what they were doing? After learning where he was, Bette headed out to her car in the dark night.

When she arrived on the scene, Marco was nowhere in sight, and his truck was being loaded onto a tow truck. She confirmed that the truck was hers and she'd given Marco, one of her English as a Second Language students, permission to drive it and take it to a mechanic to determine if he wanted to buy it. Standing beside her car talking to the two deputy sheriffs, she assumed Marco was in the back of their big Ford SUV. She only listened with half of her attention as he gave her a ticket for allowing an unlicensed driver to use her truck. She and Marco had decided to put his truck in her name as the insurance was much cheaper as a second vehicle on her policy. Marco paid her promptly every month.

Now, as she stared at the deputy's black car trying to make out Marco's silhouette inside, her mind was on him being hauled back to Mexico, and all the loose ends he was going to leave behind – his full-time job, the men and women who called for his help on weekend projects, his bank account, all the stuff he'd been collecting at yard sales to take back, and now his truck was impounded.

"He has a valid Mexican driver's license. Why can't he drive with that? I've driven in Europe with just my U.S. license."

"Not legally," the deputy sheriff said. "You have to have a passport. The guy driving your truck didn't have a passport or green card so even though the truck is registered and insured, he can't drive it. Without some documentation from their home country to prove a foreign license is valid, there is no way to ensure that drivers have had proper training, driver's education, or gone through the testing process."

"Why are you towing my truck?"

"Because he's not licensed to drive in the U.S." The deputy continued, "If I cite him for not having a license, tell him not to drive the truck, then I leave, he could drive after I left and cause harm. I'd be liable." Bette wondered why Felipe hadn't gotten his car towed before he sold it. Maybe because it was the police and not the sheriff?

She was more interested in Marco, however, and as she was signing for her ticket, she asked, "Can I speak with Marco?"

"That's up to you. He left walking down that road." He turned and pointed behind him.

The tow truck pulled out in one direction and the deputy sheriff the other, leaving Bette standing alone on the dark road. The bright light and noise of the construction site she'd driven through raged behind her. She drove down the street and found Marco looking dwarfed beside a massive cottonwood tree. He got in the passenger seat.

Bette reached over and rubbed his shoulder. "*¿Que pasó?*"

"They just pulled me over. *Por nada.* For nothing. I didn't do anything." He told her about driving down Wagon Wheel Road, carefully weaving through the maze of orange and white traffic barrels. He'd bumped along the dirt road in his gray-and-silver Toyota truck, obeying the flaggers as they stopped him to let the big yellow machinery lumber past. Just as he was making his turn, flashing lights reflected off the rearview mirror into his eyes, and he pulled over beside a nursery.

"I drive your truck all the time," Bette said, "and I've never been pulled over."

"I didn't do anything. *Nada.*" Marco repeated. His lips clamped down tight into a thin white line.

"They told me I can write a letter to try to get your truck out sooner than thirty days, but it's going to cost a lot, and we both have to go to court," Bette said.

"¿What does it say on my ticket?" he asked, pulling the pink paper out of his wallet.

Bette flipped on the overhead light. "Just driving without an authorized license."

"¿Why'd they pull me over?" he demanded, his voice rising.

"Marco, they're cops. They can pull you over for any reason they want. Maybe you didn't use your..." She didn't know the Spanish word so mimed flipping on her blinker.

"No. I follow all the rules. I obey." He turned from her and looked out the window into the frigid night.

The next day Bette hand-delivered a letter requesting a hearing to get *her* truck out of impound sooner than the required thirty days. When the deputy called, his next available time slot was Sunday. Four more days of impound fees and she would have to pay a hundred and fifty dollars in cash or cashier's check for the privilege of a hearing. It seemed like a scam. She felt sorry for the immigrants who didn't have the money or who didn't understand the system.

When she showed up at the jail on Sunday, the front door was open, but everything else was locked tight. She wandered around the vacant halls, the sound of her boots clacking on the linoleum floor. Finally she saw two women out the back door and followed them.

After waiting for a minute in the vestibule, one of the women said, "Push the buzzer if you want to speak with someone." She was leaning against the wall, smoking, and appeared to be in her early twenties. Her companion looked about Bette's age but was missing a molar on the right side. Bette felt thankful that she had never lived a life that led her to feel knowledgeable about the jail system.

Two deputy sheriffs that weren't the ones who had given her the ticket met with Bette in an empty hallway. Standing there handing over the pile of cash felt more like a drug deal than a hearing.

"Do you know why he was pulled over?" Bette asked.

"The report says 'white light showing from the rear,'" the deputy said. "It could be that there's a broken taillight or the reverse lights are wired wrong and go on when it's in drive, or maybe the license plate light is angled wrong."

"It's my truck, and I'm pretty sure those things aren't wrong, but I'll check." Bette explained to these deputies, too, that she had let Marco drive the truck for a few days to see if he wanted to buy it.

"There's a state statute to get unlicensed drivers off the road which was updated in 2005," the deputy said. "We find a reason for the stop, and then we check their license." Why hadn't I ever been pulled over while driving the same truck, Bette thought. "If your truck gets pulled over again with an unlicensed driver, you can't get it out of impound early," he warned.

**

At the courthouse, Marco agreed to pay his fine of eighty dollars rather than protest his ticket and have to return again and lose more time from work. So far it had cost him four hundred and sixty-eight dollars for the towing, impound fee, his ticket, and Bette's hearing. She wasn't interested in paying a hundred and fifty dollars for her ticket and also wanted to argue her case in front of a judge, so the clerk set another date for her case. She was going to point out that she'd driven in Europe with no special license and had assumed that the U.S. respected other countries' drivers' licenses as well. She would explain that Marco was pulled over because the deputy said there was a white light showing from the rear. Since then they'd checked, and there were no broken taillights, and the reverse lights didn't go on when the truck was in drive. It could only have been the license plate light which wasn't broken and came standard with the truck.

Searching for the cause of the problem, Bette had gone to an auto parts store, and the attendant told her he used to be on the police force and that cops are always happy when they could see the license plate numbers, even when the plate light might be too bright. It was preferable to not being able to see the plate to run the numbers. She was sure the research she had done would sway the judge to her side, but in the end, she never got the opportunity to speak with him.

Bette sat in the courtroom for an hour, listening to other people present their side to the judge. Then the police officer would present his view. When it was her turn, the deputy sheriff didn't show up for the hearing, so her ticket was dropped. She was left wondering if he would have shown up if it had been Marco there and not her.

That night she told Marco, "I got off. *El sheriff* never showed up, so I didn't have to pay."

"¿What did this solve?" he asked.

"¿*Qué? No entiendo.* ¿What do you mean?"

"I can't stop driving to work because they gave me a ticket. There aren't any buses in this town," Marco said.

"I know. And it's too far to ride a bike. You're..." How to say stuck? *Pegado?* Glued?

"And so are all the other Mexicans around here who work like me framing houses, doing concrete, sheetrock, plastering..."

"And stuccoing, painting, roadwork..." Bette flipped into Spanglish.

"Landscaping, cleaning..." he continued.

"Ironing at the dry cleaners, cooking in restaurants, roofing, babysitting." She wanted to scream but instead said, "It's complicated, Marco."

"I don't want to be driving on the road with bad drivers, either," Marco said, "but if they won't let me take a test and get a license, what can I do? I have to go to work." There was a longer silence this time. They both knew that the same thing had happened to Fernando, but he had lost his car because the impound fees were more than his car was worth by the time the thirty days were up, so he just didn't go get it.

"I'm sorry," Bette said again. "I can't fix it, Marco."

***

Filling her water bottle at the hydration station at work the next day, she was telling Cat about the results of the hearing, when John overheard them.

"They should have drivers' licenses," he said about her time in court.

"I agree, but they can't get them here."

"Then they shouldn't be driving."

"Talk later," Cat said and walked back toward her office.

Bette wondered where his intensity was coming from but continued on. "We allow undocumented immigrants to buy a car, to register and license that car, and to buy insurance for it. But not to drive it?" She felt her hands making their way to her hips. "That's a system designed to make money but not confer any rights."

"Don't you sound lawerly? Are you saying our government deliberately set out to rig the system?"

"It is Arizona, isn't it?" Bette was at a loss. Where had Mr. Liberal gone? She took a moment and then said, "I like to think of what I do as advocating for those less fortunate."

John started to say something then snorted and shook his head. He turned and started to walk off, but Bette was right behind him. She stopped him by placing her hand on his shoulder.

"I don't want to fight with you. What's going on?" She led him to her office.

"My brother is a cop in Phoenix. They went in to raid a house where they were harboring immigrants, and his partner got shot." Bette raised her hand to her mouth. "He wasn't killed, but my brother feels guilty, and it's affecting his life." John added, "I just think they should come here legally."

"I am so sorry about your brother," Bette said, but thought better of telling him about the many years-long process it required to come here legally and then only if you could prove you were worth something to the U.S. John's mind seemed made up, and he left her office with a scowl on his face.

***

That Wednesday in her ESL class, Bette gave her students the ABCs of getting pulled over by a police officer. She noticed that they paid close attention and asked more questions than when she taught them about ordering in a restaurant.

"Pull to the side of the road, turn off your radio and engine, and roll down your window." All eyes were upon her. "Turn on the interior light and put both your hands on the steering wheel when he comes to the window." She demonstrated all of the steps and ended with her hands held out in the air in front of her.

"¿Why?" someone asked.

"Policemen are afraid of being shot. If they can see your hands, they have less stress and may be nicer to you." She was speaking a mixture of Spanish and English, wanting to make sure her students understood. She told them that two officers had been shot in Tucson recently, both by undocumented immigrants, and the police were extra nervous now.

"The officer will want three things: your license, proof of insurance, and auto registration." She wrote these on the board and got help from her more advanced students to explain what these were. They practiced saying the words without the usual laughing and side comments. She provided as much info as she could from her limited knowledge of the police because of her privileged place as a white, middle-class woman.

"There are three states that give drivers' licenses to undocumented immigrants." She heard pens scratching behind her as she wrote them on the board. Could she get Marco to New Mexico to apply for one? First, they'd need an address. And residency. Time to move?

***

The next night she and Marco invited the guys over to play games, and Bette talked Tracy's partner, Don into coming over. Tracy was in Flagstaff doing a class for continuing education credits, so Don was free. He was one of the many people she knew who said they spoke a little Spanish, but when it came down to it, all they could do was order food and beer. Restaurant Spanish. Don was the only one, however, who agreed to do things with her when her Mexican friends were over. Must have something to do with his bubbly extroverted personality.

Bette had grown up playing a lot of games with her siblings and missed passing evenings that way so had been working to teach the guys how to play Clue, Yahtzee, and Tripoli.

"Oh, Marco, you look like a lion," she said when he arrived home from work. "A lion after a day of sleeping."

Marco put his hand to his hair which was smashed flat in places and sticking up in others. "My hat," he said in English. He carried the five-gallon bucket of water from their shower outside to the back deck then dunked his head in it. He shivered and sucked in his breath.

Bette kept the bucket in the shower to collect the water as it was warming up. She estimated it took about two and a half gallons to get the water the right temperature. As she was pouring it on her bushes, Marco combed his hair. They'd paid for him to have his hair cut at one of those quick places once and Bette had watched closely so she could learn how to do it. She had been cutting his hair ever since and was pretty good at it, though she kept trying to convince him to go back to get it properly shaped again.

"No. You do a good job," he would always argue.

Tonight she ushered him back inside as the temperature had dropped and he sat on a chair in the middle of the kitchen for a haircut. "¿How was work today?" she asked.

"Good. We're working on a house at Arizona Ranch."

If there was ever a place that needed to learn about water conservation, that was it. They had planted long rows of cottonwoods on either side of the county road leading to the development, which besides being too close together, were a terrible tree for that dry location in the arid high desert. Were people going to haul their shower water out there?

As she buzzed away with the clippers, Marco told her about the new house. He held his arms in a circle as wide as he could make showing her the size of the beams they were installing.

"Hey, hold still. ¿Why don't they use a...a machine?" She demonstrated, turning her arm into a crane and moving the clippers around and placing them on his head.

Marco laughed. "They have us."

"¿How many guys lift one?"

"Five or six."

Bette looked at Marco's bellybutton pooching out as he sat there shirtless. He'd had a hernia years back wrestling some cow, and it had never been repaired.

"*Cuídate, por favor*, honey," she said. Telling him to be careful was the mantra she always sent him off with.

After the haircut and a shower, Marco made guacamole. While Bette laid out the Clue game, she said, "Marco, I'm going to drive Rosa and her children down to Mexico."

At once the questions came flying at her like knives in a circus act. ¿Why don't they take a bus? ¿What does she need a car there for? ¿Why can't one of her brothers come up for them? ¿Do you know how dangerous it is for women and children to travel alone through Mexico? ¿What if the car breaks down? ¿Don't they know how busy you are? ¿Why are you always helping others?

"There is corruption everywhere," he continued. "Even the post office." Marco was still upset that the box of Christmas presents he had mailed to his daughters in Mexico had never arrived.

Bette didn't know what to say and was saved by the guys' arrival. Enrique had returned to Mexico telling her that the economy was going to tank with the new employer sanction law going into effect and he was not about to spend all his savings here paying for living expenses as the jobs dried up. But she had expected at least his two nephews, Fernando and Mateo to come for games. Instead of Mateo, Luis accompanied Fernando. Never the most talkative teenage, Fernando was more terse than usual and didn't give Bette any information on the missing Mateo.

Her grilling of Fernando was interrupted when Don arrived wearing a bright Guatemalan shirt over actual blue jeans for a change. "This isn't your ordinary guacamole, Donaldo, so be careful. *Esta picosa.*"

"That's how you say spicy?"

"Yes. Watch out, or you'll get hot hiney."

"I haven't played Clue in twenty years," he said. "Sheesh, thirty. You'll have to explain it to me."

"Me either," Bette said and proceeded to tell him what she'd read earlier in the evening.

"Hey," he interrupted. "You're speaking Spanish."

"I am? I didn't even notice."

"You said a few sentences in English then switched to Spanish."

"Wow." She started again but had only gotten a little ways into the instruction when he stopped her again.

"You're doing it again," he laughed.

"Really? Cool. I'm to the point where they're getting mixed up in my head."

Marco loved Don's full-throated eruption of a laugh booming out of such a small man, and he tried to imitate it after seeing Don with Tracy at their home. Tonight Bette managed to get Marco out of his foul mood during the evening by having him mimic the laugh. Hearing Marco's efforts, Don boomed out his laugh again, and the two of them sounded like Santa Claus in stereo.

"Donaldo," Marco said in English. "She's wanting driving to Mexico with another women and children. Think is good idea *o* no?"

"Not Mexico City," Bette said. "Only close to there." There was no way she was going to drive in that city.

"Are you going with Rosa?" Don asked Bette.

"Yes, over a long weekend. She wants to go home. Do you know anything about driving in Mexico?"

"I've only driven in Baja. How far is it to where you're going?"

She explained as much as she knew while Marco spoke with the others in Spanish. They weighed in that they thought it was dangerous because of bad roads, corrupt police, and men who would take advantage of them at gas stations and if they had problems.

"What do you think, Don?" she asked.

"I don't know. You need to ask more people who've been there."

Marco shook his head, his fears validated.

CHAPTER 17

Coconut fried shrimp with a curry coconut sauce
Tequila scallops in *poblano* oil and tequila
Cucumber salad with sesame and rice vinegar
Feta confetti dip with roasted red peppers, fresh herbs, and garlic oil
Fried artichokes with panko breading and horseradish cream
Papas con queso with cheddar, scallions, and sour cream
Saffron croquettes with rice, goat cheese, and herbs

Bette met Cat at a restaurant later that week which featured creek-side dining and tapas, tiny appetizers that were two dollars off during happy hour.

"Happy hour. Whoever came up with that name? And where's the creek?" Bette asked.

"You are in a foul mood. It's winter. Did you expect to see flowing water?"

"Sorry. I don't know whether to beat the shit out of something or cry."

The waitress arrived to take their orders.

"I've had the black bean cakes with *chipotle* cream sauce," Bette said. "They're heavenly. How about those?"

Cat agreed and ordered another item. Bette added two more.

"Jeff always orders the lamb kabobs or eggplant topped with beef and fennel. It's nice that you and I can order vegetarian."

"All I want to do these days is eat. I feel overwhelmed with it all." Bette's eyes teared up, and she took a gulp of her hot tea to push the lump back down in her throat. She was glad Cat wasn't the touchy-feely type because if she'd reached over and touched her arm, Bette would have started crying.

The first of their tapas arrived – warm goat cheese balls nestled on basil leaves with honey drizzled over it all and a sizzling bowl full of sautéed mushrooms and garlic cloves. Bette bit into the crunchy panko coating and felt the warm cheese flow over her tongue.

"Wow, this is heavenly," Cat said.

"Comfort food packed into an attractive bundle." Bette picked up a basil leaf and ran it around the plate, gathering honey. "My favorite of the guys who always hang out at my home, Mateo, he got arrested. He's in the county jail."

"They're going to deport him?" Cat asked.

"I think so." She put the dripping leaf down, her food losing its flavor. She'd watched teenagers like Mateo and Fernando arrive in the U.S. and come to her English class as shy, respectful young men. Then after their confidence grew with time, they took on more of the traits and looks of those who had been here longer, wearing their pants wider and lower and driving flashy cars with music blaring. Mateo had stopped coming to her ESL class, and the last time she saw him at Garcia's Market Bette had barely recognized him. His pants were low-riders and had splits up the legs to make them hang lower over his large, clean tennis shoes. He had on a Levi jacket with the collar and cuffs turned up and a white bandana around his neck. Another bandana, black, was tied around his head and topped with an oversized flat-brimmed baseball cap that had a huge sparkling dollar sign on the front. Mateo was with two friends who looked like variations on his theme. One had on a skull-and-cross-bones tee-shirt and a black web belt that hung down past his knees. The other wore a gold watch with a too-big band that rotated on his arm. All three had large earrings but hardly any facial hair. Bette had hugged Mateo near the check-out counter like he was a nephew, not caring if he was embarrassed.

"¿Where have you been? I've missed you," she had said.

"I've missed you, too." The sweet smile he gave her seemed incongruent with the persona he was trying to create.

"Please come to my house. ¿Okay?" He'd agreed but had never shown up. Bette guessed that it wasn't as comfortable for him since his uncle Enrique had returned to Mexico to build his house. Why hadn't she gotten Mateo's phone number and worked harder at talking with him about what he was doing, the choices he was making?

Where had the young man gone who never drank at fiestas, helped her in the kitchen, and always did his ESL homework? Marco had explained that without his parents' or uncle's presence to stabilize the influences of the new culture, he had probably tried to take an easy route to make money. He'd been arrested for selling drugs.

"Do you think he was using them?" Cat now asked.

"No," Bette said. "I never saw him use them or evidence of that. He didn't even drink. He still has his landscaping job, too, I think."

Why her favorite? Bette knew that Enrique had tried to act as a father to his nephews while they were in the United States. Mateo was going to catch hell when he got back to his home, and Enrique found out.

"And then Marco lost his job."

"That sucks. You going to be his sugar mama now?"

"With Marco? Not bloody likely. That guy is here to make money, not to skate along." Bette thought back to earlier that week when she had looked up from her green ruler which was marking lines on the general ledger as she entered them into the computer and saw Marco standing motionless in the doorway. He was illuminated by the morning sun streaming in from the window beside her so she knew he wasn't there because of snow or rain. He stood with his hands hanging at his sides still wearing his jeans and work boots with his blue parka zipped up and his black hair peeking out from under his tan striped stocking cap. "*¿Qué pasó?*" she asked.

"No more work."

"*¿*What do you mean? The law isn't..." How to say *in effect yet?* "The law isn't here."

"Robert called us all together this morning and told us he had to let us go."

Bette stood up from her chair and reached for Marco, pulling him into a hug. She put her arms around his shoulders and held on tight, burying her face in his hat. Slowly he raised his arms and put them around her waist. He'd had steady work with Robert's construction company for many months, and now, nothing. When she pulled back, she had tears in her eyes. Marco was stone-faced, jaw tight.

"We started to unload our tools, but eScott hollered, No, no. Come over here. We lined up in front of Robert, and he told us he had to let us go because he was worried about his family. He said that if he got caught with illegal workers they would fine him and take away his business and put him in jail."

"I don't believe him," Bette said.

"He was crying."

Maybe his tears were real. He had been generous at the Christmas party and seemed genuinely at home with his undocumented workers. Maybe he was sad because his profits were going to be cut in half if he had to hire legal carpenters. Or perhaps this was just his reaction in panic after the law had been passed and he would rehire them when things calmed down.

"Marco, you're going to find more work. You have lots of connections and a good work history. You can work with Jimmy or Chuck or *la esposa peligrosa*." She'd said that last name to make him smile but it didn't work. Bette knew that Marco was thinking that there was a world of difference between a few days here and there and a forty-hour-a-week dependable job, especially with the new employer sanction law-making people skittish about hiring undocumented workers.

"¿What did the others do when they heard?" she asked.

"Nothing. They just stood and looked down at the ground."

"¿No one argued with him?"

"No. He gave us our checks, and we packed our tools and left."

"Is he going to go back to Mexico?" Cat's question brought Bette back to the restaurant, her tea now cold, the cream sauce on her potatoes a solid white, sticky mass.

"I don't know. I think he's waiting to see how things play out with the new law." Cat had met Marco but didn't know him except for the stories Bette told. Now she relayed the strength of Marco's determination, his natural confidence, and his belief that he was lucky. No telling what would happen.

"I, however, want to scream, knock over bookcases, break glass. Everything is changing. There's no stability, no predictability."

"The fears of the logical bookkeeper."

"Busted." That and a childhood of constant change.

"You look so calm on the outside. You need to let loose, girl."

"I beat up a file cabinet this morning. Does that count?" She smiled at Cat as she popped a clove of garlic in her mouth.

"That's a start. What happened?"

"John cornered me in my office today."

"Cornered? Did he want to follow up on the almost-fight you guys had in the hall?"

"That was something, wasn't it?" Bette said.

"Are you sure you like the guy?"

"Not so sure anymore. He wanted to have a come-to-Jesus meeting, to get me to see the errors of my ways." Bette crossed her arms over her chest, thinking back on it, the creepy feeling she'd gotten when he had closed the door to her office.

"You can leave that open," she had said. "People can't hear us."

"That's okay. I want privacy for our talk."

Our talk. Could there ever be a worse way to start a conversation? We need to talk was such a guaranteed sign that things were rocky, that unpleasantness was on its way. Bette mustered a quick smile to encourage him to get it over with.

"I'm guessing you know how much I like you," John said, prompting a more authentic smile from Bette. "And I think you feel the same about me."

Don't tell me how I feel, Bette thought, then tried to relax as she listened to John list their similarities. He reminded her of their shared love for the environment which extended beyond merely hiking and camping to actively working to protect it. Her mind went back and forth between being flattered that he knew and liked so much about her, to feeling pressured by his urge to get her to commit. Had he forgotten about their black and white differences regarding immigrants?

"It was like he was trying to close some deal," she said to Cat, "like some salesman."

"Ew."

"What about the kissing and building of passion and then the talk? Down the line. Like years down the line."

"In your dreams. Was he trying to get you to dump Marco?" Cat asked.

"Yes, though he didn't say it like that. But that was the gist."

"Give us a try," he had said. "You can't have a future with someone who isn't here legally."

"He's right, you know," Cat said.

"Well, what if I don't want to have a future? Just some fun? Is there anything wrong with that?" Bette's mind went back to her office. "He tried to psychoanalyze me, and you know how I hate that. Get out of my head."

"What'd he do?"

Bette relayed how John had talked about how good she was with children. "Look at the artwork on your file cabinet," he'd said. "You love children. Don't you want to build a life with someone legal and start a family?"

"A family?" Bette had said. "I don't want children. Whatever made you think I want kids?" But as she said it, her thoughts went to Isa and Gerardo, to kayaking, doing homework, swimming. To pushing *los tres tres* on the swings, playing dress-up with Mari.

"But I've seen you with them," he said softly. "You'd make a wonderful mother."

Now she said to Cat, "Couldn't he see that I can like something and not have to have one of my own? Just because I like my Mexican families doesn't mean I want to have my own. I like your pets, but you don't see me with one, do you?"

"I keep trying," Cat said, smiling.

Bette told her how John had tried to figure out what had happened in her childhood to make her so jaded about children. "I told him it had nothing to do with my childhood, even though it does a little, but rather that I had other outlets for my creativity."

"I bet he called you selfish."

"You've heard that before, too? Yup, I said, I'm selfish. I find that's the best response to that dart intended to wound. Just claim it."

Bette knew how much she gave to the world because she didn't have children. If people wanted to think she was selfish, then so be it. She was the one working to make a better world for more than her own family. The world could use more aunts.

"He idolizes his brother and wants a model life like his. I can't give him that. We broke up if you can call it that. We weren't really anything anyway, in my mind."

"But you were hopeful. I saw that."

Bette nodded her head. "Yes, I thought there was something there and that when Marco left, we might see where it would take us."

"How'd it end?"

Bette relived John pulling her into a deep, delicious kiss which she savored a long time before pushing him away. She was tingling all down the front of her body, but she walked to the door, opened it, and ushered him out. "I think he was pissed when he left, but my brain was a little foggy right about then."

"I can imagine," Cat said.

The waitress moved plates around and set down the black bean cakes with *chipotle* cream sauce. *Hombrecitos*, Bette thought. The little men were going to be kicking around in her stomach soon. "I don't know if I can survive the intensity of these emotions. Mateo in jail. Marco losing his job. My friends all moving away. The promise of John over. How can this be happening?"

"Usually you let go of relationships so lightly. Something's changed."

Bette glanced over at the faux finish on the orange walls, and a long line of past lovers paraded through her mind. She'd been in love with many and smiled at the memory then frowned when she thought of the breakups.

"No, I don't. Remember how miserable I was over Mike? I have pain when I end a relationship, but I'm not willing to live with someone if I'm unhappy," Bette said.

"Many people are, Bette. Happiness comes and goes," Cat said. "It's called marriage."

"I love my single life. Can I call myself single if I have Marco?"

"Maybe you like it because it's easy, short-term."

Bette looked up as a caw drew her attention. A raven was flying by, then another, and another. She suspected these were the same ones that traveled over her house in the evenings, heading home to roost for the night.

***

Bette wanted to talk to Tracy, who always seemed to have helpful insights that Bette had trouble seeing, but she was busy the next day and couldn't meet for a hike. Bette decided to take her mishmash of thoughts on a country drive. The winter days were just long enough for a hike after work and time in nature would be a balm, helpful friend or no. Pulling her car off on a dirt side road, she sat listening to the engine tick as it cooled then put on her backpack and headed out. She hadn't hiked far when the pull of the grassy areas between the junipers made her spread out her sheet and lie down. With her head in the shade nestled into her backpack and her body in the sun she sank into the silence, broken only by birds and an occasional car in the distance. A flock of bushtits chirped by and she watched them hop from tree to tree, hanging upside down against the icy blue sky. She popped a hard purple juniper berry in her mouth and tried to see if she could taste gin. Nope. Only a light currant with pine undertones.

It was nice out here. And easy.

With Marco, she had love and companionship and a roller coaster of emotions but never this weight of potential failure hanging over her. Bette turned her head quickly as she heard the burbling calls of a flock of piñon jays. They seemed like such happy birds, always twittering and traveling in a group. She smiled and lay still, hoping they would come close enough for her to get another chance to see these rare blue birds moving through life as a family.

Was she making a mistake with John? She thought of how happy she was with Rosa and Felipe's children, with Amaya's two boys, with Mariángela and her new sister. Was she throwing away a pretty good fit because she wouldn't budge on her plans to never have children? Maybe he would be the one to change. And if he spent time with Bette's Mexican family, surely he would broaden his view on undocumented immigrants.

Perhaps it was better that Rosa and her family were returning to Mexico. Isa and Gerardo would never be able to drive or work legally in the U.S. No student loans for college. Reconnecting with their strong family ties in Mexico was probably better, even if it meant Bette was going to have to learn something new, how to live with the pain of being the one left behind.

Her father was curious about the next bend in the road so he had moved the family across the western U.S. from state to state. After the awkwardness of being the new kid on the block or trailer court as was more often the case, she usually managed to make friends. That was at least until she was a teenager and the neighborhood kids who had been friends since childhood weren't necessarily open to new friendships. She'd always been thankful, however, that if someone had to end the friendship, it was going to be her, by moving. Bette had a new place to look forward to and wouldn't be living with a broken heart in the same old setting. Her pattern wasn't working this time, as her new family was leaving her one-by-one. The cost of family just might prove too steep this time.

CHAPTER 18

Sarg Hill Care – Sandhill Crane

Qestral – Kestrel

Grot – Egret

Gris con negro y su cola es blanco

Bette didn't get to see Rosa come into her own until they arrived in her home town of Huehuetoca, four days after they entered Mexico. She had expected it to happen as soon as they crossed the border at Nogales, but it was a timid Rosa who spoke with the customs officials. Because she hung back in the office at the border, Bette spoke to the man in her faulty Spanish and explained that they wanted to declare the items they were bringing into Mexico. He responded to her in English so that Bette then had to translate it into Spanish for Rosa. Back and forth she went, translating for two native Spanish speakers. Why wasn't everyone laughing at this ridiculous situation, she thought. Finally, the two spoke directly to one another without their intermediary, and they learned that Rosa wouldn't have to pay any duty for the van-full of items they were bringing in because the value was less than what was allowed – three hundred dollars for each Mexican citizen and fifty dollars for Bette, the tourist. The tourist? As if.

They left the office and returned to the van which was parked outside under an awning. The vehicle couldn't have been more tightly packed, and Gerardo and Isa looked like Eskimos in fur-lined ruffs as they sat in the back seat with items piled behind and beside them up to the ceiling. There was a little gas-powered motorbike deep inside the van under bags of clothes and shoes which were gifts for the extended family. Emergency tools, oil, antifreeze, and a spare tire were near the back hatch. Grocery bags of popcorn, chips, tuna, canned fruit, and salsa were precariously balanced and had to be rearranged after the first few turns leaving Warren. A blue five-gallon water container was wedged between Rosa's feet which was one of Bette's few requirements. It would last almost her entire stay in Mexico.

"We made it," she said to the kids as she slid the door shut. "Now on to legalize the car."

Thankfully, Bette had run this circuit with Catalina earlier in November when Nemecio was deported so knew how to navigate the city and remembered the three places she would have to drive to in order to finish the paperwork. When they made the first of these stops and stepped into the agency that legalizes cars, the four people in the one-room business looked their way. Again, Rosa was silent, so Bette said, "*Estámos amigos de Sergio de los estados unidos. Ella desea legalizar su coche.*" The one man in the room smiled, came over and shook their hands. He said that Sergio had called him that morning telling them to expect Rosa's arrival. Bette felt giddy, thrilled to just speak out in another language without practicing the line first, and be understood. Rosa handed over her car title, and Bette accompanied one of the young women to the parking lot where she took a picture of the van's VIN number.

While they waited for the paperwork, Bette and Gerardo played twenty questions. She glanced around her and was struck by the contrast between the computers and fax machines and the bare-walled, cement room with mismatched furniture. It was actually a little like Rosa's home in the dilapidated little triplex full of Gerardo's remote-control cars, Isa's dolls, a fancy television, and crystal knickknacks.

It was tee-shirt weather in Nogales but had been quite cold when they left Warren the day before. Amaya and her husband had joined them in the gravel parking lot as they added Bette's items to the already full van. Rosa asked, "*¿Ya, listos?*" several times and Bette said she was ready though she didn't want to be. Rosa went to hug goodbye to Amaya and handed her tightly-wrapped new nephew to Bette. Soon all three women were crying, and the men stood in silence looking at their shoes.

Later, when Rosa and Felipe emerged from the house with the children where they had gone to say goodbye in private, they were all red-eyed, and Gerardo and Isa climbed into the backseat and sat quietly weeping. As they drove off, Bette asked, "*¿Is it okay if we say a prayer for safety?*" Rosa readily agreed, and they were silent for a minute offering up their individual prayers for protection.

They continued this habit each morning of their journey, and their prayers were answered as the overloaded 1997 Pontiac Windstar with over one hundred and fifty thousand miles performed like a Subaru. Now, after two more stops to legalize the van, change dollars to pesos, and find lunch of *gorditas* stuffed with *nopales, queso, y elote*, they headed deep into Mexico.

***

"¿What are those called?" Bette asked Rosa as they drove past huge milky white greenhouses. Men and women were walking alongside the buildings wearing clear plastic raincoats over their clothes and also hats and gloves. She hoped it was for moisture in the greenhouse rather than chemicals because the protection did not look substantial.

"*Invernaderos*," Rosa said.

"¿Would you write that in the notebook?" Bette asked.

Rosa wrote, *invernaderos, donde cuidan y alimentan las plantas que dan frutas o verduras* in the orange spiral notebook that Bette was using to document their trip.

"*Gracias, mi secretaria*," Bette said.

"*De nada, mi chaufer*," Rosa replied.

That first day the kids watched a movie on the tiny screen in the stereo compartment of the van. Gerardo leaned forward between Bette and Rosa's seats, like a turtle sticking his head out of a huge shell. They drove through a town where vendors were offering bags of fruit and tortillas in the center of the road by the *topes*, the monster speed bumps in Mexico. Bette pulled over after she heard Rosa and Gerardo exclaim over *la caña*. They bought a bag for ten *pesos*, about a dollar, and Rosa asked the man if he had *chile*.

"¿*Chile Colorado*?" he asked, and came back with a container of red powder which Rosa spooned over the pieces of sugar cane. The one-inch chunks of cane were less sweet than Bette had imagined, and juicier. It ran down her chin. Her secretary was there with napkins.

The highway was better than the horror stories she had heard. So far. The lanes were narrow and bumpy in places, and there weren't any shoulders, but it was four lanes and traffic moved along far faster than the speed limit. In several places Bette saw men using machetes to clear brush from the side of the road. In another area a tractor was clearing plants by scraping the soil. It looked like it must have made many passes over the years because the shoulders were so steep that a car couldn't pull over to fix a flat or let an engine cool off if needed. Coming upon people riding bicycles on the highway, always against traffic in the left lane, was the worst. Even with no shoulders on either side and cars whipping past, the men and boys on their rickety one-speed bikes looked oblivious to the danger, pedaling slowly with their hands resting lightly on the handlebars.

Seeing the men with their horse-drawn carts in the meridian between the four lanes was a much more pleasant experience. Often the horse would be untethered and munching on grass while the man cut weeds, piling them on the cart. Not for the first time would she wish Marco were with her to answer her questions and explain things. Did the men earn money clearing the brush, or were they using it for fuel? Maybe to feed their animals? Marco would thrive being the knowledgeable one.

They were still in the desert, but it looked different from the one in southern Arizona. A new type of saguaro cactus started appearing along with organ pipe cactus and leafless trees with white blossoms on them. Bette would have liked to stop and take a closer look but kept driving while things were going well. There wasn't anywhere to pull over, anyway.

Every time she saw *los federales* with their machine guns and black-masked faces Bette got an involuntary shudder, but she proceeded through the checkpoints without any problem. Rosa explained that they were more interested in people headed north, with drugs. Bette was glad she would be flying home. There was something not right about a glowering teenager holding a machine gun.

They arrived in Guyamas, their second night's destination and first in Mexico, in time to walk along the waterfront before dark. Bette breathed in the moist fishy air and enjoyed watching the pelicans fly in long, low formations just above the sea.

Their motel that night was clean and quiet, had a big covered porch with comfy lawn chairs, and cost thirty-two dollars for two twin beds. While Bette played *Ocho Loco*, Crazy Eights, with the kids, Rosa made *tostadas de atun* topped with spicy Valentina hot sauce. If Rosa and Gerardo were uncomfortable sleeping head-to-toe on a twin bed, Bette had no idea. She didn't hear a thing until the next day when a rooster woke her and Isa in their little bed.

***

The fog that morning was thick, and the world came in and out of focus as they moved southward. A truck crammed with men standing in the bed emerged from the fog followed by a semi-truck full of chickens. They were near the sea, and the plants began to have thicker and denser foliage. Bette and Gerardo figured it must be sugar cane stalks hanging off the sides of another laden truck. When the fog thinned, she pointed out scores of vultures sitting on the huge power lines, some with their wings spread out to the sides like cormorants, warming themselves for the day's gliding. It was tough for a bird watcher to be driving in a new land without being able to stop and identify the species. She rattled off what she wanted to remember to Rosa and later read her notes in the orange journal. Slipped in amongst notes on the birds, terrain, and road conditions, Bette read, "I don't know how she can see." Fog was a usual occurrence when Bette had lived in Oregon so it didn't seem quite as opaque as it must have to Rosa.

"*Mira.*" Bette said. "*Vaqueros.*" Both children leaned forward and looked at the cowboy herding his cows. The farms around Ciudad Obregon looked lush and healthy and Bette was envious of the coulees full of water. As they approached Los Mochis, the right lane of traffic filled with slow-moving semi-trucks, so Bette stayed in the passing lane, slowing herself. She crawled past more and more trucks and realized that this was more than congestion when they had all stopped.

"*¿Qué hace?*" Bette asked.

"*No se.*" Rosa said.

Bette thought it was another *federale* stop so drove cautiously past the line of trucks. Should she be pulled over behind them? Rosa had never driven in Mexico, so wasn't much help. Maybe Marco was right, and she was being naïve, thinking two women and children could travel to central Mexico alone. All of the drivers were out of their trucks, some brushing their teeth, others lying in hammocks under their big rigs. Fifty, sixty, seventy lined each side of the road. Finally they saw a big white sign, professionally lettered that said, "We want to work. Please government, let us work." Rosa figured out that the men were on strike in protest of all the road checks for drugs in their cargo. Earlier in the day they had seen a long line of northbound trucks queued up to be inspected. There, too, the men had been out of their cabs, smoking and waiting.

"When we took the bus north to come to the U.S., we were stopped by *los federales* for inspection," Rosa said. "We had a bag of fruit, and they cut open every orange looking for drugs. They ruined them all."

Catalina reached up and placed her arms around Bette when she stepped out of the van in Novalato, Sinaloa. Nemecio was there, and he shook Bette's and Rosa's hands in greeting. Their town was near the ocean, so the six of them and one nephew got into Nemecio's car, the one Bette had driven across the border to return Catalina to her husband, and headed out to the beach for dinner. Bette sank into the backseat and her mind drifted away from the conversation, only being drawn back when Catalina pointed out mango orchards and coconut palms that lined both sides of the road. She watched the houses zip by, wondering what it would be like to live in one of them, her laundry laid over the front yard fence, a dog scratching in the dirt, flowers dangling from vines climbing the trees.

Bette ran her hand over her hair and knew they were close to the ocean because it felt like satin rather than straw, and the skin on her arm was like butter, not its normal construction paper. Arizona had desiccated her.

She'd been expecting a town but what they drove into was a one-street fishing village. Both sides of the one sandy road were lined with small seafood restaurants. The ones on the ocean side were open stalls with the kitchen in the center surrounded by counters and stools. Baskets of pink, red, and white flowers hung from the palm frond roofs. White fishing boats were beached in the shallows in front of the cafés.

The restaurants on the other side of the road had waist-high walls on three sides and a full wall in the back, blocking the view into the kitchen. The cinder block walls of bright yellows and oranges had murals of flowers and birds painted on them. Catalina chose a place at the end of the street where they had an open view of the ocean. They were the only customers and seated themselves at a long table covered by a red-flowered oilcloth. Bette would never have assumed the restaurant was open if she had been there alone, but after a few moments, a woman in a housedress came out to take their orders.

"¿*Hay más*?" Bette asked when a large, lightly-breaded and pan-fried fish was placed on their table.

Catalina smiled at her. "*Si, Betty. Pescado saranolcado* is famous here, and this is a thank-you dinner for all you did for us." Bette had already eaten a large tumbler of the freshest *coctel de camarón y pulpo* she'd ever had. Unlike the shrimp cocktails she was used to in the U.S., this was a fluted glass full of shrimp and squid mixed with chopped onions, tomatoes, and cucumbers, all floating in a thin red mixture of clam broth and tomato juice with sliced avocados placed on top. Bette poured on hot sauce and ketchup and squeezed lime over it like Rosa demonstrated. She ate it with saltines and washed it all down with red hibiscus juice. Where was she going to find room for the famous fish?

After dinner, they rolled up their pant legs and walked in the water amongst the beached fishing boats and fishermen in their knee boots mending nets and talking in the setting sun. The warm water and the softness of the air eased Bette's tension. Two days down, two to go. She watched Rosa and the children wiggling their toes in the sand and wondered if they felt a connection through their feet into their mother soil. Is this what home felt like? Bette imagined Marco back on his own land and saw an authoritative man, returning with money, stories, and confidence to create a better life for his daughters.

She would have liked to spend some quiet time mulling over these thoughts, but the night wasn't over. They squeezed back into Nemecio's car and drove to *el centro*, the center of town. First they stopped by an outdoor stand, *un puesto*, that made fresh *churros*, the long, ridged Mexican version of a donut that Bette adored. The owner of the *puesto* had a metal drum with a threaded wheel on it that he cranked with one hand which squeezed out a tube of *churro* dough. With the other hand he cut it every eight inches and let the dough fall into hot oil. A woman scooped them out after a bit and rolled them in cinnamon sugar. Bette ate one as soon as she and Nemecio got back into the car and it was hot and delicious.

When they arrived at *el centro*, they stopped at the church and entered from a side door. There was a mass in progress though it could hardly be heard over the music from outside as it reverberated around the thick walls and high ceilings. Maybe there were cathedrals on the east coast of the U.S. this big but nothing Bette had ever seen. It felt more accurate to call it *una iglesia* than a church. The sound of that word seemed to fit the solemnity and enormity of the structure, not a box-like church. There were statues of *La Virgen de Guadalupe* that Bette recognized from Rosa, Amaya, and Luna's houses, other mystery saints, and a huge crucifix of a bloody Jesus in a skirt. What did he have on in U.S. churches? A loincloth? She made a mental note to check when she got home. Bette kneeled with the others in one of the pews and offered up a prayer of thanks for their safe passage so far and asked for continued guidance and protection.

They exited through the front door and were blasted by the sound of a high school brass band playing at full throttle, tuba included. Catalina explained that today was *Santa Teresa's* day, and they were honoring her.

Bette walked with the group around the square, stopping at various booths to look at the wares being sold. Rosa purchased dried fruit in earth-tone hues for their trip. As they left the open-air market they stopped at *una nievería*, an ice cream store, and Bette had a glass of strawberry milk. It was icy cold with chunks of fresh strawberries in it but must have worked diligently to find a way around all the food in her stomach.

Catalina and Nemecio were living with her parents and brother until they could build a home of their own, but even with the house crowded, they found room for the four visitors. Gerardo was given a room of his own, but he chose to sleep on the floor at the foot of the double bed where Rosa, Bette, and Isa were. Before she dropped off to sleep, Bette rubbed her extended stomach and decided she was never again going to do anyone a favor. She couldn't afford the new clothes she was going to have to buy for her expanding figure.

***

On the third day, Bette was lulled into a false sense of confidence because the drive was so beautiful, and some of the roads had shoulders. They could see the ocean from the highway in many places, and there were *barcos muy bonitos*, large, beautiful fishing boats out in the sea. The land was rolling and when they crested a rise and caught glimpses of the sparkling water they pointed and called out to each other, "*¡Mira!*"

As they entered Mazatlán, barefoot, dirty boys in ragged clothes were lined up at the intersections washing windows. When they saw the *gringa* in the car, they dug through their pockets and held out U.S. coins to Bette and rattled away in Spanish.

"*¿*What do they want?" she asked Rosa.

"They want you to give them *pesos* for their coins. They can't use the U.S. coins here, so they are useless."

Bette did the math as quickly as she could, adding a zero to the quarters and dimes in her hand and gave them *pesos*. The drivers behind her were tolerant and didn't honk for her to move along. The children also asked for empty bottles of water, but Bette only had her refillable hard plastic quart bottle.

"Some of my friends say that you shouldn't give money to children washing windows. That they only do that to bring the money home so their father can buy beer."

"No. This is all these children have," Rosa said. "Maybe their dad drinks some, but they need money to eat. They can't go to school because they don't have money for uniforms and books."

"For me," Bette said, "it's such a little bit of money, and I can't see into these children's lives to know if they actually need it or not. And look how clean our windshield is. No more dead bugs."

They drove past *agave*, corn, and *nopale* farms that day, in creatively shaped patches tucked here and there, up mountain slopes and in valleys. The dusty blue, spiky *agave* plants looked like stitching on a quilt in their neat, straight rows. In many farms there were pyramids of corn stalks, drying in the sun. On one section of that day's journey the main *autopista* was closed for construction, so they detoured over to side roads. Bette tried to figure out why so many overpasses were being built along this route out in the middle of nowhere. No towns, just a few houses clumped together now and then. Later when they were back on the main freeway she saw a *vaquero* herding cows over one of the overpasses and realized they were for people to use to move around the freeway that had been built through their land, not on and off ramps like she was used to in the U.S.

It never failed that they got lost in the larger cities. "¡*Oiga*!" Rosa would call to seek someone's attention at a food stand to get directions. Bette took pride in being an excellent navigator, but where were the road signs in this country? It didn't seem like the tiny, narrow streets they were directed down could actually be the right thoroughfares, either. Often they were.

They stopped at a little outdoor cafe in Tepic and were told they had *quesadillas y tostadas de carne asada*. Gerardo had wanted *tortas de carnitas,* but they'd settled on the first *puesto* they'd found with easy parking.

"It's similar," Bette said to him. "*Quesadillas* are like bread, and it's meat." She'd never been allowed to select her own food growing up, especially when traveling. They ate out of the cooler.

"But it's beef and not pork," Gerardo replied.

"Ah, *si*." To Bette, it was all meat, and she couldn't yet understand the differences in flavor that would make Gerardo pine for *carnitas*. The meals came on plastic plates and had *bolsas de hule* – plastic bags – over them so that they wouldn't have to be washed. Such a creative way to handle no water for cleaning up.

"The food is *muy rica*," Gerardo said and smiled at Bette. Both kids were being so good and not whining or complaining at all. Bette was sure they must be bored, but they didn't show it. In the car she had taught them to play I'm Going to Grandmother's House, and they went through Spanish and English versions of that. They also snacked during the long drive. Rosa would pour them bowls full of popcorn and then drizzle Valentina hot sauce over it. Sometimes they'd each have their own can of chunk pineapple or apricots, drinking the juice down and eating the fruit with a fork. For Bette it was a grand adventure, but for Rosa and the children they were going home to their land, their customs, and their family.

On the last stretch into Guadalajara Bette saw men sweeping the *carretera*, the freeway, with brooms, leaving little piles of rocks and dirt to be picked up later. If she got to make this trip with Marco, she'd have a conversation with him about why his country didn't have machines to do this. Was it better to provide jobs for people? Along the road, tall cactus plants grew with vines climbing up them. As they approached the city the road got steeper, and the car's temperature began to rise. They waited at a gas station for it to cool then headed into two hours of madness.

CHAPTER 19

Familia de Rosa

Rodrigo y Rosemaria (papás)
1. *Ignacio y Luna con Rodrigo (20), Mari (4), y Anali (1) in Arizona y Luciana y Lucía (17) in Mexico*
2. *Oscar y Alma con Vicente (8) y Alan (4) in The Bronx*
3. *Isidora y Gabriel con Fiorella, Ramiro, y Fabiana*
4. *Rosa y Felipe con Gerardo (10) y Isa (6) in Mexico y Arizona*
5. *Alonso y Regina con Gael y Antonia*
6. *Adriana y Emilio con Luis (12) y Teresa (10)*
7. *Carlos y Amaya con Javier (4) y Estevan (1) in Arizona*
8. *Maria y Christian con Pablo (4)*

All she wanted to do was to take the bypass and get from the west side of Guadalajara to the east, find a hotel and put her feet up. Bette had printed out maps of the city from the internet but what Rosa now held showed no relation to the maze they entered. Arriving in rush hour while it was raining after nine hours of driving didn't help either, and they were stuck in a thick traffic jam from a nasty car-truck accident. *Gracias a Dios* it wasn't them. When they were moving again they headed down the six-lane divided highway hoping they were on the right road but not really able to tell because the signs were so terrible. Or simply lacking. There were stoplights on the highway and covered overpasses where pedestrians were crossing. And then the highway ended and turned into a dirt road. Just. Like. That. They followed it for a while before Rosa found someone to ask for directions. Bette swore the man had never driven a car in his life.

Back and forth down that highway they went. Soon, Bette recognized certain factories, learned where to watch out for ponds of rainwater that had accumulated on the road, and what each of the exit signs read. She felt like the guy in the Kingston Trio song who gets stuck on the subway without sufficient fare to get off. Charlie and she went back and forth, back and forth. It was getting dark, and after being caught at a stoplight on a side road for twenty minutes, Bette decided they'd take any exit into the heart of the city and stay at the first hotel they found. She didn't care what it cost, she was going to pay tonight, not Rosa. Just let her stop driving.

It took another half an hour, but they found a hotel in Tlaquepaque, the old part of the city. Bette finally felt like a tourist in their fancy hotel with the little monkeys in the open courtyard, a bar and restaurant, and English-speaking front-desk help. She saw herself enjoying a romantic evening there with Marco if she could ever find this place again, and if he didn't return home without her. She forced the lump out of her throat and back down, hoping it didn't lodge in her heart. And with John...what would that be like? Would he even come to Mexico? What was she thinking? She was done with him.

After they'd hauled their stuff upstairs and settled into their big room, Rosa, Bette, and Isa walked around the old town while Gerardo stayed behind and watched TV. The rain had stopped, so they window shopped in expensive stores, then found the *Mercado*, the open-air market. The roasted ears of corn they ate were impaled on rough sticks and coated with mayonnaise, lime, *queso*, and *chile*. They bought *tortas de patos*, pigs' feet sandwiches and carried them home for dinner. The thin red salsa the cook had spooned over them was just the right amount of spicy.

"This bread is different from the *tortas* we get in the U.S," Bette said. Maybe fresher? Less sweet? Gerardo smiled at her and nodded. No wonder he craved *tortas*.

Bette and Rosa leaned side-by-side out the second-floor window that evening and breathed in the fresh air. The rain clouds were thinning, and stars were starting to peep out in the dark sky. "My mother gets up early every morning to make tortillas for the family," Rosa said. "It was my older sister Isidora who helped but sometimes I filled in. She'd call to me, 'Wake up *mija* and see the tortilla star. It's only out for a few moments.'"

"You must be excited to see your family."

"Especially my mother and sisters."

"Tomorrow."

"Thank you, *amiga chula*," Rosa said, and reached over and gave Bette a rare hug.

***

After more *Oigas* and *Discúlpames* by Rosa the next morning, they at last made their escape from Guadalajara. Most of the people had no idea how to direct them out of the city, but at least no one sent them down the wrong road like the night before.

They didn't stop for breakfast until they were well out of Guadalajara and firmly on the *autopista*. Bette wanted that city far behind her. It felt freeing to be back on the highway, especially in the early morning with hardly any cars around. As they crested a mountain, Bette saw a little pueblo off to the right.

"*Mira*. ¿Do you want to eat there?" she asked Rosa.

"*Si, si.*"

They exited, and Bette took note of the turn to get back on the highway. She drove slowly down a tree-lined road with farmland on both sides, her head swiveling back and forth taking it all in.

"¿What's that?"

"*Es una hacienda.*" The two-story rambling mansion surrounded by tall stucco walls looked more like a little village to Bette than the home of one family. Marco had told her that his hometown used to be surrounded by massive haciendas, but they had all been replaced by factories. How sad to have witnessed that, the ancient trees cut down to pave parking lots.

When they came to the edge of town, there was a *puesto* on their left, so Bette parked on a side street. Theirs was the only car in sight. This was how she had imagined Mexico outside of tourist contact, and she wanted to walk down the narrow cobblestone streets and explore. What did their town square look like? And the church? But this was the day she would deliver Rosa, Gerardo, and Isa home so didn't want to delay their reunion.

They took a seat at one of the three white plastic tables in front of the food stand under a large tree, and the cook came to take their order.

"¿What do you serve?" Rosa asked.

"*Birria.*" That was it. Bette was figuring out that these little stands had one specialty and that's what you ate. Bette had no idea what type of animal it was from.

They ordered two tacos each then Rosa returned to the van for her phone. From his place in the *puesto*, the cook asked Bette if they wanted *cebollas* on their tacos. She answered yes on two orders but not on the ones for the kids. He didn't scrunch his eyebrows or ask her to repeat herself or turn to Gerardo for interpretation. They'd understood each other and Bette felt like she had earned a gold star. She approached the booth then and watched him preparing their meals. He had a large metal pan full of stewed meat that looked like it had been slow-cooked all night. Pulling off chunks of meat with tongs, he then whacked them into fine pieces on a chopping block that was indented into a shallow bowl shape. She got up the nerve to ask him if it had started out flat, and he said yes. She was speaking Spanish in Mexico to a stranger and was being understood. The day was starting off well.

They washed their hands at a faucet in the yard coming up out of the soil, then ate their tacos, sharing a bottle of apple soda that Gerardo pulled from a blue-and-white cooler under the tree.

Back on the road, the highway took them through beautiful mountainous land dotted with farms. Pine trees appeared in the state of Michoacán as they climbed higher in elevation. On the other side of the mountains, they stopped along the freeway and bought fresh strawberries in a homemade basket. It was the basket Bette wanted, but the berries were heavenly.

"¿How much longer?" Isa began asking. This was the first time she had gotten a little antsy. Bette taught her to say, *Are we there yet?*, like U.S. kids asked their dads.

"Rosa ¿Would you make me a family tree so I can start to get to know the names?" That kept the kids occupied for a while as they worked with their mom to remember all of their cousins, aunts, and uncles.

As they got closer, the main freeway ended, and they moved to a two-lane, winding road. Bette saw a group of women kneeling to scrub their clothes outside in a communal washing area. She had seen something like that at the mission in Santa Barbara, but it was from a time when the Native Americans washed the *padres'* clothes and was no longer in use.

"I want to go home," Gerardo said. They were all anxious to get there when they came to another freeway, this one six lanes.

"Okay, Rosa, we're close. ¿Which exit should I take?"

Rosa stared at her for a moment then said, "I don't know. I never drove when I lived here."

Bette was weary of driving, and they hadn't eaten a real meal since breakfast, only snacks. She pulled over under an overpass then after peeing and stretching she felt better and got back in the van. While she cleaned her hands with antiseptic gel she asked Rosa if there was someone she could call for directions.

Rosa phoned and got help from her father, or so Bette thought because she called him *Compadre*. When they pulled off at their exit, Gerardo who had been leaning forward between them pointed and said, "¡There! ¡There they are!" Bette parked behind a line of cars, and the tears and hugs started. Rosa's sister, Maria was there with her husband and son, Pablo. Maria looked like Rosa but thinner, and wore tight jeans with a turquoise blouse and spoke with a soft girlish voice. Her husband, Christian, aka *Compadre*, was chunky with a round, flat, smiling face. Rosa's four-year-old godson Pablo gave Bette *un besito*, a little hug and kiss that made the weariness of seventeen hundred miles disappear for a few moments.

At Rosa's parents' house, more relatives were waiting and helped to unload the van. What would John think if he could see the joy of this family? Would his stance on immigration soften or would he remain adamant that they should all leave? Rosa's brother Alonso looked like one of the brothers Bette knew back in the U.S. Another soft-spoken sister, Adriana, was there with her two tall children, Teresa and Luis.

Gerardo took off with his cousins and came back with a two-liter Coke bottle full of gasoline for the motorbike. They took turns pulling the crank until it belched out a blue plume of smoke and choked to life. All the neighborhood kids took turns driving it and giving rides to Pablo. Bette, the former tomboy, loved seeing Teresa ride it by herself.

"Rosa," Maria said, "You left *La Virgencita* outside." Bette looked at where Maria was pointing and there on a fifty-five-gallon metal drum amongst pots of flowers was a wooden box with a picture of the Virgen of Guadalupe in it. It had ridden in the glove compartment from Warren and Rosa had set it outside when they were unloading the car and forgotten it in the hubbub.

"She wanted to see her Mexico," Bette said.

There were a few moments of silence in which Bette thought she had said something offensive and then smiles and laughs erupted.

That evening eleven of them sat tightly around two tables. One was in the living room and another in the enclosed garage/ porch/ laundry/ water/ partial kitchen whatever room. What did they call this place? Three metal doors with substantial locks led off from this room to the living room, kitchen, and Rosa's parents' bedroom. The one sink in the house was in this room with a plastic barrel of water beside it and a little wooden box in front for shorter people to stand on to wash their hands, dishes, and clothes. The most fascinating aspect of the room was a square opening in the ceiling that led to the roof, leaving the room vulnerable to rain and the heat of summer. The dirty white poodle that lived on the roof looked down on the activity below, making everyone laugh at his curious little face.

That night Bette ate a red broth soup of potatoes, carrots, and tiny dried shrimp called *caldo de camarón* with soft rolls and tried not to think how difficult it was going to be for someone to wash the dishes without hot water, let alone running water. She enjoyed listening to stories about the U.S. which poured out of Rosa, but tears threatened as she realized how much she was going to miss her friend, Gerardo, and Isa. The fantastic chocolate cake topped with shaved chocolate curls helped her forget her sadness a bit. It was a cake only made at this time of year. Lucky Bette. It was as large as a pizza pan, about two inches high, and dense like a specialty flourless cake with a thin layer of softened peaches in the middle.

Rosa's mother was an hour and a half away in Mexico City, taking care of her own mother who was quite old and lived with Rosa's aunt. Bette wanted to just drift off to sleep after the big meal and long day but knew she needed to join them to meet Rosa's mother and grandmother. She left the cheery lemon yellow walls of the house behind knowing she could relax in the backseat of Christian's car while someone else handled the stresses of driving in Mexico.

This was the second time on this trip that Bette had been in a passenger car with seven people stuffed into it. Now it was Bette, Rosa and two of her sisters, and a niece and nephew pressed together with Christian into his VW Golf. She felt cozy and protected nestled amongst family as they entered the freeway headed toward Mexico City. Like Guadalajara, things became busier as they approached the city, going from six lanes to eight with cars cutting around each other and slowing in the left-hand lane to make U-turns, *returnos*. That's where they were when Christian leaned on his horn as a driver hit their car on the right side.

CHAPTER 20

p a _ e _

oñtsbrghlm

Christian screeched the car to a stop right there on the freeway in the fast lane which created an uproar of honking as cars veered around them and the white van that had hit them.

"*Tranquilo, mi amor. Tranquilo,*" Maria said to her husband when he returned to the car, slammed it into gear, and took off after the van. When they exited the freeway, everyone got out except for Bette and four-year-old Pablo whom she clutched firmly on her lap. It was dark, and Bette hoped she wasn't passing her fear through to the child. Cars were blaring at them for obstructing their way, and many people stood nearby watching the scene, waiting for their buses. Rosa came to the window and told Bette that Christian was arguing with the driver about paying for damaging his car, but the drunk passenger was angry and complicating the negotiations.

"*Necesitamos la policia*," Rosa said, looking around. "Bette ¿Can you move the car up a little, so we don't block traffic so much?" It was a stick shift with a catch in the clutch, but she got it to work. As she was setting the handbrake she heard yelling and scuffling and hopped outside to help break up the fight between Christian and the drunk man. Bile rose in her throat, and she swallowed hard. With four women, surely the guy would have to back off, but Bette saw that another man had his arms around the struggling drunkard, holding him back. Christian's face was grimaced in pain, and he gripped his upper arm.

"You're going to have to take us to the hospital," Rosa said to Bette. Maria ushered Christian into the back seat, and the others slid in gently around him. "None of my sisters know how to drive."

Bette rammed her coat behind her back because the seat wouldn't stay forward and even with her long legs, it was a stretch to reach the clutch. As she was adjusting herself she saw the drunk man take off his shirt, wrap it around a big rock, and walk toward them.

"*¡Sale! ¡Sale! ¡Sale!*" Rosa hollered. The man began running toward the car, so Bette pulled across three lanes of traffic while learning to use the sticky clutch. She had to wait for a break in traffic to make her U-turn and finally zoomed off just as the crazy man reached the car and slammed his rock down on the trunk. *Gracias a Dios* he didn't break a window or get hit by a car himself. This is insane, she thought, then she caught herself and started chanting the prayer of protection Tracy had taught her. *La illaha illa 'lla' hu.* All that exists is God.

Darecho, darecha. Shit, which was which? Right or straight ahead? Straight ahead or right? Now that she was under fire, she regretted not learning the difference. *La illaha illa 'lla' hu.* Rosa was conferring with Christian for directions, then rattling them off to Bette who was trying to understand while crossing traffic and making funky turns which she would never consider in the U.S. She wove down lane-less roads and maneuvered around and through the biggest potholes she had ever seen. People went through red lights because there were police officers directing traffic, some stop signs weren't obeyed because traffic lights had been turned on, there were unlit streets completely absorbing the dim headlights, and minivan buses zooming in and out of it all. If Marco knew what she was doing he would give her a blistering lecture like he did his niece. She would welcome it, just to get out of this mess.

At the hospital, Bette missed the entrance, and instead of driving around who knew how many blocks to get back, she drove the wrong way into the exit. After dropping off Christian and his wife, a man whom Bette thought was going to yell at her instead helped her turn around in the small space and park without having to go back out into the maze of maddening streets. As she was backing up into the spot, the man whistled as a sound guide, just like she had seen Fernando do when he was guiding Sergio's trailer into her driveway to load Catalina's belongings. Such a small, comforting thing gave Bette her only smile during the stressful night.

Inside, the emergency room was full of people waiting for service. Many family members were sitting on the scarred and chipped floor, but Bette found a vacant spot where she could lean against a wall. There was a sign posted above the receptionist area that listed the prices for various medical services.

"Rosa ¿Does Christian need money to see the doctor? I have."

"No. He received a thousand *pesos* from the driver who hit us." A hundred bucks. That wasn't even going to cover the damage on the car and who knew how much the hospital was going to charge.

After waiting for an hour without being seen, Christian told them they were going to find a different hospital. Oh no, Bette thought, please not more driving in Mexico City.

This time Christian gave directions from the front seat with Rosa helping with the language from the back. They raced along, making their way to a nicer part of town with high-rises interspersed with glittery billboards advertising jewelry and perfume. But still the roads were crowded with speeding cars. Many of the larger arterials had three lanes each direction for fast-moving traffic separated by a meridian of trees, and then two more lanes where traffic went a little bit slower for access to the stores. The transitions from three-lane over to two-lane and back were nerve-wracking but Bette thought she did okay. Maybe when she got to know Christian better she would ask him for his memories of the experience.

At the second hospital, Bette drove up the lane for ambulances because she didn't want to pass up the entrance again. A woman came up to the car and took Christian away and told Bette where the parking was across one of those three-and-two plus three-and-two roads. No way, she thought. Instead they parked on this side of the street in a no-parking zone, something Bette would never do in a U.S. city, but it didn't faze the women at all. She wondered if these non-drivers knew what they were doing or if they would emerge from the hospital to find their car not there. If Bette had to locate a towed car at the end of that long day, she was going to find a quiet little alley and curl into a ball and do it in the morning.

The waiting room was as crowded as the last hospital but cleaner, had better lighting, and more seats, though all were full. People were camped out on the floor with blankets, and Bette found her own spot on the linoleum near the pop machine. Pablo and his cousin Teresa played quietly while they waited another hour for Christian to come out with his arm strapped to his chest. It had been dislocated in the fight.

At one point during the wait, two men had come in and gotten people's attention. "*Discúlpanme.*" One of the men told the seated and standing crowd that he and his brother-in-law were there on behalf of his pregnant wife who needed medical service, but they didn't have enough funds. He talked on and on, and then a woman sitting in one of the chairs spoke up saying she knew him and this was true. Or at least that's what Bette thought was going on. He passed a baseball cap around to collect money, and since Rosa added something, Bette did, too. Thank God she lived in a country where people were accepted for emergency care, regardless of their ability to pay. The thought of having something wrong with your pregnancy and not being able to go to a doctor sounded nightmarish.

The dented Golf was waiting for them when they emerged at midnight so they sardined back in and Bette drove them home. All that and they never got to see Rosa's mother. When at last she turned the engine off for the night, she wanted to kneel and kiss the ground.

***

The next morning Bette made tea with the electric immersion coil she had brought with her, then climbed the homemade wooden ladder through the opening to the roof. Poochy greeted her with much tail wagging and straining on his leash, but she stepped around the dirty, matted dog and his poop and perched on a short cinder block wall to take in the vista. The land rolled away to the north and east until it came to mountains. There were a few houses clumped about, and she could hear roosters crowing from somewhere to the left. Off in the distance a man was singing out, ¡*Gas*! He was selling the replacement tanks like the ones downstairs hooked to the stove.

Rosa had told her she could rent nearby for sixty dollars a month, but Bette would want a place with a roof like this. That would cost more, but there weren't enough windows in the houses to meet Bette's desire for light. Here she could plant flowers and vegetables in pots and be away from the scads of dogs and yet still be outside. All the male dogs had their testicles, so odd to see, and they were always running around barking. Bette would want to have a slingshot to carry with her when she walked to town, not to hit them, as if she could, but to make them run away.

"We're going to walk to the market," Rosa called up to Bette.

"*Espérame, espérame,*" Bette said, happy to use one of the new phrases she'd learned on this trip. It was a small crowd that awaited her including Isa and Rosa, her father, and sister Maria with her son Pablo, survivors of last night's adventures. Gerardo was off playing with his cousins where he had spent the night. He was home.

On their way to *el centro* Bette stayed close to Rosa's father who twice picked up rocks and threw them at dogs that were getting too close. They walked single file on a dirt path alongside open fields dotted with pyramids of corn stalks then behind the backs of buildings. The fences of cactus and bedsprings were functional and delightful to see, but there was trash everywhere. As they neared the downtown area, they crossed a footbridge, high above a small river whose banks were covered with trash and smelled of open sewage. Maybe this was where the odor was coming from that occasionally wafted past the house. Bette looked back at Rosa to see if she noticed the smell and saw Maria toss a Kleenex down the bank.

The stalls at the open market were still waking up when they arrived, and Bette felt like she was stepping into the Land of Oz. They wound their way down narrow walkways between booths where men were cutting huge chunks of meat off of stiff pigs with pointy feet and hanging cows while others washed the floors. People were arranging their wares getting ready for the day's customers and she almost hit her head several times on low-hanging ropes, poles, and goods while gawking at the market's riches – an entire table full of blender parts, colorful school supplies, toys and candy, hardware items, skimpy bras and underwear, and fruits and vegetables piled high.

She felt like she was being led around by a ring in her nose but it was only the smells that kept drawing her head one direction or the other: pigskin crackling and sizzling in a huge caldron of fat, griddles covered with blue tortillas, pots of tamales with steam rising off of them that smelled of earthy *masa.*

Rosa's dad passed many perfectly adequate-looking stalls before he finally stopped at one and asked the vendor what type of *tamales* she had. *Rojo, verde, rajas*, and *dulce*. Bette sat on a short, plastic stool and ate a *tamale de rajas* stuffed with *chiles*, tomatoes, onions, and cheese and sipped a hot grain drink made from rice, water, sugar, and cinnamon. She wrapped her cold hands around the *etole* in the Styrofoam cup in an attempt to warm them. A bit farther into the market, Rosa bought Bette a *Oaxaqueño* which was similar to a *tamale*, but the *masa* was filled with chicken cooked in *tomatillo* salsa and then steamed in a banana leaf instead of a corn husk. The smooth texture slid right down Bette's throat whispering *more* as it went.

"Betty," Rosa said. "¿Do you want to see my land?"

"*Sí*, Rosa. *Sí.*" But she also wanted to linger to see how that young man so deftly cut the stickers off of a *nopale* cactus pad at a vegetable stand. Wouldn't Marco be surprised if she could prepare them for him when she returned?

They retraced their route and came to Rosa's sister Adriana's house where she lived with her husband and two children, and now apparently Gerardo. The kids must be off with the motorbike.

"This will be wonderful," Bette said. They were standing behind Adriana's house at Rosa's land. "It's so close to your family." It was a five-minute stroll from her parents and ten to her favorite sister, Maria's place. Behind Rosa's land, a cinder block house was being built, and they approached it to see the progress.

"*Hola*, Emilio," Bette said. He was the rail-thin husband of Adriana and was working with two other men placing cinder blocks atop one another building an exterior wall. A woman was in a corner of the roofless building cooking over an open fire.

"*Hola*, Betty. This is my brother, Martin, and this is his house." The man reached over from the cement mixing box and shook her hand. "This is my sister, Josafina, and her husband, Pablo."

"Your house looks very good," Bette said. "I want to help Rosa and Felipe build their house when he returns."

"You can learn," Emilio said.

Bette watched as Emilio's brother-in-law spread cement on a row of cinder blocks and set the next one in place. A string was pulled tight to guide him in getting the height correct. What she also wanted to do was build a house of straw and mud but didn't know how hard it was to locate straw in this part of Mexico. It would be so much warmer in the winter and cooler in the summer than the un-insulated cinder block houses they were accustomed to. All these kids living without heat worried her.

"It must feel good to build your own place," she said to Emilio.

"*Sí*. With your own hands you create a home." He held up his cement-flecked hands and smiled at her. Bette thought often of building her own home but knew she would never have enough money as a single woman living in the U.S., a job changer at that who couldn't decide where to settle.

"That's my field there," he said and swept his arm out in an arc. She wanted that pride to show in her face, too. Her field of corn for her sheep.

***

When they got back from breakfast, Rosa told her they were going to try to make it to Mexico City again to pick up her mother. That sounded okay, well sort of, after the night before, until she learned that she would be the driver. There were ten this time in Rosa's van – Bette, Rosa, Gerardo, Isa, Adriana, and her two children, Maria and her son, and their father Rodrigo. They would be eleven when they came home with Rosa's mom, Rosemaria. The traffic was not as heavy, and it was daylight, but driving was still so different from in the U.S. Definitely two hands on the steering wheel at all times with cars, semi-trucks, bicycles, buses, and horses on the roads, all going at different speeds and passing each other willy-nilly. There were monstrous speed bumps, potholes, and cars and pedestrians entering the road from both sides. And those *returnos*. It seemed like she was always making U-turns to head the other way. Where were the overpasses in this country? Bette had to regularly remind herself to let go of her death grip on the wheel and shake out her hands. *La illaha illa 'lla' hu.*

Rosa's mother was staying with her sister, Maritza, while they took turns caring for their mother. Seeing Maritza's house was worth the drive. That and Rosa's mother-in-law's home which was right around the corner. Maritza and her husband lived next door to and above the *farmacia* they owned. Bette entered through a door off of a busy street and found herself in a lush world of green lawn, bougainvillea, roses, and other flowering bushes and hanging plants – a garden oasis amidst the bustling city.

She wanted to stretch out on the grass but turned instead to meet Rosa's mother.

"Thank you for returning my daughter to me," Rosemaria said. She took Bette's hand and pulled her into a cheek kiss.

"*Tu no puedes ser la mamá de Rosa. ¿Estás su hermana?*" Bette couldn't believe that the thin, smooth-skinned woman greeting her was Rosa's mother and not her sister, the mother of eight children. Rosemaria smiled, but Bette caught herself too late and apologized for using the informal *tu* form of the verb instead of *usted.*

"It's because I only use the *tu* at home and haven't learned to use *usted. Discúlpeme.*" There it was again, asking for forgiveness using the informal command. Rosemaria took her hand and led her inside to meet her mother, a little apple doll of a person, wrapped in a floral pink fleece blanket and propped up in bed by a mountain of pillows. After her family members gave her *un besito* on the cheek, she started moaning, over and over.

"¿Are you in pain?" Rodrigo, Rosa's father, asked.

She stopped moaning, and in a clear, strong voice said, "No." Everyone started laughing, including Bette who understood the humor for once.

Maritza invited Bette upstairs to her home above the pharmacy for *un cafecito*, a little coffee and a snack, which her maid prepared. Bette was going to use that word with Marco when she got back, and he would laugh at her use of the special Mexican term. Maritza's house was modern with tile floors, an up-to-date kitchen, plenty of windows, and indoor plumbing. If Bette had known, she would have waited instead of going in the door-less room near the grandmother, within earshot of the entire family.

Here there was another floor above which had a clothesline and a small room with a real washing machine and ironing board. Bette looked out from the roof and turned in a slow circle. Nothing but city as far as she could see in every direction.

Rosa's mother-in-law's house, Felipe's childhood home, was merely one block away but was on the other end of the economic spectrum. Her walls were unpainted gray cinder block adorned only with a painting of the *Virgen de Guadalupe*, crosses, and rosaries. All of the other homes Bette had been in had yellow and orange and pink painted walls, or at least white over stucco. But it was the garden that brought this home to life. Coffee cans had been nailed to the cinder block walls that enclosed the courtyard and were overflowing with plants and flowers. Larger pots and buckets lined the walls and were filled with flowers, trees, and vines. Bette wondered how many little refuges like this were tucked behind walls throughout the city. It would be impossible to tell because the houses all abutted the sidewalk and were closed off to view by high walls and gates. She would have loved to linger a while here, sip a cup of hot tea, and listen to the singing of the caged birds but she had to drive the group back.

***

That afternoon back in Huehuetoca, Bette had a discussion with Emilio, Rosa's brother-in-law, while they were eating their goodbye dinner at a restaurant. He said that Mexicans love their children more than North Americans. Bette had heard this same sentiment stated in the U.S. You love your pets more than your kids. She might have believed it before but not now after being in Mexico. It was her first time in a developing country, so she recognized that parents didn't have control over issues of unsafe drinking water and open sewers. She saw that they were unable to send their children to school if they couldn't afford uniforms. And because she was a guest and didn't want to offend she kept quiet, but her mind rattled off her rebuttal. Is it loving your kids to drive like maniacs, so the streets aren't safe for pedestrians? And what about those loose dogs that threaten and bite? She could feel her hackles rising so took a slow breath and looked around her at Rosa's big family enjoying each other's company. Not until much later would she realize how ignorant she was about Mexico. It was then that she would offer thanks that she hadn't spoken her un-informed thoughts.

There were ten of them together eating *quesadillas, sopes,* and *gorditas* all made right in front of them by two women working on a huge *comal,* maybe five feet across, heated below by tanks of gas. Bette's *quesadilla* was topped with sautéed mushrooms, onions, and *nopales,* thin slices of cooked cactus exactly like she wanted to prepare for Marco.

"¿Would you like to try a tortilla?" Rosa asked her.

"*Por supuesto.*" This would be the third time she had eaten a freshly made corn tortilla in this little town, and they had all been a little different in taste and texture. Rosa handed one to her and to Teresa, her ten-year-old niece sitting next to Bette. As she bit into the hot, slightly doughy tortilla she decided that this was her favorite, at least until the next one she ate. She watched Teresa, then added a little salt and roasted salsa *roja* to the last of hers. Heaven.

That night she and Gerardo taught Teresa and Luis to play *Ocho Loco* and Hanged Man, and the four of them sat in the garage room – the water room? – and laughed and played cards and ate the last of the popcorn with hot sauce drizzled over it. Their grandfather sat close, but they couldn't get him to join in though he ate his share of popcorn.

"You have good luck, tonight," Gerardo said to Bette in English.

"I know. It's fun to win. Are you going to school tomorrow with your cousins?"

"No. Mom needs to go first."

Bette glanced up and saw Rosa's two sisters and brother-in-law looking over at them. They had never heard Gerardo speak English.

"Keep studying English. Okay? Try not to forget." Bette smiled and touched Gerardo's shoulder. He returned her smile, and Bette's heart gave a little squeeze reminding her of the new term she had learned this week, *un dolor insoportable*, an unsupportable pain.

***

Rosa's mother woke Bette before dawn like she had requested, so she could watch her make tortillas. The day before they had each carried a bucket of corn to the *molinera* and waited while it was ground into masa. This morning, Rosemaria made a fire in the tin stove out of trash, corn cobs, and pieces of a pallet. In no time at all, she had a rhythm going of rolling the masa into an egg-sized ball in her left hand, smashing it flat with the metal press, flipping it back and forth between her palms, then placing it onto the stove. Bette tried it after much coaxing, but hers tended to cling to her hand and tear when she tried to lay them on the hot surface. She decided to stick with sampling, which she was excellent at, and just be with Rosemaria near the warm stove on the quiet, dark morning. Bette could see stars out the opening to the roof.

"¿Can you show me the tortilla star?"

Rosa's mother smiled and nodded. She took Bette's hand in her own flour-covered ones and raised her arm toward the sky, pointing at the star. Bette felt her heart constrict and tears fill her eyes at the warm, motherly touch.

"Gracias," she said as she wiped a tear from her cheek, leaving a small smudge of masa.

By the time the rest of the family awoke, the stack of fresh tortillas was six inches tall and growing. There were twice that many when they loaded them into Bette's backpack, presents for Felipe and Rosa's two brothers and their families back in Arizona.

She entered Mexico City later that morning and for the first time wasn't driving. It was Rosa's brother Alonso who drove her to the airport in the van. The city was big and hilly and rolled on forever. In some places, there were seven lanes of traffic in each direction. Were there places so convoluted in the U.S. that you had to go in circles to get anywhere? On the drive in, they bought four kilos of *mandarinas* for ten *pesos* – about one dollar for nine pounds of delicious juicy fruit. Pablo sat on Bette's lap and played with the leaf he found on his orange, humming happily to himself.

As the conversation buzzed around her, Bette let her concentration drift and thought about living there. It would be simpler, but could she be happy without her Anglo friends? Washing her clothes outside on a cement scrub board like the other women wasn't a problem, and she was already used to hanging them on a line. She would bring down her solar shower so she wouldn't freeze like she had done that morning taking a sponge bath and washing her hair from a five-gallon bucket. But what about the trash? Bette had watched, and flinched, as a man took the plastic covering off a new antennae he'd bought and let it drop to the ground though the trash barrel was less than twenty feet from where he stood. The trash in the U.S. seemed accidental, as if it flew out of the beds of trucks, but maybe she was being naïve. It grated on her sense of aesthetics and seemed to indicate something larger.

But she could get away here, or maybe even move toward something for a change, rather than always leaving. She wanted to participate in a *quinciñera*. Not just anyone's, but Teresa's, the little tomboy's fifteenth year stepping into adulthood celebration. And she wasn't ready to let go of her friendship with Rosa. They had gone religiously to the YMCA in Warren until Rosa had lost quite a bit of weight, then slowly gained it back. When talking to her sisters this weekend, she told them how many kilos she had lost, then said she had missed her *grasa*, her fat. Looking at Bette, she smiled and said, "*Mis llantas.*" My tires. Bette would miss her friend.

She wanted more than ever to talk to Marco to get his perspective. About everything here. She had wanted to see his daughters, but it was too hard to get to their town. Would he make her feel terrible because she had been in Mexico and had spent all the time with Rosa's family and not made the effort to see his daughters? The conflicting feelings were too much, too much, and the tears fell as she watched the city roll by.

CHAPTER 21

To: Bette
From: Marco

I'm sorry for don't can company a you travel to Mexico. I'm wants
May be one day. Travell, company – toggeder.
Im now you like ice-cream
Im bay one for you with a lots love.
No encontre ice cream *de soya, pero te compre uno con chocolate que*
se que te gustara, y es de lith (dieta) para me guerita.

Muchos besos, Marquito

Bette checked her cell phone for messages as soon as she got off the plane in
Phoenix. There was an unexpected call from her father. He didn't even know
she'd gone to Mexico, they talked so infrequently. She guessed he must have
sensed she was on the road and wanted to come along vicariously. A sweet
message from Marco. After texting to let him know she was back in Arizona,
she relaxed in the back of the shuttle van for the two-hour drive north. She
gazed out, watching the dry landscape roll by. There must have been rain
lately as the ocotillos had red blooms at the tops of their sticky branches and
the saguaro cactus looked like plump *churros*. When the van crested the rise
to the upper elevation where she lived, Bette inhaled deeply as the expanse
of open land spread out on both sides of the highway. This was her favorite
time on the drive north when she felt like she was coming into her part of
Arizona.

She had now lived in Arizona for ten years, longer than anywhere else in her life. All of the hiking she had done in the state had given her a sense of place she'd only experienced once before when she lived in the Northwest and kayaked its endless waterways. She had not felt at home under the gray skies there and until recently had thought that Arizona was home. But the politics of her state were what she was having trouble tolerating now.

A text came in from Cat, checking to see if she was safely back in the country. They set a date for a margarita night at a Thai restaurant later in the week, and Bette reminded herself not to mention the treatment of pets in Mexico. It was hard enough on Bette, the pet-less person. Cat would implode with anger. Bette didn't want to put herself in a situation where she had to defend an entire culture. She'd had enough of that already with undocumented immigrants. She was not about to take on the country. Let those *paisanos* do it, another cool word she had learned for fellow countrymen and women.

Marco met her at the shuttle, both a good and a bad sign. It meant he didn't have work that day, but it was wonderful to have time to talk with him about his homeland.

"Let's go home and have *un cafecito*," she said.

"Oh, *qué Mexicana*," he replied, smiling.

He felt so good, so natural with her arm around his shoulders, his arm around her waist. The coffee would have to wait until they saturated themselves with one another again.

The gifts she brought were welcome, but what he really wanted were the homemade blue corn tortillas. She let him talk her into pulling out a few inches worth, hoping that Felipe and Rosa's brothers weren't told ahead of time how many to expect.

"I'm sorry I can't see your daughters," she said, still struggling with the conditional tense. She explained she had tried to, had called Enrique to see if he could come and pick her up and drive her down. It was a three-hour trip, each way, and Enrique hadn't wanted to because he had a bad cold.

"It's okay, *chaparita*," Marco said, not going on a rant about Enrique. "We'll go together." He pulled her onto his lap on the big, comfy chair, and she bombarded him with questions about his homeland.

***

"Do you want a glass of wine?" Tracy asked her the next week. Bette was sitting at their kitchen table while Tracy and Don made dinner.

"No, thanks. But could you make me a cup of black tea?"

"Ooh, black tea," Tracy said. "Dangerous."

"I need a little something different."

"I've got just the one," Don said, opening the cupboard and pulling out jars and tins.

"Nothing flavored, please."

"No, no. This is a Chinese brand that's not at all sweet."

"How was it in Mexico?" Tracy asked Bette.

"It was…different. Not what I expected. They were very poor, but they didn't seem to notice. I guess if everyone's like that it seems normal." Bette told them about seeing the lack of water in the houses, no heat, and washing clothes by hand outside on cement scrub boards. She relayed how she wondered how Rosa could have chosen that over the comforts of the U.S. It was the pull of family, they agreed.

"But they also have things that I don't, like big TVs and a few pieces of fancy furniture. It's all crammed into one or maybe two rooms, beds, dressers, couches all in one room."

"Just choices we all make," Don said.

"And they love their children in very demonstrative ways. I can't remember my dad ever hugging me, and here's a culture where fifteen-year-old boys carry around their one-year-old cousins." She shared with them a scene she had witnessed at a community center where the parents of young children were playing a game with their kids. The dads and moms would hop up a basketball court with a rubber ball gripped between their knees, the child running alongside encouraging them. Then they would run back down the court with the child holding the ball, to hand it off to the next parent-child combo. "Everyone was laughing and cheering and participating, no matter what size or age of the parents. And they're always calling their children *mi amor* and *mi vida*," Bette sang out in loving tones. "It was pretty sweet." It had made her think of John and wonder why he was so against Mexicans when they epitomized the loving family he professed to want. If only he could broaden his experiences and open his heart a bit more.

"I'm hoping that when Tracy and I move to an intentional community, my son and his family will join us. Wouldn't it be great to get to be a grandparent all year long?" Don smiled at Tracy and set Bette's tea down. "Was it beautiful?"

"Thank you." Bette paused. "Well, no, not really. Not like how I imagine those coastal resorts in Mexico are. The roads were mostly dirt except for the main ones, and there was lots of trash. And graffiti everywhere. And it smelled like sewer a lot of the time. But it had its own beauty if you looked closely. There were blossoms on trees and pots of flowers on roofs and around people's doors. And I could spend days exploring in the markets. They were amazing and cheap, too."

Tracy turned from the counter where she was cutting up cooked beets for a salad. "What would you miss if you lived there?"

"Hmmm. Lived there? I guess I would miss talking about politics and books and nature. Let's see...how many houses was I in? Six, I think, and not one had books in it. I don't think they read or hike or birdwatch."

"You're making a pretty general statement about an entire country after meeting only a few people. There may be lots of kindred spirits that you just haven't come across," Tracy said.

"Maybe if you knew other Americans there it would work out. I think they have intentional communities in Mexico, too," Don added.

"I wouldn't want to live in one of those ex-pat places. I don't think it would feel like Mexico. In Huehuetoca I was the only *gringa,* but nobody made a big deal about it. What I need is a gay birder who has money and wants to go to Mexico," Bette said. "Then, I wouldn't have to worry about those relationship issues, and I could travel with the security of a male partner."

"Have you given up on men? What's Marco think about that?" Tracy asked. "I can't believe that you, of all people, would be without a lover."

"You make me sound like some sort of tramp. I'm just all confused. About Marco with his daughters. About John, Mr. Almost Right." There had been a letter from him when she returned home, apologizing and wanting to get together again. She had ignored it and so far had managed to avoid him at work.

Bette looked down at the stew and poked around with her spoon. Chunks of yams, turnips, carrots, mushrooms, and white tofu floated in it. "Is this that Moosewood recipe? I love this soup." Could she find miso or tahini in Mexico? Balsamic vinegar and Darjeeling tea? Not in Rosa's town.

"We thought we'd make you something as far from Mexican food as we could find," Don said.

"*Gracias.*"

After dinner, Tracy and Bette sat in the living room near the pellet stove while Don improvised at the piano.

"Everything's changing here," Bette said. "At our ESL class on Wednesday, there were only four guys. Four. We normally have twenty-five or thirty. It's the new law that just took effect. My students and their families are going to other states or back to Mexico."

Bette thought back to that week's ESL class.

"They laid off the entire kitchen staff at the Hungry Lion last week," Robin had said. "And the dishwasher at the Golden Garden." Bette already knew that Rosa's nephew Rodrigo had lost his job as a prep cook at Takamoto's.

"When I was at Walmart there weren't any Mexicans shopping there," Gretchen said. "It was kind of creepy." Voldemort was going to be in trouble, too.

"It'll likely regulate out a little once the initial panic is over. I heard on NPR that the state doesn't have enough money to enforce the new law," Robin said. "I bet they focus on Phoenix first."

"Tell that to the employers," Bette said. "All of my friends have already lost their jobs." The silence that followed that remark was broken when their first student arrived.

"Good evening, Jesus. Where is Gustavo?" Barbara asked about his brother, who always accompanied him.

"Went to Mexico."

"And you? Will you return?"

Jesus smiled and shrugged his shoulders.

Bette worked with him one-on-one that evening since there were more teachers than students. He was in his forties and was a determined student, spending time reading the bilingual newspapers Bette brought him from Flagstaff or Phoenix when she made trips there. When she asked him how his week was, he lost his usual smile and spoke quietly to her in his improving English.

"I work same job for three years. Fifty hours a week. Now my boss tell me he pay me eight dollars an hour, not twelve. He say, you no like, go to *desempleo*."

This was a wrinkle Bette hadn't thought about – employee abuse by employers who knew they had their workers up a creek without a paddle – no more legal recourse for unethical practices. She felt her pulse start to quicken. "What are you going to do? Go back to Mexico?" Bette knew that this wasn't likely as he was sending money home to put his two children through a university. Whenever he spoke about them, his eyes beamed.

"Maybe I move to other state."

Maybe I move, too, Bette thought.

"Who's leaving?" Don asked, bringing her attention back to her friends.

"My Mexican and Guatemalan students. The employer sanction law has screwed up the entire system. It's the toughest in the country now."

"I missed that," Don said.

"Most people who don't associate with undocumented immigrants don't know what's going on." Bette relayed a story from one of her students who worked at Kentucky Fried Chicken. "She says normally they use twenty boxes of potatoes every day, and they're down to three, and they used to sell five buckets of macaroni salad, and now it's less than one."

"I had no idea that many people were leaving."

"They have to. There's no work. I don't know what our state's thinking. Who's going to make up the lost revenue in sales tax?"

"What's Marco going to do?" Don asked with his back to them, still playing.

"He's not sure. He's still finding some work right now and I'm guessing he'll hang on as long as he can. A while back, I called on a few construction jobs for him, but they all told me they need guys with papers. Legal papers."

***

When Bette got home, Marco was lying in bed, and she paced back and forth beside the bed as she brushed her hair. "Only one of my students still has his job, but now he receives less per hour. Everyone else lost their jobs." Marco whistled under his breath then patted the bed beside him.

"Sit *chaparita*, let me." He took the brush from her and began to stroke her long blond hair.

Bette had thought he was good from practicing on her hair, but after returning from Mexico, she wondered if it was experience from his daughters. "There was a lot of...*fabuloso*...hair on the little girls in Mexico," she said. She wove her hands together and Marco supplied the missing word for *braids*. "*Si, trenzas*. In..." patterns, shapes... She gave up searching for the words and used her hands to show him on her head. He laughed and agreed. "¿Did you make *trenzas* on your daughters?"

"No, my wife did, but I will learn when I return." He pulled firmly on her thick hair, supporting her hair with his other hand. She let her head be moved with the force of the tug. He scooped it up and brushed the underside. Little mewls of pleasure escaped her. She tapped her foot on the floor in delight like a dog getting its favorite spot scratched and it made him laugh.

"¿How long before you go back home, *mi cielo?*" She dropped in one of the new terms of endearment she had learned. My heaven.

"I don't know, *miel.*" He gave her one right back. "I talked to Rafael, and he has work for me one day a week. And Loba on Saturdays."

When Rosa was preparing to leave, Marco had taken over her cleaning job at the log cabin mansion in the woods. He had gotten a little grief for it from one of his construction job friends, but the money was worth more than his pride. Now Bette looked forward to his coming home from cleaning with stories about the little two-year-old who lived there, Cole. Last week Marco had reported that Cole said, 'No more clean, Marco. No more wet my floor.' He had wanted to play, and Marco's cleaning was getting in his way. Marco had set Cole's feet on the mop head with his hands gripping the handle and pulled him along as he scrubbed the floor. Squeak went the mop and squeal with delight went Cole. Bette loved seeing this softer, paternal side of Marco which hadn't appeared when he had been a powerful construction worker.

He finished her hair, lustrous and shiny now, and they snuggled close to one another in bed.

"Come with me to Mexico."

Marco pulled away and rose up on one elbow so he could look into her eyes. "¿You're asking *me* to go to Mexico with *you?*"

*Me, te, lo, la, le, se...*those pronoun placements were so different in Spanish than in English and still challenged her, but she knew what he was asking. "*Si, mi tesoro.*"

"¿What about my daughters?"

"*Tia.* I can be their aunt." She wiggled upright in bed, bouncing a little and said, "I can live close in my own place with a rooftop garden growing flowers and vegetables. I can walk to the little stores crammed with everything imaginable." She mimed that part and hoped he understood. She was fascinated by the huge, mysterious world she had barely begun to explore, but which also frightened her. It was so unruly, so unregulated. Was it more that she hated the racism in Arizona or that the pull of the new, the unknown, was so strong? Did it matter?

Marco slipped his hand down between her legs. "*Pulpo,*" she said, giving the octopus tentacle a playful slap then squeezing it with her thighs so he wouldn't remove it.

"You can teach English," he said. "Lots of people want to learn."

"¿Are they better students than you?"

"Me speak English," Marco said.

"Oh, *si Señor, qué bueno su ingles.*" They laughed together.

"¿Can you help me get to Rosa's town to see the three threes?" The thought of not seeing her expanded family was painful. Would Marco share her? "I..." *Would*...How to say that dang conditional tense again? Try another tack. "When I live there, I want to live with Rosa's family some time, too."

"I can drive you." He took her face in her hand and kissed her tenderly. "You will love our Mexico."

EPILOGUE – 2018

Bette turned the radio off with a snap of her wrist, silencing Trump's senseless bluster. "Done with you." She downshifted to second and started scanning all of the signs screaming for her attention in both English and Spanish. Why so many? Why so big? It was as if they were trying to keep her out, rather than guide her in. Even though she was now fluent in Spanish, the amount of signage seemed designed to confuse. Was this Mexico's attempt to subliminally, ineffectually, keep U.S. citizens out?

Orange fifty-five gallon barrels and concrete dividers were funneling traffic into different lanes. Which was hers? It would have made the drive down to El Cerrillo, Mexico more direct if she had crossed in El Paso, Texas rather than Nogales, Arizona but she had opted for the known over the expedient. She let memory guide her now and found her lane then crossed the border. Just like that. Green light, you're in. No passport check. No visa application then denial. No dogs running around sniffing. No people peering into her car. No photos. No fear.

Bette found the downtown bypass and drove carefully, cautiously toward the mall, aware of the cargo she carried and wanting to protect it from discovery. Many sets of English as a Second Language textbooks in various levels, reams of handouts, and study manuals were all safely tucked in the trunk beside whiteboards and pens. To disguise her printer, she'd wrapped it in tee-shirts and stuffed it in a black plastic bag along with several printer cartridges removed from their boxes. There was a box bulging with cooking ingredients – balsamic vinegar, tahini, herbs and spices, Thai red curry paste, capers, wasabi, powdered buttermilk, rice pasta... Tucked in behind it all were bags of gifts for Rosa, Amaya, and their children, now all teenagers – soccer and tennis shoes, leggings, hair straighteners, backpacks, and older model phones and iPads.

With everything hidden inside the trunk, she hoped she wouldn't stand out as a mark for *la mordida*, bribes, or worse, robbery. In the backseat was a cooler with road trip food, a five-gallon jug of water, and a small suitcase with traveling items. Nothing to raise suspicion, she hoped. When she and Marco had traveled down ten years ago, the back of the pickup truck had been piled high with his goods from the U.S. The brown tarp they had covered it with did nothing to deter those who wanted a piece of that wealth. Now Bette wondered if her U.S. license plate would flash a big arrow at her car, making her vulnerable on this drive south.

Ni modo. She was here. Bette parked in the mall lot, said a prayer of protection for the car and her future, then headed inside to find Marco.

ACKNOWLEDGMENTS

I am grateful to my many friends for their continued support, encouragement, friendship, and wisdom. You are too many to name – how blessed I am to be able to say that – but I trust you know who you are.

There are some people I would like to thank in particular, however, who helped me in specific ways as I wrote this book. Thank you Cathy Righter and Vicky Young from the bottom of my heart for reviewing and editing so many drafts, thus shaping the final novel. To Terril Shorb for brainstorming and gentle guidance while off-trail hiking in northern Arizona. It would be hard for me to express how central the three of you are to my work.

Thank you Sean Souders and Azima Lila Forest for the exchange of edits and encouragement to seek publication. The women of my writers' group provided varied and comprehensive critiques, and I am indebted to their wisdom: Las Mubdis, Katherine Feist, Barbara Williamson, Beatriz Giraldo, Elaine Jordan, Colette Ward, and CR Bolinski.

I couldn't have written this without my many ESL students who opened their lives, hearts, and homes to me. *Gracias por hacer mi vida tan maravillosa.* To Beatriz Giraldo and Socorro Rico a heartfelt *gracias* for guiding me with the Spanish.

How did I get so lucky as to have my sister and brother and my nephies and new nieces? Thank you for always making me laugh and for letting me build upon the stories in your lives. I love you all. Thank you Sally for your continued love and support.

Finally, to the women of The Village, my special Albuquerque family, and Kristina who keep my heart happy, I offer boundless gratitude and love.

NOTE FROM THE AUTHOR

Word-of-mouth is crucial for any author to succeed. If you enjoyed the book, please leave a review online, anywhere you are able, even if it's just a sentence or two. It would make all the difference and would be very much appreciated.

Thanks!
Abbey

ABOUT THE AUTHOR

Photo courtesy of Rachel Owen

Abbey Carpenter was born in Seattle, Washington and raised in the West. She graduated with an M.A. in Sustainable Community Development from Prescott College and has worked, taught, and volunteered in the areas of social justice and environmental sustainability. Her stories and essays have been previously published in *Muse It Up*, *Sustainable Ways*, and *Read It Here*. She has traveled widely in Mexico and currently lives in Silver City, New Mexico.

Thank you so much for reading one of our **Women's Fiction** novels. If you enjoyed the experience, please check out our recommendation for your next great read!

City in a Forest by Ginger Pinholster

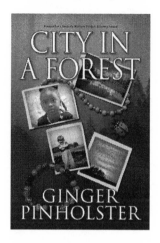

Finalist for a *Santa Fe Writers Project Literary Award*

"Ginger Pinholster, a master of significant detail, weaves her struggling characters' pasts, present, and futures into a breathtaking, beautiful novel in *City in a Forest*.
—IndieReader Approved

Made in the USA
Coppell, TX
08 February 2020